# Abruzzo Intrigue

## A Hardy Durkin Travel Mystery

**By: Bluette Matthey**

**BLUE SHUTTER PUBLISHING**

Blue Shutter Publishing

# Abruzzo Intrigue
A Hardy Durkin Travel Mystery

Author: Bluette Matthey

Library of Congress control number on file with publisher.

ISBN-13: 978-1-941611-01-2

Dedicated in loving memory to:
Emerson, a Prince among Cats

Hikes:
Day 1 Santo Stefano
Day 2 Hermitage of San Bartolomeo
Day 3 Scanno
Day 4 Villetta Barrea
Day 5 Pescara
Day 6 Navelli Plain
Day 7 Caramanico
Day 8 Castrovalva

A page from
Hardy Durkin's
Diary

# PROLOGUE

*Hardy Durkin leads a hiking tour into Italy's Abruzzo region where they experience the area's culture, food, and history. There is a good deal of exposure to the region's religious and spiritual past, and one of the members of the tour group struggles with an odyssey of the soul that ends in redemption. Some of the cast of characters are who they seem to be, but most aren't. A member of the group, a grieving widower, plans to steal one of the Vatican's most precious religious relics, The First Eucharistic Miracle, from the Church of San Francesco in Lanciano. The book is a collision of values and traditions while hiking through the oft-overlooked beauty of ancient Abruzzo.*

# CHAPTER 1

"I figure the time is right for a real Italian restaurant in Winston-Salem. Nuthin' chi-chi or over-the-top-expensive; just good, rustic peasant food. Which, considering the state of food in the States right now, is almost exotic. Know what I mean? Food that tastes real. Not the stuff that looks and tastes like plastic cuisine."

Hal Lambeth was waxing large on his favorite topic: food. And, more specifically, his passion at his current stage in life: bringing good food to the public table. 'Hale Hal,' so called due to his hearty, hale-fellow-well-met persona, had been in the food and beverage business for thirty years. Someone else's food and beverage business. Now, at age fifty five, Hal had decided it was his turn, so he was going to open his own establishment, a themed restaurant. Since Hal's mother was originally from the Abruzzo region of south/central Italy, it seemed only natural that Abruzzo and its foods would be the starting point for Hal's endeavor. His mother, may God rest her soul, had died recently and left Hal a nice-sized nest egg for his inheritance. What better way to honor his mother, and carry out what he saw as his destiny, than to open an Italian restaurant in the true spirit of presenting his best and most cherished?

"So, the way I see it …" he droned on.

The recipient of his discourse, Winifred Bradford, had mentally drifted away from Hal's conversation three minutes ago. Winifred, who really answered to Winnie, felt her brain dying as she stood under the deluge of Hal's self-validation. She wasn't above just walking away, but since this was, after all, the let's-get-acquainted dinner for their walking tour through Abruzzo she was disinclined to stiff a fellow wayfarer their first night out. She continued to nod and purse her lips, normally signs of attentive listening.

"Winnie, darling," her twin sister, Tillie, sang out, as she waltzed up to where she and Hal were standing on the terrace looking out toward Gran Sasso, which means 'Great Stone,' the glacier-clad mountain that is the centerpiece of the Gran Sasso National Park in central Italy. Clad in a muted-print, jersey jumpsuit, her lanky, five-foot six-inch frame had the litheness of a dancer. "I really must show you the view from the other side of the terrace," she said. "Hal, you won't mind if I steal her away for several minutes before the sun goes down, will you?" Tillie had seen the very slight arching of her sister's eyebrows from across the room. A movement that would have gone totally unnoticed by anyone else, to Tillie the gesture was akin to rolling one's eyes: Winnie was bored and needed bailed out of her present social dilemma. As the twins glided away, their silver-maned heads, both worn in short bobs, joined conspiratorially, Tillie gently pinched Winnie, "You owe me one, kiddo."

A Japanese-American couple, Dennis and Teresa Fujimoto, hung somewhat shyly on the edge of the group. "I hate these get-to-know-you affairs," Teddy hissed to her husband. "It's always the worst part of any group tour. I didn't come on this trip to mingle with people I hope never to see again and could care nothing about." Teddy was a fairly successful but painfully shy fabric designer. She and Dennis, both forty two, lived in Philadelphia, where Dennis had set up his dental practice after graduating and interning at Penn. Both were originally from the West Coast. Dennis' maternal grandfather had been in the legendary WWII 442nd all Japanese-American combat unit and had served in southern Italy. This was their main reason for their trip to Abruzzo. That, and the fact that Abruzzo wasn't Philadelphia.

"Just relax, baby," Dennis reassured her. "Your apprehension hangs over you like a cloud."

'That's encouraging,' Teddy thought. Aloud, all she said was, "Great."

"Have another drink. Can I get you one more sherry, or would you like to try one of the local wines? The Cerasuolo from this region is supposed to have a subtle grape flavor with a highlight of cherry."

"Yes," Teddy agreed, "I'd like to try the local wine." Dennis went off to get her wine, leaving her feeling vulnerable. She sighed. He was such a people person and could talk to anyone. He'd never known a stranger, a quality that had drawn her to him when they'd first met. His outgoing personality became her armor, and allowed her to pretend an ease among strangers which dissipated instantly when he wasn't with her. She started to turn her back to the group, a defense mechanism, when she heard a voice at her side.

"You look like you don't enjoy these first night meet-ups, either."

She turned back and found a young woman with prominent cheekbones and dark complexion at her side. Dark, thick hair; large, brown eyes. 'Native-American,' Teddy thought. 'About my age.'

With a somewhat embarrassed smile and downcast eyes, Teddy nodded. "I never get used to them," she admitted.

"I'm Lucy Quickstreet. Are you the couple from Philadelphia?"

Teddy's face registered brief surprise.

"I always read the information sent out about my fellow travelers," Lucy explained. "You two seem to be the only couple on the trip, aside from the twins," she added, nodding toward the silver-haired duo. "I didn't mean to intrude, but you looked a bit lost."

Teddy realized she'd been thrown a life-line of sorts and, gratefully, she grabbed it. "Not at all, Lucy. My name is Teresa ... Teresa Fujimoto. Please, call me Teddy." They shook hands. It was a solid handshake, and it broke the ice between them. "So, where are you from, Lucy?"

"Originally, Maine. But I manage at the Foxwoods Resort Casino in Mashantucket, Connecticut. My daughter attends Middlebury College in Middlebury, Vermont, where our tour leader graduated from. Which, I guess, is why I chose this particular tour company."

Dennis returned with drinks in hand and a welcoming smile on his face as he rejoined his wife and her new acquaintance. "Hi! I'm Teddy's husband, Dennis."

"Lucy Quickstreet, Dennis. Nice to meet you."

Dennis turned to his wife. "I've asked Peter Fynch, another member of our group, to join us."

Lucy spoke, "Well, I'll see you two later ..."

"No, please stay, Lucy," Dennis urged. "I just thought he looked a bit forlorn is all. Don't run off."

Teddy spoke up, "Oh, do stay, Lucy. That's just Dennis for you. He positively collects people." She nodded soundly to emphasize what she'd said. At that moment a good-looking man, handsome in a non-descript, plain sort of way, ambled up to their group. He looked prematurely gray compared to his unlined, smooth complexion. There was a stoic, proper air about him.

"Ah," Dennis said, "here he is now. Everyone, this is Peter Fynch, from Nashua, New Hampshire. Peter, this is my wife, Teddy, and this is Lucy Quickstreet, another member of our group." Lucy's interest-ometer registered a jolt as she eyed Peter's clean-cut good looks. He pretended not to notice

"Lucy was just telling me that our tour leader went to the same school as her daughter, in Middlebury, Vermont," Teddy announced.

"That's right," Lucy said. "He was quite the BMOC, from what I heard. He was the school's star pentathlon athlete and an excellent marksman. When he graduated from Middlebury he went into the army and was stationed in Germany with military intelligence. SIGINT. Signals intelligence, I think. Plus, he kept up with the military's version of the pentathlon and placed near the top internationally. Speaks at least four languages. Quite an amazing guy for a tour leader."

Dennis whistled appreciatively. "Sounds like a warrior. This should be an interesting trip."

"And you know this how?" Peter asked. There was a slight edge to his voice. For an instant Lucy felt as though she were being challenged and bristled. "Hardy Durkin is a legend at Middlebury College. They've even named a track field after him, informally."

Just then their larger-than-life tanned tour leader, Hardy Durkin, strode into view. His lanky, muscular six-foot-four physique commanded their attention with his air of assurance. The dark blue, intelligent eyes, set in a handsomely proportioned face, topped by thick, chestnut-brown hair, assessed, in an instant, the atmosphere surrounding his tour group members. Turning his head slightly, like he wore giant, invisible, antennae, he picked up the 'weak link' in the party and headed over to strike up a conversation.

The object of Hardy's attentions was a lone, odd-looking man, fiftyish, who leaned against the stone wall of the terrace, drink in hand. His face was rather like an axe, with wide-set gray eyes. Intelligence set his features. Something like an aura shone from his façade, giving him the appearance of a worldly-looking ascetic. He manifested aloofness, but his eyes were constantly watching, assessing.

"Father Gossett?" Hardy questioned, his hand outstretched.

"Please, just Kelvin," the man responded, meeting Hardy's handshake. "I gave up the Father bit when I left the priesthood," he explained.

"Got it," Hardy responded. "So, is this your first trip to Italy?"

"Heavens, no," the ex-priest replied. "I've been to Rome many times, but this is my first visit to Abruzzo."

"Have you done walking tours before?"

"If pilgrimages count, yes, I've done several. The longest was from Santiago de Compostela, in northwestern Spain, to Rome. Seven, no, eight years ago. It was done it total silence. Took me three months. It changed my life, profoundly."

Hardy whistled. "Well, I won't have to worry about you keeping up on our walks, will I?" he grinned. 'Aha,' Hardy thought, 'I begin to understand why you opted to pay for a single supplement to have your own room on the tour.' "I visited the cathedral in Santiago de Compostela two years ago ... very impressive. Although not a pilgrim, I attended the weekly service for the pilgrims. The incense burner they swing back and forth through the transept is really something. It takes eight men to pull the rope on it. They call it a ... um ..."

"A botafumerio," helped Kelvin. "It means 'smoke expeller.' That particular incense burner weighs close to one hundred and eighty pounds. Historically, the swinging incensory at Santiago de Compostela was put in use during the 11th century when many of the pilgrims, tired and unwashed, arrived at their destination smelling pretty badly. Also, it was believed that the smoke from the incense had a purifying and protective effect during times of plague. And, of course, the burning of incense is itself an important part of the liturgy, being a form of prayer to God." He paused. "Which is, I'm sure, more than you ever wanted to know about the incense burner," he laughed apologetically.

"Not at all," Hardy replied. "I found the cathedral and its place in the Church's history fascinating. I also was very moved by the people who go on pilgrimage. A ritual of simple faith that has stood the test of time and, in fact, still offers hope and comfort in a world that seems to have gone off kilter."

Kelvin threw a somewhat suspicious look at Hardy, wondering if he was having his leg pulled. He saw, however, that his group leader was sincere in his speech, and adjusted his opinion of Hardy accordingly.

"Mr. Durkin?" someone spoke from behind.

Hardy turned and recognized Amy Snoddard, a Special Education teacher from Silver Spring, Maryland.

"Hi, Amy!" he returned. "And please, it's just Hardy.

"O.K., Hardy. I apologize for being late, but ..."

"Hey, not a problem, Amy. Tonight is low key and very informal. Totally off the clock, except we do need to start dinner on time or Antonio, the owner, won't let me bring any more groups to his fabulous family-style feast. Oh, excuse me. Amy, this is Kelvin Gossett, one of ours. Kelvin, Amy Snoddard."

Amy's blue-gray watchful eyes gave Kelvin a detached once-over. 'A decent sort,' she thought, approvingly. Athletic and almost mannish-looking, Amy had never married and harbored a suspicion of people in general and men in particular. Her best friends were two Blue-Russian cats, Ivan and Emma, who were being looked after by a highly trusted cousin in Gaithersburg. "Pleased to meet you, Kelvin," she said, giving him a nod.

"Can I get you something to drink, Amy?" Kelvin offered.

"Um, no ... I think I'll wait until dinner. Thanks."

Almost on cue Antonio and a young girl, probably his teen-aged daughter, entered the terrace, each bearing a large platter of salumi, cured meats from locally raised and slaughtered free-roaming pigs. Antonio's family had been preparing their own salumi for many generations, a tradition he upheld seriously and sacredly. The smoked, peppery aroma from the salumi drew everyone, en masse, to the three tables which had been pulled together into one long buffet. Carafes of Montepulciano d'Abruzzo and Cerasuolo, the famous wines of Abruzzo, had been placed on each table, both excellent accompaniments to the salumi. Talking subsided for several minutes while the company of hikers delved into the food. Antonio stood back, pleased at the appreciative response to his charcuterie platters. The next course was the typical Abruzzese maccheroni alla chitarra in a spicy tomato sauce. The pasta is so-called because it is rolled out flat onto a square box with strings, shaped like a crude guitar, or chitarra and the strings of the 'guitar' cut the slab of egg dough into pasta noodles.

Next came an assortment of crepes filled with savories, cheese, or vegetables, some of which were baked and others which had been stewed in a meat broth. A polenta in a spicy sausage ragu. And lamb, locally raised, in a creamy cheese and egg sauce, served with roasted potatoes. The wine was continually replenished. The combination of good, glorious food and wine worked their inevitable magic. Conversation flowed, burbled, and surged on a tide of good will all round. No one was excluded; no one held back. A group that had been strangers two hours ago had transformed into a brotherhood.

As coffee was being served, an overweight Italian in his early forties appeared at Hardy's side. Dressed in somewhat wrinkled chinos and a short-sleeve Oxford shirt, left untucked, he stood smiling deferentially. Lightly rapping the side of his water glass with his spoon, Hardy called the group to attention.

"Let me introduce you all to one more member of our band of travelers. This is Giuseppe, our driver for the duration of our trip and a native of Sulmona." Hardy then went round the assembled diners making brief introductions. Giuseppe nodded and bobbed at each name, beaming an engaging smile.

Kelvin the ex-priest, always taking everyone's measure, thought, 'Shifty-eyed bugger; over-solicitous.'

Amy Snoddard's private reaction to the driver was, 'Looks like he's always on the take.'

Peter Fynch figured Giuseppe was probably connected to the Mob.

All three were correct in their assessments.

After the diners were sated and somewhat tipsy, Antonio reappeared and was met with a round of applause and hearty 'bravos' from his audience. When the acclamation had subsided Hardy spoke, "Antonio, you've really outdone yourself, my friend. What a feast!"

Antonio demurred. "This was only a meal, really. A feast is what we in Abruzzo call la panarda. It is a meal prepared to honor Saint Anthony and consists of thirty five to fifty different dishes. The whole village turns out and eats all night long. That is a feast. But I am honored that you enjoyed your meal and hope you will visit us again."

\*\*\*\*\*

# CHAPTER 2

Hardy Durkin, owner of Durkin Tours, had brought his latest group of middle-aged-plus hikers to the region of Abruzzo in Italy for a ten-day tour. His clientele were usually upper management and professional kinds of people who loved to decompress by hiking through spectacular natural scenery and living simply but well while doing so. They were folks who didn't mind a healthy trek during the day, but expected good food and their creature comforts at day's end.

Hardy, who had started out as a computer geek in a cubicle working for a company specializing in GPS applications in New Hampshire after active duty with the Army's SIGINT brigade in Germany, had decided there was far more to life than working in a rabbit warren. As a result of this realization, during his last year of Reserve duty he had created a nice niche business of catering to the adventurous spirit who craved quiet solitude with nature while hiking, but at night wanted a hot shower, soft bed, and the kiss of civilization nearby. He'd started Durkin Tours, and never looked back. Now, at the age of twenty eight years, Hardy could safely say that his business was a success and so was his life, if one measured success by happiness and self-satisfaction.

*****

Italy's Abruzzo region is considered the 'Green Heart' of Europe and is one of the wildest and most beautiful areas in Italy. Bordered by the Apennines on the west and the Adriatic Sea on the east, one third of the region is preserved as national or regional parks which are home to woodlands, an endless variety of wildflowers, birds, and butterflies, and a haven for bear, chamois, wolves, eagles, large cats, and other vanishing species. These natural riches are preserved in the national parks of Maiella, Gran Sasso, and Abruzzo, the regional park of Sirente-Velino, and numerous smaller reserves.

Although the region of Abruzzo is considered to be in southern Italy, it is really where the north and south of Italy meet. Historically an empty, sparsely populated region, Abruzzo became even less dense after World War II when people quit the land and the practice of sheep farming, with much of the population immigrating to America. Medieval villages in the mountains located in the national parks lost much of their citizenry, but recent efforts to carefully and authentically restore the villages have resulted in a modest increase of population and growth in the tourism industry. Scattered throughout the region are abandoned castles, remote hermitages, hilltop villages, old farmsteads, and some truly remarkable abbeys and churches. Two thirds of the region of Abruzzo is mountainous, and the highest peaks in Italy, outside the Italian Alps, are here. The mountains give way to hills planted in vines, olives, and orchards, and then come the plains of the coastal areas which meet the Adriatic in Blue Flag Beaches, beaches which set the standard for being environmentally friendly and clean.

Although far from the madding crowd, Abruzzo does attract ardent tourists in small numbers. It has become a special haven for those who love mountain tourism and skiing, a mecca for beachgoers since the beaches along the Adriatic are some of the best in Italy, and Abruzzo also beckons those who appreciate art, history, and religion.

In early history, Abruzzo was comprised of several different Italic tribes which lived apart from each other until they unified to resist the encroaching Roman Empire. They finally succumbed to conquest and became citizens of Rome.

After the fall of the Roman Empire Abruzzo changed hands many times, but it was under Charlemagne's rule that Christianity grew and the abbeys, cathedrals, and monastic retreats were built. Charlemagne was followed by Norman rule, several other Houses and Kingdoms, and then the Spanish took over, followed by the House of Bourbon and, finally, the unification of Italy. The various regions, however, still retain their identity and importance in the lives and minds of the people who live there. When asked where you are from, the most important part of the answer is your town or village. You are not Italian first, but Abruzzese from Scanno, for example.

Abruzzo is the rustic heart of Italy ... it is Italy the old way ... it hasn't changed for centuries. The foods are simple but sublime; their preparations are artisanal and unforgettably succulent and fragrant, and very, very fresh. Abruzzese cuisine is an undiscovered treasure among Italian cooking. The inspired ways, in which the freshest ingredients are combined to create unforgettable dishes that startle and delight the palate, boggle the taste buds. Theirs is an ancient gastronomy based on what they grow, raise, and catch ... uncontaminated and unpolluted.

*****

# CHAPTER 3

The bed and breakfast inn Hardy had chosen for the tour's stay in Sulmona, located in the historic old town just off Corso Ovidio, the main street in the small city, was a real gem. Sei Stelle, or 'Six Stars,' was the best of all bed and breakfast worlds: the rooms were tastefully decorated with an old palazzo feel and were clean, large, and modernly comfortable. The owner and his family were delightful hosts and went out of their way to be welcoming and helpful. From its balconies you could watch the city come to life each morning in Piazza Garibaldi, with Apennine peaks brooding in the background. Also visible and very much a part of the old town is an ancient medieval aqueduct, seen in some of the rooms of the bread and breakfast as a cut-away feature.

The members of the tour group assembled for breakfast at the pre-arranged hour of seven o'clock, arriving in pairs and singles. It was unusually early for the group to gather the day after arrival but all members had agreed to do so, graciously, since there was some business to attend to before the actual hikes could begin.

They had the option of dining in the small dining room or the interior courtyard. On a fine, June morning, with the sun already a benign, smiling face, they had chosen the courtyard. There was a sleepy but excited buzz among the guests as they breakfasted on fresh-baked goods, sweet and savory crepes, fruit, yogurt, and, of course, coffee. Not your typical Italian breakfast.

With breakfast pretty much over, Hardy stood to begin his housekeeping speech. "Before we actually head out for our first hike I want to examine everyone's equipment to make sure we're all ready for the rigors of the trail. I need to see the items listed under #2 on the 'Things to Bring' sheet which was sent out as part of your tour packet. Let's meet back here in ten minutes. Bring your hiking shoes, socks, raingear, hats, walking poles, buddy packs, trail snacks, sunscreen, insect repellant, and water bottles."

There was a collective groan from the group. "I know, I know," Hardy assured them. "We all want to hit the trail, but experience has taught me that, to quote my mother, 'An ounce of prevention is worth a pound of cure.' Ten minutes, everyone, please."

This was the aspect of leading tour groups that Hardy tolerated. The parenting, as he thought of it. It was, however, the responsibility of leading a tour; that, and collecting the signed liability wavers and pay-in-advance fees. Oh, well … this unpleasant detail would soon be dealt with and the fun could begin.

The Japanese-American couple, Dennis and Teddy, was the first to reappear with their equipment. No problem there. Hardy commented favorably on their choice of footwear and told them they were good to go.

Next came Kelvin Gossett, the priest who'd completed a three-month pilgrimage. Kelvin got a pass, as well.

When Hal Lambeth showed up sporting sneakers for his hiking footwear the alarm bells started going off. When the sneakers were followed up with ankle-high cotton socks Hardy knew he had a problem. "Hal, we're going to have to fit you out in more suitable gear," Hardy informed him. "Most of your supplies are OK," he fudged, "but we need to upgrade your basic gear a bit. The kind of miles we put on our feet, you need more substantial equipment."

A look of doubt washed over Hal's face. "Not to worry," Hardy assured him. "There's a store nearby where they stock what you need. I'll go there with you when I'm done checking everyone out." The doubt on Hal's face settled into a pout, but he nodded his agreement.

Amy Snoddard's gear checked out fine, but Lucy Quickstreet needed walking poles. The ones she'd brought along were for someone much shorter and couldn't be adjusted for height. "Lucy," Hardy explained, "if you use the ones you've got your back and hips will be killing you by the end of the day. Trust me. We can find you a pair that are the appropriate height, and they really won't cost that much." She gave him a smile and a 'thumbs up.'

The twins, Winnie and Tillie, displayed their gear with a superior air that bordered on obnoxious. They thrust it forward for Hardy's inspection like a show-and-tell exhibit, while glancing and sniffing in Hal's direction, signifying they thought he was an idiot. Their meaning was fairly obvious to everyone. Hardy had to admit they did have top-of-the-line stuff, however, and crossed them off his list.

Last up was Peter Fynch, waiting in his well-bred, patient manner. His equipment was the best in the group and well-cared for, Hardy could tell. But, unlike the demonstrative arrogance of the twins, Peter was totally unpretentious and retired, modestly, when Hardy approved his gear.

"Right," Hardy said, looking up from his list. "That's everyone." He paused, considering. "Giuseppe will be picking us up in front of the B&B at half past ten, sharp, to drive us to the starting point of our first hike. We'll be doing walk number ten, a ten kilometer walk between the medieval village of Santo Stefano de Sessanio and the castle of Rocca Calascio. It's about a three and a half hour hike; please make sure you have water with you. Our hosts furnish us complimentary bottles of water, so don't be shy. It's a loop walk, so half way through, at the Refugio della Rocca, you can get a really decent meal. Or, bring your own snacks, whichever you prefer. This area is susceptible to stormy summer weather, but it looks like that won't be a problem for us today.

"I need to take Hal and Lucy out for a few pieces of gear. There are all sorts of shops and cafes within walking distance, since we are in the old part of Sulmona; feel free to explore for a bit. Sulmona is the birthplace of the poet, Ovid, so you will see reminders of him around the city.

"Today being Saturday, it's market day in Sulmona and the Piazza Garibaldi is filled with almost two hundred vendors selling everything from fresh produce to fresh fish, handmade crafts, clothing, you name it. It's an easy opportunity to experience the local culture and glimpse the personalities that make markets so special. I usually pick up meat pies to carry along for a snack." He thought a moment, then asked, "Any questions on converting Euros to dollars?" Shrugs and shaking heads answered him.

"Piazza Garibaldi is an important social hub for the city of Sulmona. Every summer it is the location for a Palio-style horse race and medieval festival known as the Giostra Cavalleresca. On the south side of the Piazza is an old aqueduct which dates back to the twelfth century. It should be easy to spend a few hours exploring on foot and is almost impossible to get lost.

"One last thing, Sulmona is famous for their candied almonds, which the Italians call confetti. You know, the pastel-colored, sugar-coated almonds. Well, this is where the process was perfected, so you see the endlessly hued candies sold in shops here everywhere. They actually make a decent trail snack. That's all for now; enjoy, everyone. And remember, ten thirty, outside the B&B, ready to go."

With that, Hardy headed off toward the shops along Corso Ovidio with Hal and Lucy in tow. Dennis, Teddy, Amy, and Peter headed off toward the market in Piazza Garibaldi. The twins decided on visiting some of the nearby boutiques and cafes along Corso Ovidio, and Kelvin ambled along in their wake.

*****

As scheduled, Giuseppe pulled up in front of Sei Stelle at twenty minutes past ten in a fifteen-passenger, air-conditioned Mercedes van decked out with a refrigerator and mini bar, leather seats, flat screen television, Hi-Fi rack, and DVD player. The van was both spacious and comfortable. On one side of the aisle ran a row of single seats; across the aisle the seats were in pairs. There was a wide, bench seat across the back of the van.

The Bradford twins were the first to board, and they commandeered the dual front seats behind the driver. They immediately began settling in, defining their territory. Hardy took the single seat in front so he could watch where they were going and also stretch out his long, bronzed legs. Kelvin sat directly behind Hardy, and then came Amy and then Lucy. Across the aisle, the seats behind the twins remained empty. Dennis and Peter sat in the next row, with Peter at the window. Teddy sat on the aisle, behind her husband and across from her new friend, Lucy.

Hal stood back as the rest of his group boarded the van for Santo Stefano. He had decided to stay in Sulmona to gradually break in his new hiking shoes instead of heading straight into a designated hike and risking blisters or other foot impediments from new footwear. He would spend the rest of the day prowling among the various eateries in the historic district, expanding the inspiration for his business venture.

*****

# CHAPTER 4

The van headed northwest on the SS17 toward
the village of Barisciano, where they turned
onto SP7 which would take them to their
starting point of the hike, the medieval village
of Santo Stefano di Sessanio. On the way to
Barisciano, they passed through the hilltop
town of Navelli, renowned for its production of
the best quality saffron in the world, Red Gold
saffron, extracted from the vast fields of
crocuses which grow on the Navelli plain.

When the group reached the SP7 at Barisciano
they entered one of Abruzzo's three national
park areas, the Gran Sasso. The road from
Barisciano to Santo Stefano di Sessanio snaked
six miles around mountaintops and over ridges
before straightening on its way into one of the
most beautiful medieval villages in Italy.

Santo Stefano di Sessanio was once a Medici
possession, indicated by the Medici coat of arms
emblazoned on the entrance to the town square,
the Porta Medicea. Due to the Medici's powerful
influence in the wool trade, the village had

prospered as a major area for raising sheep and had been a focal point of the transhumance, the seasonal migration of the sheep between the summer pastures in the mountains of Abruzzo and the winter pastures on the plains of Puglia. This migration of sheep and shepherds had continued for centuries but changed when the world's wool market prices fell. The wool trade was dealt an additional blow by the post-world war emigration from the region.

Today, Santo Stefano is most noted for growing organic gourmet lentils. It is an old, rare variety of lentil that thrives in the poor mountain terrain, growing conditions which contribute to the high iron content of the legume. It is a lentil prized by the best chefs in Italy.

Guiseppe dropped the group at the entrance to the village, since it is an area to be explored on foot or Vespa, and drove around the village to the north, agreeing to meet them at trail's end. He had cousins scattered all throughout Abruzzo, and Santo Stefano was no exception.

The group tumbled out of the van enthusiastically, invigorated by the crisp, clear mountain air carrying the scents of a cultivated landscape and sheep farming. Collectively, they stretched their legs, then individually and in small groups or pairs set off through the village, feeling transported back centuries in time. It was glorious to be alive!

Like a self-contained unit, the twins rushed off in a clear attempt to be free of the rest of the tour group. "The trail to Rocca Calascio starts on the north side of the village where the road junctions," Hardy called after them. But they neglected to acknowledge his advice and forged off on their own.

"Not very sociable, are they?" commented Amy, as she caught up with him. Hardy fought down his impulse to agree, and instead changed the subject.

"Have you been to Santo Stefano before?" he asked.

"No, this is my first time. Lovely little place."

The picturesque village was pristine, the cobblestone streets and vaulted alleyways looked like they had just been swept clean. Terra cotta pots and planters bursting with flowers hung from balconies and decorated stone stairs and entrances to shops and homes throughout the village. Contented cats sunbathed everywhere. It was enchanting. They had stepped back into the Middle Ages.

A fortified hill town built around the year 1000, Santo Stefano di Sessanio had been almost completely abandoned by the middle of the twentieth century. The houses, built together, form the exterior wall that protects the village. These houses were built very high, with thick walls and small square windows, making it easy to defend. The entrances to the stables and barns could only be accessed from outside the town; the living areas for people could only be entered from the narrow streets of the town's interior.

Sitting atop a hill in the middle of a huge valley, the medieval village offers beautiful views of the tapestry of the surrounding Abruzzo countryside. Composed of stone houses with flower-filled balconies topped with terra cotta tile roofs, the ancient village is arranged around meandering narrow lanes paved with stone and joined together by stone archways, many of them tiled with floral motifs. The labyrinth of little streets, here and there meeting in tiny piazzas and sun drenched courtyards, converge near where a lookout tower used to stand.

Hardy and Amy waited for the rest of the group to catch up. "A wealthy businessman from Milan is undertaking major restorations in Santo Stefano and it has become a magnet for elite tourism as well as a center for craftsmen and artisans," Hardy explained. "An earthquake in 2009 caused a total collapse of the village's pride and joy, a crenellated lookout tower built by the Medici in the fourteenth century. Thanks to the town's visionary patron, the project to rebuild the watchtower is well underway." They strolled to the area where the shops began.

"There are some really talented craftspeople who've set up shop throughout Santo Stefano," he continued, "so I know you'll want to spend some time exploring. The pottery is on this street, straight ahead, and there's a weaver's shop where they work on handlooms just around the bend. The weavers produce some stunning wool blankets and throws. The lace maker does very fine work, and there are several little shops that specialize in local, traditional foods like salamis, honeys, jams, mountain cheeses, homemade breads and, get this, jars of wild saffron. Everything you need for a hearty peasant meal. You can find cafes tucked here and there if you want a coffee. It's best to pay in Euros. Some places accept dollars but you pay a premium to use them.

"The starting point of our walk is on the north side of the village. There is a stepped, cobblestone ramp which takes you to where the road junctions. Why don't we meet there in, say, an hour. That is, for those of you who want to walk as a group. If you prefer to walk on your own, that's OK, too ... the trail is pretty straight forward. There is, as I mentioned, a really good place to eat at the half way point, at the Rifugio della Rocca or, if you want, you can buy some of the local foods and make a picnic of it along the way. At any rate, I'll be at our rendezvous point to start the walk to Rocca Calascio. In the meantime, enjoy delving into the village of Santo Stefano."

They ambled off in the same general direction, cameras at the ready, but their paths soon diverged as individual interests dictated. Hardy headed for one of the shops selling local delicacies to stock up on his snack rations and then found his favorite caffè on Piazza Medicea for a strong cappuccino and a healthy dose of people watching in the sun. 'Life couldn't get much better,' he mused.

His attention was caught by a furtive movement off to his left and he turned his head to see Kelvin the ex-priest duck into an archway across the piazza and then poke his head out as though he were spying on someone. Hardy followed the direction of his stare and saw Dennis and Teddy browsing through a display of linen goods on the cobblestone outside one of the artisan shops. When they moved on, Kelvin artfully followed. It was obvious he was stalking them.

After watching this scenario for a few moments Hardy stood up suddenly, a movement deliberately calculated to attract Kelvin's attention. When Kelvin glanced in his direction, Hardy waved his hand, beckoning him to his table. Shooting a quick look at the disappearing Japanese-Americans and looking as though he'd been found out, Kelvin sauntered over to Hardy's table looking slightly sheepish.

"Sleuthing so early in the day?" Hardy opened.

There was a brief, embarrassed silence. "Just having a bit of fun is all," Kelvin lobbed back. "It's a game I often play ... this village with its winding streets is a perfect forum for cat-and-mouse." He quickly changed the subject. "Have you used our driver, Giuseppe, before?"

It was a sudden question. "Ah, no, Kelvin. This is his first time with me, actually. The driver I normally use had to cancel at the last minute and Giuseppe stepped in to take his place ... we're lucky to have him. This time of year everyone is usually booked in advance. Why?"

"No reason," Kelvin answered. "Just curious about my fellow travelers."

Hardy looked at his watch. It was time to head to the meeting place for the walk to Rocca Calascio. He finished his cappuccino and counted out some change to leave on the table. "I need to start for the trail head," he explained to Kelvin. "You coming?"

*****

# CHAPTER 5

Assisted suicide is legal in Switzerland, and several companies facilitating assisted suicides have gone into business to meet the needs of the developing niche market. These assisted-suicide companies cater to Swiss citizens and those beyond Switzerland's borders, giving them the infamous moniker of 'suicide tourism.'

A significant percentage of those opting for death-on-demand have no terminal or progressive illness. They choose a date on the calendar, and on that day they either go to a clinic to end their life or someone ready to help shows up at their door, allowing them to end their life at home.

The practice is, of course, hotly controversial, and has stirred heated debate on both sides of the argument. One Swiss company, in particular, has come under investigation and public scrutiny for charging exorbitant fees for their assistance in production-line death, and was even caught dumping large numbers of crematoria urns containing ashes from its former clients in a local lake.

Raymond and Christine Devaux, from Neuchâtel, Switzerland, owned and operated Un Choix Meilleur, a senior citizen home that emphasized a commitment to healthful living in old age. Un Choix Meilleur, as its name implies, stressed a positive approach to eating well and wisely, and promoted a genuine, loving outlook on life: A Better Choice. The Devauxs frowned on assisted suicide and maintained it is beyond man's authority to decide the hour of his death. In short, that is a determination for God to adjudicate.

The Devauxs organized bus tours to some of the religious shrines of Italy for their more able-bodied seniors, which included some gentle walks to visit quaint churches and shrines off the beaten path. Thus far, they had visited the Cathedral of Turin to pay respects to the famous Shroud of Turin, thought to be the burial shroud of Jesus, as well as numerous relic sites in Rome, among which were several glass-enclosed incorruptibles. Incorruptibles are the bodies of dead saints which, somehow, have escaped deterioration and decay.

Presently, their tour group was en route to the small town of Lanciano, in the region of Abruzzo, to see the holy relics of the first and greatest Miracle of the Eucharist of the Catholic Church. The Catholic Church teaches that, after consecration, the wafer and wine of the Holy Communion actually become the Live Flesh and Live Blood of Jesus.

According to the story behind the Lanciano miracle, in the eighth century in the small Church of St. Legontian a Basilian monk was preparing to sanctify the unleavened bread and wine in celebration of the Holy Mass. The monk doubted the true presence of the flesh and blood of Jesus in the consecrated host. After pronouncing the words of consecration "...This is My Body ... This is My Blood" the monk saw, before his eyes, the host become a living piece of flesh and the wine turn into real blood, which split into five globules of different sizes and shapes.

This Host-Flesh and Host-Blood can be clearly observed, today, in the Church of San Francesco in Lanciano. The Flesh, which has the same dimensions as the host wafer used today in the Catholic Church, is encased in a round gold-silver lunette between two crystals, and the Host-Blood is contained in a chalice of crystal. Both are mounted on an elaborate monstrance designed in silver, and displayed on the altar of the church.

Over the past twelve centuries many bishops from the same diocese as the church in Lanciano have authenticated the relics. No surprise there. However, scientific investigations, performed by an eminent Professor in Anatomy and Pathological Histology and in Chemistry and Clinical Microscopy in the 1970's and again in 1981 yielded the following documented, scientific analyses: the Flesh and Blood are real, belong to the Human species, and have the same blood type-AB; The Blood contains proteins and minerals in the same proportion as that found in human blood; and the preservation of the Flesh and Blood, which were left in their natural state for twelve centuries, exposed to atmospheric and biological agents, is a most extraordinary happening.

The Devauxs happened to believe that this living Flesh and Blood at the little church in Lanciano was a source of continuing miracles, particularly the miracle of healing. They reasoned that, if the hem of Jesus' garment could heal, how much more powerful would His living Flesh and Blood perform in this capacity. To that end, Raymond, Christine, and their charges were going to Lanciano by faith, expecting a miracle. At least that is what Raymond and Christine told the senior citizens on the tour. They were heading to Lanciano to not only see the First Miracle of the Eucharist; they intended to steal it.

Raymond and Christine's group had arrived in Sulmona mid-morning on Saturday when market day was at its peak. Sulmona would be their base as they visited churches and other interesting sites in the Abruzzo region. They checked into Hotel Stella, a nicely refurbished hotel in the medieval part of Sulmona within easy walking distance to the Piazza Garibaldi. The hotel was contemporary in furnishings, and the baths were very modern and beautifully tiled with all the amenities Swiss senior citizens would expect. An added benefit of the Stella was that the tour's twenty-two passenger bus could be parked next to the hotel.

*****

# CHAPTER 6

Hal Lambeth had watched the van depart the bed and breakfast on its first day of hiking and grinned with satisfaction. "That worked out perfectly," he congratulated himself. He had the entire day to see to 'business,' as he called it. And it wasn't the restaurant business.

He set off along Corso Ovidio, passing Piazza Garibaldi on his right with Saturday's market in full swing. The huge square was filled with shoppers strolling amongst the many vendors on a perfectly glorious, sun-filled morning. The air was alive with hawkers' cries and a plethora of delectable aromas from the various baked goods, cheeses, and charcuterie. Corso Ovidio was lined with charming old buildings sporting graceful arches and stone balconies enclosed in wrought iron containing a variety of small shops, boutiques, and cafes. He felt conspicuous, and silly, wearing his madras pork pie hat but it was his means of identifying himself to someone he'd never met before. He was so intent on his destination, Café des Artistes, that he almost walked right by its entrance.

The caffè was only half full at this time of morning, so he had his choice of seats and lodged himself at a small table for two near the rear wall. He was right on time. Hal doffed his hat, placing it on the table's edge where it couldn't possibly go unnoticed, and ordered a caffè corretto with just a drizzle of grappa. He was suddenly overwhelmed with a sense of the old country and felt a kinship and warmth for his mother's humble origins.

So lost was he in his musing that he neglected to notice a scowl-faced man in his forties approach his table. It was the man's stale cologne, mixed with sour sweat, that woke him from his reverie and Hal looked up, startled.

"Signore Paolini?" the man queried.

"Yes," Hal assured him, "I am Mr. Paolini."

The odd little man switched to English. "Signore DiSalle asks that you accompany me," he said. "This way, please," he added, motioning to the rear of the caffè.

Hal placed two Euros under the edge of his saucer, grabbed his hat, and followed. They passed through a rear door of the caffè, into an aisle leading through a storage room and exited onto a narrow alley out back. Turning left, then right, and left, again, they arrived at a tiny piazza, surrounded by old, three-story limestone buildings divided into roomy apartments on each floor.

Hal followed his escort diagonally across the little square to an archway-fronted grey apartment on the ground floor. The heavy recessed door, ornate in carved wood, swung open on large metal hinges, groaning slightly. The two men entered and the little man, standing to one side, said only, "Signore Paolini," and ducked back out the door, nodding at the doorkeeper as he left.

The concierge ushered Hal through a decorated, double wooden door off to the right in the entrance hall. Hal, hat in hand, found himself standing in a handsomely furnished room with floor-to-ceiling windows overlooking a modest-sized but well-landscaped garden. The heavy, faded velvet sepia drapes had been pulled back and secured by satin braided cords with thick, tasseled knots on the end, allowing natural light to flood the room. An Italian Regency cabriole leg desk in walnut oyster burl graced the far end of the room in front of the garden windows.

Behind the desk, his back to the window, sat an elegantly dressed man, hair graciously graying at the temples. He was almost dandyish in his immaculate light gray suit and pale pink dress shirt with Italian silk tie and matching pocket square.

Before Hal could take another step into the room he was set upon by two men who professionally and thoroughly frisked him and then stood back, nodding at the man behind the desk. Hal was completely disconcerted by the search and wondered, briefly, if he was making a mistake.

"Mr. Paolini?" the man behind the desk queried.

"Yes ... er, no. Well," Hal stumbled, "my name is Hal Lambeth, but my mother was Maria Chiara Paolini ... my grandfather is ... was Vincenzo Alfredo Paolini, from Sulmona."

At mention of Vincenzo Paolini the man behind the desk's face lit with a warm smile. "Aaah!" he uttered. "Vincenzo's grandson!" He rose from his worn leather desk chair, moved out from behind his desk, and approached Hal, arms outstretched.

He grabbed Hal by the shoulders and leaned forward, cheek-kissing him on both cheeks. Hal, somewhat taken aback, stifled his embarrassment and went with the flow. Standing back, the older man studied Hal's face. "Yes," he told himself, softly, "you have your grandfather's pudgy nose and his hazel eyes." Thus satisfied, he inquired, businesslike, "Now, Signore Lambeth Paolini, how can I help you?"

"Well," Hal began, nervously clearing his throat, "I was hoping you and I could go into business together."

*****

Armando DiSalle was a disarming, handsome sixty-year-old native of Sulmona, Italy. His tanned, squarish head with strong jaw line was almost devoid of wrinkles and the skin on his face was taut and youthful looking. His graying hair was abundant and always perfectly trimmed and styled, as was the hint of an abbreviated pencil mustache that followed the curved contour of his upper lip.

Armando could have passed for everyone's favorite uncle. He'd married at the age of nineteen and pledged his heart and fortune to his young bride who, deciding his fortune was inadequate, gave her favors to an older, wealthier merchant. Cuckolded and silently enraged, Armando DiSalle had bided his time and, when he deemed it the right moment, strangled the love of his life and stuffed her body in a vat of sulfuric acid ... a lupara bianca or 'white shotgun' death where the body disappears, dissolved in acid. Two days later it was as if she never existed, which suited Armando just fine.

Something twisted and perverse took hold of Armando after he killed his Concetta. Heretofore a mild-mannered, hot-blooded son of an Italian farmer, Armando found he enjoyed inflicting death and fear on people, and began to practice regularly on opponents while he built his fortune and reputation as a drug dealer shuttling heroin between Albania, Milan, and points west through the region's main port town of Pescara. Funds from the drug trade were then funneled through his construction and trash collection enterprises as a means of laundering his illegally gotten wealth.

His success in the illegal drug trade caught the attention of the Casalesi clan of the Camorra in Caserta Province in neighboring Campania. DiSalle was becoming wealthy and the Casalesi wanted let in on the action. DiSalle realized he was no match for the well-established crime family so he agreed, purely in the interests of self-preservation, to open his fledgling organization to the Casalesis and operate under the sanction of the Casalesis clan.

The Camorra, or Neopolitan mafia, has been in existence since the mid-1800's, originating as a prison gang in Naples. Once out of prison, the gang members recruited more members, forming clans, which continued to grow more and more powerful.

Because of its gang origins, the Camorra differs from the Sicilian mafia in that its structure is horizontal while the Sicilian crime families are pyramidal with the most powerful position at the apex of the pyramid. When top Camorra leaders are imprisoned or killed they are easily and readily replaced with new leaders and clans germinating from the demise of the fallen, rather like a flatworm regenerating itself.

The Camorra is more egalitarian; it is not uncommon to find a thirty-year-old heading a clan with fifty-year-olds working for him. The clans act independently of one another, often feuding among themselves and gaining wealth or influence at the expense of each other. It is not a crime organization based on blood relations, as is the 'Ndrangheta, or Calabrese mafia. While the 'Ndrangheta gets its strength and impenetrability from the blood relationships and marriages that make up its crime families, the Camorra values its members on what they do to advance their criminal interests ... it's all about their street value.

Unlike the Sicilian mob, which operates somewhat like a men's club, many women hold positions of power within the Camorra, giving rise to madrinas, or godmothers, in the various clans. In Neopolitan society, which is matriarchal, women typically raise the children and run the household, which puts them in charge of family monies. With Camorra women these skills easily translate to controlling interest rates for loan sharks as well as paying local kids to keep a lookout for the police. Raising children, steeping them in a life of crime, and arranging marriages for their offspring provide the women opportunities to strategically increase their clan's influence, social prestige, and even create new clans. Also included in their duties are processing drugs, i.e. cutting and repackaging cocaine and heroin in their kitchens, and looking after crime bosses in hiding.

Increasingly, as their men are killed or imprisoned, the wives, daughters, sisters, and sisters-in-law are moving into leadership positions, wielding guns, commanding executions and committing murders themselves. They have the clout, and they hold the reins. And they, too, are being gunned down and going to prison.

The Camorra initially specialized in cigarette smuggling and received payoffs for all cigarettes smuggled throughout Italy. The Sicilian mob convinced the Camorra to use its established cigarette smuggling routes for moving illegal drugs. Not all leaders of the Camorra agreed to this conversion to drug trafficking and the Camorra Wars ensued in the 1970's with nearly four hundred men murdered and those opposed to drug smuggling the losers.

The big money maker for the Camorra came in 1980 when a devastating earth quake hit southern Italy. The Neapolitan mafia skimmed thirty two billion Euros from state reconstruction funds when they landed many of the reconstruction contracts with the aid of their political patronage.

Through brutal violence, political connections, and local leadership, the Camorra embeds itself into the basic fibers of Italian society, exercising influence and control at local and national levels, using their network to continually extend their domination and increase their wealth.

In the 1990's the criminal clans of the Camorra moved into the business of waste disposal in the region of Campania, with disastrous results for the environment and health of the local population. The Camorra's total disregard for public and environmental safety should be considered crimes against humanity.

Heavy metal, industrial waste, and toxic chemicals are often dumped along roadsides and burned, releasing toxic waste and fumes into the air and soil. Dangerous waste is mixed into cement slated for construction and the waste is now part of buildings all over Naples. Slurries of PCB have been misrepresented as fertilizer and compost and spread over agricultural lands. One result of this gross, deliberate negligence is a liver cancer rate among men that is 2.5 times higher than the national average in an area of Campania known as the Triangle of Death.

Armando DiSalle's primary motive in meeting Hal Lambeth was greed, pure and simple. The 'Vincenzo's grandson' routine had been an emotional touch to bond with the stupid American and gain his confidence; nothing more. He had nothing to lose and everything to gain if things worked out with the American fool.

He'd been looking for an entré into shipping illegal drugs into the United States for months and exporting Italian groceries to an American restaurateur was perfect. When Hal presented his business proposal to Armando it afforded DiSalle the opportunity he'd been looking for and even though he thought Hal a bit of a buffoon he was a buffoon DiSalle could control, IF he could be trusted. So Armando had clapped Hal on the back in camaraderie, shaken his hand with gusto, and sent him on his way giddy with the prospect of making a lot of money in a very short time. No problem.

"Put Black Maria on him, now," DiSalle had told his majordomo, Ugo. "I want to know who he talks to and where he goes; if he's a rat, I want to know. Sooner rather than later. Capisce?"

*****

# CHAPTER 7

The group of hikers strolled along at a leisurely pace after leaving the village of Santo Stefano di Sessanio, modifying their gait as the trail rose in gradual elevation and then fell away again. Down the hill, to their left, the narrow fields cultivated in mustard greens and poppies were riotous in yellows and reds. There was an undercurrent of murmuring and buzzing as the insects worked the blossoms; all was right with the world.

Lucy spied Peter at the head of the group and increased her pace until she caught up with him then fell into step beside him on the narrow path. He glanced in her direction and acknowledged her with a nod and the ghost of a smile.

"So, we're from the same part of the country, eh?" she asked, breaking in on his thoughts.

"Connecticut, right?" he responded.

"Near Norwich," she replied. "Ledyard, actually. I manage at Foxwoods."

"The casino or hotel?"

"Both."

He was impressed. "A lot of money flows through that place. My wife and I stayed there two years ago; I lost my shirt on a high-limit table." She saw his face tense at mention of his wife who, everyone in the group knew, had died recently after a prolonged illness.

"Let me guess .... chemin de fer?" she asked, referring to a form of baccarat commonly called 'chemmy.' He nodded. "You're lucky it was only your shirt," she said. Their pace had slowed a bit as they conversed but Peter now picked it up again, signaling the end of the conversation. 'Well, that was a start, at least,' she thought. They continued on in a companionable silence.

The morning passed uneventfully for the hikers. They lunched at a great little restaurant near the ruins of an ancient fortress and began the trek back to where they left the van. The hike back was unremarkable and, mostly, downhill. The hikers got into a steady rhythm and made good time, arriving at the car park on the northeast edge of Santo Stefano with time to spare.

Giuseppe wasn't in the van and Kelvin glimpsed him leaning against a narrow gap in the wall of what was called 'La Buscela,' a secret place where young lovers met in medieval times to steal kisses. Giuseppe's back was toward Kelvin and he didn't hear the ex-priest approaching

"I have someone I can call for the information you seek, Signore," Giuseppe was saying. "It will cost a lot of money, what you ask ... can you get such a large sum of money?"

"Don't worry about the money, Giuseppe," was the reply. "This is worth a lot of money to us and we're willing to invest in your helping us get it. Just make sure you tell no one else about what we're doing. The element of surprise needs to be on our side."

Kelvin beat a hasty retreat to a small shop on a nearby piazza where he pretended to look through a selection of post cards, all the while keeping his eyes on the alley to see who emerged. Giuseppe came out first, slewing his eyes left and right before he stepped into the piazza.

"Oh, you are definitely a weasel, Giuseppe," Kelvin muttered to himself. He kept his eyes focused on the entrance to the alley, waiting to see if anyone else would follow Giuseppe. He was rewarded when Tillie and Winnie Bradford breezed into the little square, their jaws set, a hard look in their eyes. "And I wonder what you two are up to," he mused.

\*\*\*\*\*

Hal spent the rest of the afternoon strolling around the old town part of Sulmona after his meeting with Armando DiSalle. He stopped at two different cafes and tried several local specialties, even buying some finger food from a street vendor hawking her wares on the main avenue that ran into Piazza Garibaldi. He poked his head into a souvenir shop and tried on hats in a men's clothing store he'd discovered hidden away in a quiet courtyard.

Black Maria soon got bored tailing him. It was a child's game, following the American clown, but DiSalle had been insistent that he be watched so watch him she would.

From further south in Italy, Black Maria was a member of one of the Camorra clans and had moved into an active role in her clan's illegal activities after her husband had been gunned down by a rival clan. They'd had no children so Maria cooled her grief by a thirst for revenge, taking his place on the street to further their clan's control and influence by increased power and ill-gotten wealth.

Maria was not unattractive; not what you'd call a beauty but all five-feet-seven of her was muscle and meanness. Her darkened skin, perpetual scowl, and insatiable appetite for revenge had earned her the moniker of Black Maria and it was a name she more than lived up to. Things had gotten a bit tense in her native province of Caserta near Naples after she'd done a drive by assassination on a Vespa, so she'd been transferred to Sulmona while things cooled off back home. It was proving to be a punitive exile. She'd been given shit jobs that any idiot could do; at this rate she'd lose her street edge.

*****

The main topic at table that night, as the entire group dined together, was sacred objects and their place in society. Amy started the ball rolling.

"Italy has simply masses of religious relics, and the Catholic Church has them all under lock and key."

"What would you expect The Church to do, Amy, leave them lying around for people to pick up and handle ... and then put in their pockets and walk off with?" Dennis asked her.

"No, of course not. I mean, well, the relics should be more available to the public, I think. What good are they all locked up where no one can see them?"

"But the public can see them. Most of them, anyway," Peter volunteered. "It's true, the Vatican hides lots of loot away from the laity. Only Heaven itself knows what all The Church has accumulated through the centuries and what is stored in the vaults underneath the Vatican. You can see incorruptible saints, and various artifacts under glass. Like a museum. The Church is rather a repository for religious valuables, as it should be. A religious museum, if you will."

"But what about the poor who can't make it to Rome or wherever to see these relics?" Amy shot back. "It seems they should have access to these pieces of history and faith, too."

"Have you been to the National Archives in Washington, DC to see the Constitution of the United States?" Peter asked.

"Of course I have," Amy answered.

"Well ...?"

"But that's different," Amy persisted. "I'm not poor and I had the money to visit the nation's capital."

"It's true that Rome seems to have the market share of the church's religious artifacts," conceded Peter, "but there are lots of relics in small village churches all over Italy. The Church has made a point of maintaining the relics in the specific churches where the artifacts originated."

"We're missing something important here," Lucy interjected. "To a Native American all things having to do with our beliefs and ancestors are vital to our continued spiritual health.

"For decades the museums in the States contained exhibits displaying bones from dead Indians, headdresses, totems, masks, and all sorts of sacred objects. Indian burial sites were plundered and the bones of our forbearers hauled off to a museum, which is totally against our belief that these remains have to be cared for by their tribe and put to rest in the earth to complete the life cycle. It is a balance that must be maintained. The masks and headdresses physically embody spirits and they are not meant to be locked behind glass in a display case.

"Our Elders believe that messing around with these sacred artifacts and showing a lack of respect for them has resulted in the social woes which plague Native Americans: alcoholism, suicide, domestic violence. They believe that if these sacred objects are returned to their rightful places our people will be healed and restored. That's as a Native American. But, it makes me wonder if the same principle could also apply to the various artifacts The Church has taken possession of, as well."

"Good point, Lucy," agreed Amy. "When's the last time the Shroud of Turin has been seen? The other thing that bothers me is that The Church has total control of all the sacred objects and it seems to make a lot of money exploiting them."

"Exploiting is a rather ugly word, don't you think?" asked Kelvin. "I tend to think of The Church more as a caretaker of precious objects which have been entrusted to it."

The twins had offered no opinion to the discussion so far. Peter turned to Tillie and asked, "What's your view on this, Tillie?"

Tillie stiffened slightly and glanced quickly at Winnie, who pretended not to have heard. "I have no opinion on the matter," she finally replied. "Religion is one of those topics I avoid like the plague," she added flippantly. "Now, if you'll excuse me, I've had a tiring day and have some letters to write before I turn in for the night. She extricated herself from the dinner table and started for the door, stopped and turned back. "Coming, Winnie?"

"I'll be along shortly," Winnie replied. After Tillie departed Winnie picked up the thread of the conversation. "I've often wondered if keeping all these old bones and other relics around isn't tantamount to idolatry. Aren't they on display as an object of worship?"

"No, not at all," Peter answered her. "They serve as an example toward what we should strive in our spiritual lives. They are for the purpose of edification."

"Interesting," Winnie mused. "I know that the majority of sacred relics seem to be in Rome, but in the country side so many small churches have artifacts on display within the churches themselves. It must be a source of inspiration for the worshippers. But in today's environment I am amazed that you don't hear of them being stolen out of the churches ... it isn't like the relics are in a secure vault."

It was Kelvin who spoke, softly but forcefully. "That would be a serious sacrilege, Winnie. Your soul would be forfeit, I'm afraid."

She flashed a brilliant, phony smile. "That's a sobering thought, isn't it? On that note, I think I'll turn in for the night. Hardy, are we still on for the walk to the San Bartolomeo hermitage tomorrow?"

"Weather permitting, Winnie," he responded. To the group at large he said, "Plan on breakfast tomorrow at eight thirty or nine ... Giuseppe will be here with the van at ten and we'll leave shortly after. Everyone, make sure you have ample bottled water and some snacks. Bring your swim suits and a change of clothes, since we'll stop at a spa on the way home. And plan on a picnic lunch tomorrow."

The hikers said their goodnights and headed off to their rooms.

*****

# CHAPTER 8

The following morning when Hardy went down to breakfast he bumped, literally, into a young woman who backed into him as she was leaving the courtyard used for dining. The contents from the pitcher of milk she carried slopped down the front of her blouse.

"Damn!" she muttered, then seeing Hardy's face, hastened to add, lightly, "It's not your fault. It's just my lot in life."

She was in her early twenties, Hardy judged, and quite good looking. Blond hair, cut short, fitted her shapely head like a wind-blown cap. Her intelligent eyes were a startling aquamarine, set off by the light teal color of the silk blouse draping her graceful figure. All in all, very pleasing, he decided.

"American?" he asked. The accent was mid-western, he thought.

She nodded. "Ohio. I'm a farm girl. Visiting my uncle for the summer."

He waited for her to explain and when she didn't asked, "And who's your uncle?" She smelled like fresh lemons, he thought.

"Oh!" she exhaled, embarrassed that she wasn't making sense. "My uncle owns the Sei Stelle. His daughter, my cousin, is studying in the States for the summer so he hired me to fill in for her."

"Lucky you! Is this your first visit to Italy?"

She nodded happily. "It is," she said, "and I love it here!" She gave Hardy a brief once over. "Are you the guy with the hiking group from the States? Durkin, isn't it?"

"Yeah, but please, call me Hardy."

"I'm Honey," she told him. 'You certainly are,' he thought, 'Sweet!' She suddenly realized milk was dripping from the pitcher onto the floor in a small puddle. "Gosh! I need to clean up this mess before my aunt sees it. She's not easy going like Uncle Dante. I'll see you later, Hardy." She bustled off with her hand cupped under the pitcher to catch any drips.

"I hope so, Honey," he called after her as she ducked into the kitchen. It was an interesting development, he thought.

*****

Piazza Garibaldi was teeming with life that sunny Sunday morning. Church bells peeling out in a spectrum of pitches and tones playing different cadences orchestrated a cacophony of sounds inviting life to be lived joyously.

Giuseppe showed up a few minutes late apologizing profusely.

"I saw someone I know, Vito, down at Hotel Stella as I was driving past and had to say 'Ciao,'" he explained. "He's driving a bus for a group from Switzerland; they're heading to San Bartolomeo today, as well."

"Then let's get on the road ahead them," Hardy suggested.

*****

The hour-long drive from Sulmona to Caramanico Terme and beyond to Decontra passed quickly for Hardy's cadre of hikers. The scenery was spectacular as the van wound like a giant serpent up and down valleys and through mountain passes to the constant low murmur of quiet conversation and the 'click-click' of Winnie's knitting needles as she whiled away the trip trying out a new stitch pattern for a vest she'd designed.

Decontra is a traditional village of rustic buildings set in the heart of the Majella National Park, perched on the edge of a dramatic gorge surrounded by meadows and mountains. One story goes that the first people who lived in Decontra were outcasts and rebels from villages further down the mountain who had been kicked out by law abiding fellow citizens and sent packing.

Giuseppe parked the van near a church soon after entering the village and the group disembarked. Hardy rechecked the back pack he always wore for basic medical supplies, splints, ace bandages, and insect repellent.

The twins set off, at a fast pace, both wearing a Panama hat like the kind you buy from J. Peterman, leaving the rest of the group behind. Everyone had on a hat of some sort for protection against the southern Italian sun as it beat down from above and reflected off the rock around them. Peter and Kelvin, both avid Red Sox fans, wore dark blue baseball caps with a red bill sporting a big red 'B' for Boston. Hal had donned his madras pork pie, and Hardy wore a straw panama with wide brim and braided leather strap. Lucy and Amy both wore wide-brimmed sport hats with mesh ventilation on the sides and a back veil to keep the sun off their necks. Dennis and Teddy had matching light-weight, khaki-colored canvas safari hats.

They set out at a steady, leisurely pace. Somewhere in the distance bells tinkled on sheep as they grazed the high mountain pastures. After passing an old well that looked like a stone bee hive they rambled through meadows alive with butterflies, little lizards, and bright, showy red moths. Bees buzzed. Cicadas hummed. Larks soared and sang overhead. Flowers, including wild orchids in an array of colors, carpeted the grasslands around them and the scent of herbs perfumed the air. Occasionally, the troupe overtook other walkers or met them as they returned after finishing their hike.

They crossed over a small stream bed and the trail all but disappeared, leading them through very rocky pastureland, past a tholos, an ancient stone shepherd's shelter built in the shape of a beehive and peculiar to the Majella.

The uniqueness of the tholos is that it is a form of construction with dry stonework that doesn't use cement and relies on concentric and tapered overlapping of stones to create a vaulted building that will not collapse, contrary to accepted engineering fundamentals of erecting arches and vaults. Construction of tholos fulfilled a dual purpose: the structures were used as shelter, and gathering the stones for the construction of the tholos freed up additional grazing lands. Many such huts in the Majella are still used today, either as shelter for shepherds or livestock, or for storage.

When they arrived at the lip of the gorge Hardy paused for his group to catch up. Dennis was the first to arrive.

"Outstanding!" he exclaimed, gazing across at the band of cliffs under which a Celestinian hermitage had been built into the rock face sometime before the year 1000 AD. "How do we get over there?" There were exclamations and grunts of appreciation as the other hikers caught up and saw what had for centuries been used as a refuge for both the pious and the persecuted.

"That," said Hardy, pointing, "is the Hermitage of San Bartolomeo di Legio. Saint Bartholomew, according to the Catholic Church, is famous as a miracle worker. He is credited with curing mental health problems, headaches, convulsions, and paralysis."

He began a careful descent into the gorge, paused, and turned back. "He is also the patron saint of butchers and tanners," he added, as an aside. The rest of the entourage followed, picking their way carefully as they descended. They crossed a little river at the bottom of the gorge by way of a natural bridge made of large boulders.

They prepared to climb the path on the other side, but stood aside as a group of about fifteen older men and women, in their fifties and sixties, led by a younger man and woman, headed for the stone bridge. Spry and athletic looking, they spoke French, had an excited air about them as they hiked, and their day packs sported Swiss flag patches. Most of them clasped a tightly closed carafe of water which each person carried reverentially.

When the larger group had passed, Hardy led the way up to the left side of the hermitage to an ancient stone stairway ending at a precipitous terrace overlooking the valley below. An enormous rock roof overhung the length of the balcony. At one end of the stone veranda a small chapel had been hewn out of the rock.

Inside, opposite the chapel door, water trickled out from under a square stone and collected in a basin dug out of the floor.

"This water is considered holy and used in healing miracles," Hardy explained. "It's supposed to be effective for healing sores and wounds, and is miraculous for healing children's illnesses. It is also used as a last hope for the dying. Pilgrims come here to gather it to give it to those in need. That's probably what was in the carafes the other group of hikers carried."

Hardy backed out of the church and retraced his steps along the sculpted stone balcony to an opening in the wall.

"And this," he said, pointing upward, "is called the Holy Staircase. It leads to the top of the cliff. You can also reach this hermitage coming from another direction, from a small village called Roccamorice. The monks cut a hole through the roof of the cliff and carved these stone steps to access the hermitage from the roof. The stairway is called the Holy Staircase because pilgrims navigate the steps on their knees, while praying.

"Pope Celestine the Fifth liked to stay in this hermitage to meditate and escape to tranquility." He paused. "That's my spiel for the hermitage; I imagine you all would like some time to explore and just get the feel of the place. I'll be in one of the cells or on the balcony if I'm needed."

Dennis and Teddy went back to the little church to study the frescoes above the entrance. Hal dodged between them and ducked inside the chapel. Lucy and Kelvin stood at different points along the stone balcony contemplating the view; Peter stood at the bottom of the staircase with his back to the steps, leaning over the balcony wall. Amy was just preparing to climb the steps when a medium-sized boulder came hurtling down the opening. She gave a shout, at the same time jerking on Peter's fanny pack with all her might to pull him out of harm's way. The rock skidded over the top of the balcony's wall and down into the valley below. A fist-sized chunk of stone broke off the boulder when it hit the top of the wall and glanced off the back of Peter's head. He collapsed in a heap with a bloody gash where the stone had hit.

Lucy and Kelvin rushed over to where Peter lay; Kelvin dashed up the staircase and out of sight. Hardy poked his head out of a cell along the balcony at Amy's shout and, seeing a body lying on the balcony floor, grabbed his back pack and raced over to where Lucy and Amy knelt at Peter's side.

"What happened?" he asked kneeling by Peter. With the help of Amy and Lucy, Hardy gently rolled Peter over on his side so he could examine where the rock had hit his head.

"I don't know," gasped Amy. "I was just going to climb the steps to the top and I saw this huge rock flying through the air, right at Peter, so I shouted and pulled him out of the way. The damn thing just missed him. When it hit the top of the wall a big piece broke off and hit him in the back of the head." Suddenly, the realization hit her. "My God! If that boulder had hit him it would have killed him!"

Hardy studied Amy's face, briefly, and knew what she said was true. She was pale and trembling, her face drawn. Just then Kelvin returned and knelt next to Hardy. It was getting crowded on the narrow balcony, so Lucy moved away to give them more room.

"How is he?" Kelvin asked Hardy.

"He's been knocked out, but his breathing seems normal. Nasty cut on the back of his head, though."

He rummaged in his backpack and pulled out an Instant-Ice pack, shook it, and pressed it ever so gently on the lump growing on the back of Peter's head. Peter moaned. His eyes fluttered open, and he groaned. Suddenly, Peter started to vomit, so Hardy held his head turned to the side, keeping Peter's airway clear so he could breathe.

"Ooh, crap," he mumbled. "Where am I?"

"We're on the balcony at the hermitage, Peter, remember?" Hardy prodded.

"What happened?"

"You got hit on the head by a rock ... can you sit up?"

Hardy and Kelvin helped him sit up and propped him up against the wall under the overhang of the cliff, out of the bright sunlight. Lucy had wet a handkerchief in the holy water in the chapel and used it to sponge Peter's face. Dennis, Teddy, and Hal followed along, not realizing anything was amiss.

"What's goin' on?" Hal asked.

"Where have you been?" Kelvin asked him.

"What? Uh, we've been in the chapel, the three of us. Why? What's the matter with Peter?"

"He was hit in the head with a rock and knocked out," Kelvin explained. He looked at Amy. "Did you see or hear anything when it happened, Amy?"

Amy looked startled at his question. "Well, no. I didn't. I mean, it was so weird, the way it happened."

"Weird how?" Hardy asked her. She pursed her lips in thought.

"Well, before I saw the boulder flying down the stairs I got the impression someone was up there. But I didn't see anybody. And we were all down here."

Kelvin spoke up. "I heard a noise like someone scuttling off over the rocks. That's why I ran up top."

"Did you see anything?" asked Hardy.

Kelvin shook his head. "It was a boulder the size of a basketball, Hardy. There aren't any big rocks on the roof of the hermitage ... there's just small rocks, and scrabble." There was silence while the possibility of what Kelvin had just said sunk in.

"Where are the twins?" Dennis asked. The group fell silent; no one spoke.

'Good question, Dennis,' Kelvin thought to himself.

Teddy said what everyone else was thinking, "Those two are really bizarre, if you ask me. It's like they're always up to something." No one in the group responded verbally to Teddy's comment, but the body language spoke volumes.

'Not good,' Hardy thought. Aloud, he said, "Let's not even go there." His focus returned to Peter, who was still sitting upright. "How you feeling, Peter? Do you think you can stand up, or do you want to sit a while longer?" He pulled a can of spray antibiotic and some gauze and tape out of his ruck sack, along with a pair of scissors.

Lucy was back after another trip to the little stone church to soak her handkerchief and she was gently daubing the gash on Peter's head with it. Peter let out a low howl.

"Easy does it, Peter," she said. "This is supposed to be holy water ... good for healing cuts and wounds. Maybe we'll see a miracle and you'll be healed." She paused, and then grinned. "Anyway, it can't hurt, right?" Peter gave her a feeble but thankful smile.

"My turn," announced Hardy, spraying the antibiotic on Peter's wound in short spurts. He made a thick bandage out of many layers of sterilized gauze pads and gingerly placed it over the wound. Kelvin wound a strip of gauze around Peter's head several times, holding the bandage in place. He cut several lengths of tape and handed them to Hardy, who finished taping the dressing in place.

Next, Hardy emptied a packet of Emergen-C into a bottle of water and shook it lightly to dissolve the crystals.

"Here," he said, handing the bottle to Peter. "Drink this, slowly. It'll help replenish the salts you lost from the trauma."

Peter dutifully took the bottle offered him and sipped it, slowly. Gradually, the color started to return to his skin and his body relaxed; he was feeling a bit better. Hardy and Kelvin helped him to his feet and steadied him while he regained his sense of balance. They watched as he tottered slowly along the balcony, and then walked back toward them. Teddy, Lucy, and Amy huddled together at the far end of the terrace; Dennis and Hal hovered near Hardy.

"Do you think you'll be able to make it back to the van?" Hal asked Peter as he ambled past.

"Is there another option?" Peter asked, wryly. "Yeah, I'll make it back ... just give me a few more minutes to get my legs steady."

When they finally started the return leg of the hike Kelvin and Hardy stayed on either side of Peter while he clambered down the steps from the hermitage to the river crossing. The sun's warmth kept shock at bay for Peter, but it made Kelvin and Hardy sweat profusely as they helped Peter along.

It was a juggling act to get the three of them across the bridge of boulders. Hardy fell in the stream once and swore, but they finally reached the other side and headed up to the top of the gorge on the other side of the river.

Two thirds of the way up they stopped at a grassy spot to rest and eat the picnic foods they'd brought along. There were a few beech trees to afford light shade, and with the breeze that rustled through the grass it was a refreshing stop for everyone. The remainder of the hike to Decontra was slow but uneventful.

When they reached the van Peter hoisted himself aboard and sank, gratefully, into the row of seats at the back while the rest of the group took a short stroll through the village. He was soon asleep. Sometime later, he was awakened by voices outside the van. He caught snatches of a conversation.

"... from Abruzzo? Village ... Lanciano ... miracle in church." There was a pause and a different voice answered back, but he couldn't make it out. Then the first voice was talking again. "... miracle locked up ... visit ... time ... accessible? Secluded?"

The other voice, again too low to hear from inside the van, answered back. There was a chorus of 'thank yous' and 'ciao' and silence. But not for long. The next voice Peter heard was that of a woman, demanding, snarling. The man's voice answered back, staying low and calm. Not good enough. The woman's voice rose in anger and volume.

"Lanciano? ... What did you tell them? You're not helping them, are you? What about our agreement?" She was shot-gunning him with questions.

The man's voice was careful ... reassuring ... nonchalant. "Yes, the deal is still on. No, I'm not going back on our agreement. They're Swiss; they were just curious. Not to worry." He felt the vehicle jar slightly as someone started to step into the van, so he let his head fall forward as though asleep. He waited a moment and then peeked out from under his eyelids to see that Giuseppe had climbed on board, followed by Winnie Bradford.

*****

On the return trip the van stopped in the medieval town of Caramanico Terme for the group to enjoy the mineral waters and hot springs of Abruzzo's best known thermal resort. The mineral waters there, which are therapeutic for a variety of ailments, have the highest sulphur content of mineral waters in Europe.

"Oh, my goodness!" Teddy cooed, as she soaked in the warm, healing liquid. "I feel like I'm in a warm womb ... I don't ever want to leave," she sighed.

"This was a great idea, Hardy, stopping here," Dennis commented. To his wife he said, "We should come back next year and stay for several days ... get the whole treatment. Mud baths, massages, even the inhalation therapy."

"I'm having a massage after my soak," Hardy said. "The masseurs employed here are excellent. You won't even feel your body after a soak and a massage. Oh, and the mineral water, called Pisciarello, is a good way to detox but it is a diuretic," he warned. "The 'La Salute' is a mineral water used for digestive problems. They have both here." To Peter, he said, "If you start to feel light-headed take a few minutes to cool down a bit. And if you decide to have a massage you should probably make it a light one."

"How's the head, Peter?" Hal asked.

"Better," replied Peter. He had removed the bandage from his head and was gently soaking himself in the waters. "This is really soothing."

The Bradford twins were soaking at the far end of the pool. "What happened to you two today?" Hardy inquired. There was a bit of a delay before Tillie responded.

"Did something happen to us today?" she said, a bit stiffly.

Winnie jumped in, trying to defuse Tillie, "We visited the hermitage, same as you ... we just seem to walk faster than the rest of the group. But," she added, "we saw you arrive at San Bartolomeo's ... we were just leaving as you arrived."

"Really?" Lucy quizzed. "I don't remember seeing you, at all."

Tillie's face iced over but before she could say anything Winnie chimed in, "We left when you were peering into the chapel at the far end of the stone balcony."

"So you just missed the whole scene with Peter almost getting killed," Lucy persisted.

Tillie's face flushed with indignation. "Are you checking up on us?" she demanded.

"No, of course not," Hardy interjected, trying to avoid a scene. "But I am responsible for the safety of all of you while we're traipsing about. Peter had a close call today. I just wondered where you were. It's a legitimate concern, is all."

His explanation pacified Tillie, who then said to Peter, "It must have been a freak accident, and Peter ... I'm glad you weren't seriously injured."

It sounded patently insincere and after she said it Winnie shot a quick look at Kelvin, who caught the look and wondered, 'Maybe it wasn't an accident ... maybe Peter was the wrong target ... we're roughly the same build, and we were both wearing the same hat on the hike ...'

*****

# CHAPTER 9

At Hardy's urging Peter decided he would stay behind at the bed and breakfast in Sulmona the next morning and forego the trip to Scanno. He was feeling much, much better, but had a slight headache. Lucy offered to stay behind, as well, but Peter wouldn't hear of it. She stayed, anyway. She knew about head injuries, she said, and you just never knew. Hardy restocked the first aid supplies in his backpack, made sure everyone had sufficient water and snacks, checked that his Garmin Oregon GPS was charged, and they set off for their next hike.

The mountainous road from Sulmona to Scanno is spectacular as it weaves through the narrow, rocky Sagittario Gorge. It was left for Giuseppe to negotiate the serpentine route and blind hairpin turns, climbing almost steadily in elevation, while the tour group marveled at the panorama unfolding with every turn of the road, although the switchbacks did get a bit intense.

The sky was painted a beautiful, clear, cerulean blue; the few clouds were white balls of fluff, and the sun lit up the entire stage. Here and there flocks of sheep and their shepherds dotted the mountainsides. Very little talking was heard as the group quietly marveled at the awesome scene unfolding around each curve of the road. The only ambient noise was the now ever-present 'click-click' of Winnie Bradford's knitting needles.

When the van reached the village of Frattura at over four thousand feet they got their first view of Lake Scanno, the largest natural lake in Abruzzo, formed by a gigantic landslide from Mount Genzana that blocked the Sagittario Valley, thus creating the lake. Located in the upper Sagittario Valley, Scanno is a gateway into the Abruzzo National Park. It is an old hill town full of life. The town's proximity to Lake Scanno as a tourist and resort destination has helped the town to survive and actually thrive. The mountain town of Scanno reached its peak in the seventeenth and eighteenth centuries, its wealth a result of the area's wool industry. It was Scanno's Golden Era.

The women from Scanno, well known for their skill in warping and weaving wool, are also renowned for a unique style of dressing. Their traditional outfit, a black dress with homemade lace and colorful apron, topped off by a distinctive flat headdress, is worn by many women in Scanno today on a day-to-day basis as their regular clothing.

In the village's heyday, Scanno's landed gentry competed amongst themselves to build the most elaborate palaces, thereby establishing their local prestige according to the amount of money spent on their homes. The mix of architectural styles is fascinating. The variety of portals, columns, cornices, courtyards, and balconies are still a part of Scanno's private homes, palaces, and churches. One unique characteristic of houses in the village are the doors: no two are alike. Many homes have a main door and smaller door referred to as the 'death door,' since it was used as a means for the disposal of dead bodies.

\*\*\*\*\*

The group set out on the walking trail with Hardy taking the lead down a quiet lane leading past a somewhat decrepit cemetery on their right. After switching to a footpath they passed leisurely through woods and meadows before descending steeply toward the south shore of the lake. The lake's surface sparkled like diamonds from the brilliant sunshine. Across the lake, here and there on the meadows running down to the water, they could see flocks of sheep tended by shepherds and the traditional cream-colored sheep dogs common to Abruzzo.

They were back in civilization. They passed a beach bar, several swimming spots, and more bars and restaurants. The beach itself was fairly quiet. It was, after all, still young in the day, but here and there early sun worshippers, oiled and bare, lay basking in the sun's rays. The stillness of the lake was spotted with several paddle boats, called pedalos, plying its surface.

Hardy's group had strung out as they crossed the beach area and their pace slowed to a crawl as they gaped and gawked at the scene around them. Looking to the far end of the beach where the hiking trail paralleled the road, Hardy was sure he glimpsed the white-haired heads of Winnie and Tillie Bradford hurrying off the path from the church by the lake, heading back towards Scanno. 'Don't they ever just slow down and enjoy life,' he wondered.

The terrace of one of the hotels was doing a brisk business and Hardy recognized members of the large group of Swiss hikers they'd encountered the day before leaving the hermitage of San Bartolomeo di Legio. He decided to enjoy an espresso on the terrace, as well, and took a table in their midst. Their conversation was in French, which he understood, so he listened in shamelessly. The main topic of interest seemed to be a little church they had just visited ... 'probably the church on the lake, our next stop,' Hardy mused. The discussion broadened to churches and miracles and churches they had visited thus far. 'Aha,' he thought, 'a group of hiking pilgrims.'

Kelvin suddenly appeared at his table. "Mind if I join you?" he asked.

"Be my guest," he responded, moving his back pack off the chair so Kelvin could take a seat.

"The group from Switzerland, I see," Kelvin commented, taking in their neighbors with a nod of his head.

"They're the same group we passed in the ascent to the hermitage yesterday. I think they're on a tour combining hiking and pilgrimages to various churches famous for miracles," he explained. "At least, that's been their main topic of conversation."

"You speak French?" Kelvin asked.

"Yeah, and German. My mom is German and lives in Frankfurt."

"Your father?"

"My dad was killed, years ago, in Corsica." 'Murdered,' Hardy thought, as he remembered his trip to the French island in the Mediterranean last fall where he finally learned the truth of his father's death and brought the killer to justice, barely escaping being killed himself. The memory blocked the warmth and light of the sun for a brief moment, and then he was back in the present.

"I'm sorry," Kelvin apologized. "I didn't mean to pry."

Hardy managed a shrug. A slice of conversation from one of the Swiss hikers at the next table caught his attention.

"I wonder what has happened to our guide, Raymond. When we left him in the chapel he said he'd be along in a few minutes, but that was twenty minutes ago. Look at his wife, Christine.

She's nervous as a cat ... I can tell she is worrying about something."

"Christine isn't the hiker her husband is," came the reply from a fellow hiker. "She feels more at home in urban areas, I think. Speaking of that, when do we head for the coast and Pescara? I'm really looking forward to our visit to the Church of the Eucharistic Miracle in Lanciano."

At mention of Lanciano, Hardy noticed, Kelvin's ears pricked up noticeably and his face took on a thoughtful look as he gazed, again, around the group of Swiss travelers, committing each face to memory.

*****

After a brief interlude doing the beach scene Hardy's hikers were back in stride. They followed the water line to the far side of the beach where they picked up a trail running alongside the road to Sulmona. The trail was a brief diversion ending at the Church of the Annunziata, which is actually built out over the main road, straddling it. It is perched on the edge of Lake Scanno and the church's interior is accessible by two stairways on either side of the structure.

"What's the story behind this church?" Hal asked, as he prepared to mount the steps.

"Tradition has it that when the locals wanted to visit villages to the south they had to clamber over a dangerous piece of rock at this spot because the road was too narrow for horses to pass through. Somebody put a statue of Mary on the rock one day to afford protection to travelers, and after the statue arrived miracles started happening. So, one thing leading to another, the locals built a chapel here and put the statue of Mary on the altar. At first it was built into the rock as a tiny chapel, about 1702, but later it was enlarged and built out over the road. The neat thing is that the backdrop for the altar is the actual stone side of the mountain."

Hal had already skipped up the stairs to the tiny sanctuary. The rest of the group gradually followed. All of a sudden Hal reappeared in the doorway to the little church, yelling for help.

"There's somebody dead in the church!" he hollered. The hikers, strewn along the stairs leading up to the church, stared at him in frozen silence.

Hardy finally broke it. "What do you mean there's a body in the church?" he demanded, climbing the stairs two at a time. Kelvin hastened after him. Hal ducked back in the sanctuary to get out of Hardy and Kelvin's path.

"Just here," Hal pointed, "inside the door."

There was, indeed, a body lying on the floor, but not a dead one. The members of the hiking group crowded around the entrance to the church blocking out light and air.

"Hal," Hardy instructed, "get everyone back outside and down the stairs." Obediently, Hal shushed everyone out and down.

A slightly built but physically trim and athletic man in his late forties dressed in khaki shorts and a pale green polo shirt with some logo on the chest lay crumpled on the cold stone floor near the entrance. There was blood matted in the thick brown hair on the right side of his head and dried around his ear. His face was completely white and pinched. A thin scar ran down the left cheek, connecting to his ear lobe.

"He has a nasty wound on the side of his head, but he's still alive," Hardy said. "Help me straighten him out on his back, Kelvin. Support his head and neck while I turn him."

Kelvin immobilized the injured man's neck while Hardy gently rolled him flat on his back, supporting his back in line with his neck. Hardy listened to his breathing, watching the chest rise and fall, and checked his pulse.

"Breathing is fine." he said, "So is his pulse." He carried out a brief examination for other possible injuries but found none.

Gripped in the victim's right hand Kelvin saw a scrap of paper. He gently pried the paper from his grasp. On it were written two sets of numbers. Kelvin sat back on his heels, lost in thought as he looked at the long numbers.

"What is it?" Hardy asked, nodding at the paper. He had peeled off his ever-present backpack and found the smelling salts he always carried. With the cap removed he waved the bottle briefly under the victim's nose. There was an immediate, woozy reaction followed by a moan. The eye lids flickered open and the pupils in the blue eyes were only slightly dilated ... a good sign. The man moaned a second time and focused his eyes on Hardy.

The wounded man made a feeble effort to move but Hardy stayed him. "Who're you?" the man asked with alarm.

"It's OK," Hardy reassured him. "We found you knocked out in the church on the lake. I've just used smelling salts on you; we're only trying to help." He paused, "Do you know what happened to you?"

He looked blankly at Hardy.

"Did someone conk you on the head? Did you see anyone?"

"Uh ... Uh ... I'm not sure what happened," he replied, his eyes averting Hardy's gaze. "I guess I must've fallen and hit my head."

"What about this?" Kelvin asked, thrusting the piece of paper forward for the man to see. "Is this yours?" The man squinted, then grabbed the paper with the strange numbers on it.

"Uh, yes, I must have dropped it," he replied, "Thanks." He stuffed the scrap of paper furtively into the front pocket of his shorts and attempted to sit up. Hardy tried to stop him, but he insisted that he was OK and got to his feet, somewhat unsteadily. Hardy and Kelvin tried to assist, but he waved them off.

"You really should stay still while I clean and dress your wound," Hardy told him. "It'll only take a few minutes." But the strange man was already out the door of the church and gone from sight. Hardy stared after him, a thoughtful look on his face. He turned to Kelvin. "What the heck was that all about?"

"At a guess I'd say that was Raymond, our missing Swiss tour guide. And I think he was lying about hitting his head. Somebody whacked him a healthy blow, and I'm betting he knows exactly who it was."

Hardy recalled the Bradford twins hurrying away from the direction of the church on the lake, a memory that caused the back of his throat to start itching which, in his experience, was a harbinger of pending trouble.

"What was on that piece of paper? The one that was in his hand ... wasn't there something written on it?" Hardy asked.

Kelvin shrugged his shoulders and gave his head a shake. "Just some numbers." But they weren't just 'some numbers.' Kelvin knew exactly what those numbers were: they were latitude and longitude numbers for a place on a map. And Kelvin knew exactly where on the map: Lanciano, Italy.

*****

The remainder of the hike was uneventful. They arrived back at their starting point and decided to explore the bustling small mountain village of Scanno and have lunch before returning to Sulmona. The hikers, minus the twins, agreed to meet at the van in three hours for the trip back.

"If anyone runs across the Bradfords during your meander through Scanno, please let them know when the van leaves for the trip back to the hotel," Hardy said. "As for lunch, Scanno is famous for its cheeses, especially their fresh ricotta. Lamb and pork dishes are a safe bet here, as well. We've eaten a lot of the 'guitar pasta,'" he continued, "so if you're up for something different, try the cazzellitti, which is another Abruzzo pasta that is often served with fava beans and a fresh green. Scanno's best dessert is pan dell' orso, which is a cake made with almonds and honey and covered with chocolate. It's the one food item you have to try while you're here, trust me. That and the ricotta, particularly if it's seasoned."

"Can you recommend a good place to eat?" Hal asked.

"Honestly, Hal, I've never had a bad meal in Scanno. All of the hotels have restaurants which are very good, if you're more comfortable with that. Plus, all the independent restaurants have excellent, local dishes made with fresh ingredients. Personally, I often eat at a small establishment near the Fontana Saracco which is in front of the Church of Purgatory on the Via Abrami."

\*\*\*\*\*

Fontana Saracco, a sixteenth century fountain, consisted of two large arched bodies. The one on the left was reserved for animals only. The one on the right, for people. Its uniqueness is found in the fact that there are multiple spigots in the people side of this fountain. The spigot with the head of a king carved above it in stone was reserved for use by noble men, only. Next to this tap is another, with a head of a queen carved in stone. It was for use by noble women. A third tap, with a carved image of a shoe-maker, was to be used only by commoners of both genders. And the fourth spigot, with a carved image of a friar, was to be used only by religious people.

*****

The area in front of Fontana Saracco has always been used as a sort of meeting place for people and, sure enough, Hardy espied the Bradford sisters, tête-à-tête with Giuseppe. 'He's probably already told them about our departure time,' he thought, 'but I'd better make sure.'

He strode over to where the three were standing. So earnest were they in conversation that they didn't notice his approach and he heard fragments of their conversation.

"... slight bump, nothing serious ..."

Then, Giuseppe's deep voice, "... when do I get the money?"

And one of the Bradford's, he couldn't tell which, replied, "... the job done in ..."

Hardy didn't know what he'd tumbled onto, but that unnerving itch in the back of his throat was back. 'Trouble,' he thought. He coughed to make his presence known and plastered a big smile across his face, hoping it didn't look as phony as it felt.

"There you are," he called. "I'm glad I found you." The three moved quickly apart when they saw him; they all looked as guilty as hell, their manner stiff. He blundered on, "Giuseppe has told you, I guess, the van leaves in three hours for Sulmona?" He stated it as a question. There was an awkward silence.

'How much did he hear?' Winnie wondered.

Tillie spoke up, "Yes, we're aware of that," she said, turning toward him. Her smile was tight, her eyes cold. Hardy flinched, inwardly, at her manner. He did a double take when he saw a swollen bruise, high on her right cheekbone.

"Tillie, what happened to your face?" he blurted out.

She was instantly defensive. "I lost my balance going up the stairs to the little church on the lake and bumped it," she replied, too quick to answer.

'She had that answer down pat,' Hardy thought. "I've got some disinfectant in my back pack if you'd like me to clean it for you," he offered.

She sniffed, "Thanks, but no; it's not a big deal." The silence that followed this exchange grew long and uncomfortable.

"Uh, great. Then I'll see you at the van in three hours," he managed, and beat a hasty retreat.

Hardy felt the flush of anger and embarrassment simultaneously after the unpleasant encounter with the Bradford twins and his driver, Giuseppe. He felt like the situation, whatever it was, was out of his control. Not a good feeling when you're responsible for a bunch of people you've taken on tour. Always one to give someone the benefit of the doubt, he'd reached his limit with the Bradfords. And just what the hell was going on between them and Giuseppe? He was beginning to think the twins weren't who they said they were, but where did that leave him? And what could he do about it?

\*\*\*\*\*

# CHAPTER 10

That night after dinner Winnie Bradford made a call to the United States from her room on her cell phone.

"Everything is moving ahead as planned; the target is still in sight." She paused, listening. "No, I really don't anticipate a problem. Just make sure the money is sent, as agreed." There was a brief hesitation, then, "We've taken steps to insure that the competition, if any, has been eliminated. We've tried to keep a very low profile; tipping our hand would only invite unwanted obstacles." She listened again. "It looks like Pescara is the best route." Pause. "Right; I'll be in touch." That done, she went to fetch Tillie for a stroll through Piazza Garibaldi.

*****

Kelvin Gossett was in the sitting room of the Sei Stelle casually perusing a walking map of Sulmona when he saw the Bradford twins exit for their customary evening walk. Deftly refolding his map and stuffing it in his jacket pocket he headed nonchalantly back toward his room.

When he was certain no one else was about he picked the lock to Winnie and Tillie's room and let himself in. The sun hadn't yet set, so there was no need to turn on the light. Kelvin moved swiftly around the double room, checking the drawers and closets, and under the bed. Next, he examined the suitcases, but they were empty so he checked for hidden compartments and found none. Searching the bathroom yielded nothing. He was about to give up when he knocked Winnie's knitting off the low table near the settee. He stooped to pick it up and accidentally poked himself in the thumb. Blood spurted from the spot. 'What the ...' he wondered, examining the knitting needles more closely. What he discovered made his stomach churn. The ends on the knitting needles had been honed to a deadly, sharp point. Deliberately. He was holding an assassin's weapon.

*****

The knock on the door broke up Hardy's reflections and, somewhat irritably, he said, "Come in." He was exhausted after the trip to Scanno. 'Probably due to stress,' he told himself. His uneasiness about the twins and who they were, as well as people getting knocked on the head fairly regularly was something he could no longer ignore. Now that he'd finally decided to think it through he resented having his thoughts interrupted by whoever was at his door. His resentment evaporated, however, when the giant frame of Bernardo, his regular driver, lumbered into his small room, making it seem even smaller.

"Bernardo!" he exclaimed. "My old friend, how are you!" Hardy was always amused by Bernardo's enormous size and the fact that his name in Italian meant 'brave as a bear.' He reminded Hardy of a large brown bear, very large ... playful and stuffed-toy looking. But Hardy knew the other, dangerously loyal side of Bernardo, as well, and was glad he could count him among his friends. An enormous grin split across Bernardo's wide, homely face and suddenly he was handsome.

"Hardy, I come as quickly as I find out," he said, advancing toward Hardy with his arms outstretched to perform the customary cheek kissing. That done, Bernardo stood back, an anxious look on his face.

Hardy was puzzled, to say the least. Bernardo, his usual driver for his traipses in rural Italy, had had to cancel out at the last minute on this last tour when his wife fell and broke her ankle, requiring Bernardo to stay home and help with their family of six children.

"Find out what, Bernardo?" he asked.

But Bernardo was off, pacing Hardy's small room, wringing his hands as he went. "I tell my cousin, Armondo, to take my place ... to be your driver while I take care of things at home ... He say fine, yes, he will do it. Anything to help ... so all is good, yes? But, no! He is in hospital, with broken leg. Somebody run him down with a

Vespa and break his leg, so he, also, cannot drive for you. So who is your driver?" he asked Hardy aghast with the answer.

Hardy had been following Bernardo's diatribe with mild amusement, until he came to the part about his cousin not being Hardy's driver.

"Wait! Bernardo!" he interrupted, "You mean it isn't your cousin who's been driving our van?" He was getting a bad feeling about where the conversation was headed.

"No, Hardy. That is what I am trying to tell you. No, it is not my Armondo, who is in hospital."

"Yeah, I get that Armondo is in the hospital. So just who in the hell is this driver?"

"A man who is not a good man. No, he has ties to the Fabale family, through his brother-in-law, and they are organized crime. I don't know for sure that he is a gangster, but he is a man who you cannot trust. He is always looking for ways to make money and doesn't care how he goes about it." The alarm on Hardy's face intensified. "Oh, I don't mean he would kill someone ... not that ... but maybe he would at that, I don't know ... there was talk once that he maimed ..."

Bernardo's delivery would have been comic but for the fact that what he was telling Hardy could have such serious repercussions to Hardy's tour business and livelihood.

"You're telling me that my current driver, Giuseppe, or whatever his name is, is connected to the Mob, is that right?"

"Si, yes, Hardy. I come as soon as I hear. To warn you. And to offer to drive for you, if you want."

Bernardo's last words were a life line. "You can take over driving ... on this tour?"

"Yes, if you wish. My wife's mother has moved in with us while Claudia is recovering and I am no longer needed." The truth was that his mother-in-law was a real virago, a harpy, and his life was unbearable with her around. She sucked the peace out of his house and in its place planted strife and dissension. Her husband had sent her off to look after her daughter with a happy heart urging her to 'stay as long as you like, I'll manage.' Blessed Mother, yes, he'd manage. Bernardo pitied his father-in-law being married to the shrew, but it wasn't his duty to take her off his hands. His best option was to get away for a while and driving for Hardy was the perfect solution.

"Are you sure, Bernardo?"

"Absolutely."

"What do I do about Giuseppe? I can't just fire him because he's a crook, can I? Won't he make trouble?"

"Ah, I see what you mean." Bernardo's face creased in thought a few moments, and then relaxed into a warm smile. "Tell him that your regular driver is back and that, according to your standing contract, you are obligated to take him back immediately or the contract will be violated. Offer him a generous severance pay and promise to give him a good recommendation in the future. Also, that you will keep him in mind and refer him to your contacts in the tour business. He probably won't give a rat's ass about the recommendation thing, but it sounds sincere on your part and allows him to save face."

Hardy was relieved. "I'll tell him at once, Bernardo. And thanks. I knew there was something suspicious about him but didn't have any way to find out what. He and a couple of my clients have been unusually close about something and I've been worried about what might be going on ... perhaps his leaving will put a stop to it." He didn't really believe it as he said it, but he wanted to.

"We're heading up to the village of Villetta Barrea tomorrow morning, so plan on being here around nine o'clock, OK? Let's just hope no one else has an accident. At this point, I'm wondering if your wife had help breaking her ankle." He shouldn't have said that, he knew, from the startled look on Bernardo's face.

"You don't think ..." Bernardo began ...

"No, no, of course not. I don't know why I said that. Too vivid an imagination; too many Hollywood thrillers." At least he hoped so. "I'll see you tomorrow, at nine. And Bernardo, thanks, again."

*****

# CHAPTER 11

Honey stood at the entrance to the Sei Stelle the next morning with a large basket over her arm, handing out bottled water and left over breakfast rolls to the members of Hardy's tour group as they gathered outside to wait for their transportation. The twins literally snatched the bottles from her as they hurried out the door; their actions were so rude it was comic.

Hal sauntered up. "Hey, Honey, do you think I could have two of those pastries?" he asked. "I always seem to get hungry before everybody else."

"Sure thing," she replied, handing over two yeasty sweet rolls packed with golden raisins. 'No wonder he's such a chub,' she thought.

Dennis and Teddy were next in line. Teddy was wearing a beautiful shawl woven with multi-textured yarns in jewel and earth tones.

"What a great scarf!" Honey exclaimed. "It looks like a Hattie Rae design."

Teddy's face lit up. "You know textile design?" she asked.

"A bit," Honey replied. "It's one of my majors for grad school."

"Really? Which school?"

"I'm starting at the Massachusetts College of Art and Design in Boston," Honey told her.

"You're kidding! My mentor teaches there. He's in graduate studies. Textiles. You're bound to have him for a professor in at least one class. His name's Mike Savich ..."

Her husband, Dennis, broke in. "I hate to break this up, ladies, but we've got a bus to catch. Why don't you two get together when we get back this afternoon and continue the conversation over a latte or something."

Teddy, who had been giving her husband a piqued look at his interruption, looked back to Honey. "Yes, let's," she said, excited. "We should be back by five o'clock or so. Do you think you can get away for a bit then?"

Honey hesitated. That late in the day she usually had a ton of small chores to do. "Would it be OK if we just had some coffee here, at Sei Stelle?" she asked. "It's difficult for me to get away that late and I really do want to talk to you."

"Not a problem," Teddy assured her. Here is fine. We can sit in the courtyard." She smoothed her shawl lovingly. "Until later then, Honey," she said as she and Dennis moved past her. They were the last of the group to leave.

I look forward to it!" Honey called after her. How exciting! What were the chances of meeting a friend of one of her graduate professors in rural Italy? She wondered if she came across as a small town mid-westerner and found herself blushing. 'So what?' she thought, tossing her head. 'That's exactly what I am!'

*****

Hardy found Giuseppe loitering outside on the piazza after breakfast. He made his explanations and profound apologies, and gave Giuseppe a hefty separation bonus, which seemed to smooth over a potentially tense situation. 'That's a relief!' he thought, as he watched Giuseppe walk away across the piazza. It would be interesting to see the reactions of his clients later when Bernardo got behind the wheel. He had a nagging suspicion that this wouldn't necessarily be the end of Giuseppe but decided not to borrow trouble down the road: today's was sufficient. But, he realized that someone had gone to a great deal of trouble to plant Giuseppe in his midst. Admitting that unnerved him. Was he just being paranoid? 'What is behind it all?' he wondered. 'And who?'

*****

His thoughts about Giuseppe were interrupted when he heard someone call out his name as he stood in front of the Sei Stelle.

"Ciao! Hardy!" Honey called as she walked toward him. Somewhat absently he turned and when he saw who had hailed him his face lit with a warm smile. It was a relief to see an open countenance, void of intrigue, scheming, and bad news.

"Ciao, yourself," he replied. "Picking up the language, I see."

She blushed prettily. "I hope to. It's so expressive. I hang out on the piazza when I have free time; it's my version of cultural immersion," she joked. Turning more serious she asked, "Who was that?" nodding in the direction Giuseppe had taken.

"That," Hardy answered, "was the substitute driver for my tour. Was being the operative word. My regular driver just showed up so he'll take over starting today. Thanks God," he added under his breath.

They'd been heading in the direction of the wide steps at the far end of the piazza where the arches of the medieval aqueduct line the southwest side. When they arrived they sat down on the steps near the base of one of the arches. Hardy leaned back on his forearms, extending his sun-tanned legs down the steps in front of where he sat. He had a few moments before he headed out for the day's hike. He had just begun to relax when Honey spoke up.

"Interesting," she commented.

He waited for her to say more and when she didn't, prompted, "What's interesting?"

Lowering her voice, she said, "That woman, over there," she indicated with a short nod of her head.

Hardy followed the direction of her nod with his eyes and saw a dark-complexioned woman in her twenties standing in the shadows of one of the arches. He watched her for a moment and concluded that her nonchalance was overdone, which made her stand out among the people milling about. She was dressed casually, like everyone else, and was otherwise nondescript, but she exuded an edginess that was out of place in the casual atmosphere.

"What about her?" Hardy asked, more from politeness than actual interest.

"She was hanging around the Sei Stelle yesterday afternoon," Honey replied, "and trying to pretend that she wasn't."

'Now whose imagination was running away,' Hardy wondered. "Oh?" he said.

She heard the skepticism in his voice and flushed. "And when your group got back from yesterday's hike it looked like she was waiting to see who got out of the van." She hesitated. "She seemed focused on the overweight guy in your group, and when he sauntered off toward the shops she followed him."

"Hal?" Hardy asked.

"I don't know his name; the guy who wears the goofy hat," she said. She was starting to regret ever mentioning her thoughts. Hardy would think she was delusional or, worse, paranoid.

"Look," she began, "maybe I just imagined the whole ..." The woman in question had started moving purposefully across the piazza, weaving in and out of the crowd. Approximately forty feet ahead of her bobbed a pork pie hat, sitting atop Hal's head.

Suddenly, Hardy sat up, tensed, watching. "I don't think so," he replied, "I'd say you were dead on."

Honey followed where his eyes were focused, watching Hal being tailed by the strange woman. After a moment she said, "And the other thing is that your old driver, the substitute, met her at the fountain just after dinner yesterday evening. It wasn't a chance meeting," she added. "It was obvious she was waiting for him."

*****

# CHAPTER 12

Brigadier General Roberto Montanari loved his job. It wasn't a job so much as a calling. Montanari was head of the Comando Carabinieri per la Tutela del Patrimonio Culturale, the Italian Carabinieri for the Protection of Cultural Heritage. The Carabinieri Art Squad, for short. He, Roberto Montanari, was responsible for protecting the cultural heritage and art of Italy and combating art and antiquities crimes. No small task.

With a paramilitary force over three hundred strong the Art Squad is tasked with the immense pursuit of investigating unlawful excavations, the theft and illicit trade in works of art, damage to historically significant monuments, and illegal exportation of cultural property and fakes.

The Art Squad also monitors archaeological sites, art and antique dealers, restoration specialists, and junk shops. This specialized branch of the Carabinieri, the first like it in the world, formed in 1969, also depends on the analysis of highly skilled forensic experts in its ranks to assist in the recovery of historical and cultural items which are part of Italy's collective soul. To be fair, Montanari's men did have outside help in the form of other agencies like UNESCO, ICOM, and INTERPOL, but the bulk of the work, the grinding day-to-day slog of sifting through endless tips and clues and leads, fell to the Carabinieri Art Squad.

The Art Squad publishes the Bulletin of Trafficked Art Works and maintains a database of stolen works. Repatriation of looted antiquities has increased, internationally, and the number of stolen Italian art objects and clandestine excavations has fallen significantly with the help of improved data sharing and international collaboration, but the glory should and does go to the Italians and their dedicated approach to vouchsafing Italy's cultural wealth.

So successful is the Art Squad, and so reputable its authority and influence, it has been called into war-torn Iraq, another repository of cultural riches, to assist in prevention of the pillaging of Iraq's antiquities. Since 1990, the Carabinieri Art Squad has been active in assessing at-risk sites in Iraq as well as training personnel there, developing a system of accountability for cataloging Iraq's valuable artifacts, and recovering those illegally trafficked.

Montanari regarded his profession to guard his civilization's historical relics as a sanctified one, and his oath of office held, for him, the same exalted gravity as the vow of a priest, without a pledge to celibacy.

He had married, of course, and kept an apartment near his office in Piazza Sant' Ignazio, but his office is where he really resided. His wife, Lucrezia, saw little of him, a fact which she had accepted with grace and understanding but, at times, not a little resentment. What woman wanted to admit to herself that her husband cared more for some moldy old tapestry or dirt-encrusted statue with a missing arm than his wife?

Montanari reflected on his self-sacrificing, gentle Lucrezia as he walked the seven minutes to Piazza Sant' Ignazio. She hadn't realized the depth of commitment to his profession when she agreed to marry him but, once ensnared, had acquiesced to his long absences and contemplative silences. Dear, sweet Lucrezia. He would take her on holiday, to Sardinia, he promised himself impulsively. Just the two of them (they had no children) and leave his cell phone in Rome. Well, maybe not that extreme ... he couldn't completely sever the umbilicus to his passion.

When he arrived at the entrance to the Piazza, under which could be found remains of the Acquedotto Vergine, the aqueduct which still supplies water to the Trevi Fountain and the fountains on the Piazza Navona and ends where Rome's first public baths had been constructed by Agrippa in 25 BC, he caught his breath. He always did. The sheer magnitude of the sense of history all around him made his soul sing.

Across the ancient bricked piazza the elegantly designed baroque palace, comprised of three buildings in the shape of bureaus with shuttered windows and balconied facades, housed his base of operations for the art and antiquities squad. The warm, ochre hues of the palace buildings infused the entire square with a sense of calm.

Nearby stood the Temple of Hadrian, built to honor the emperor Hadrian, known for his cultural interests and patronage of the arts. 'Fitting,' Montanari mused. 'And here am I, inserted into this grand-civilization-on-a-continuum.'

The other significant building on the piazza was the intricate Baroque Church of Saint Ignatius, with its exquisite interior, dedicated to Ignatius of Loyola, founder of the Jesuits. 'The Jesuits … well, that was another story, wasn't it?' Montanari thought.

He decided on a brief stop at Le Cave Di Sant'Ignazio, the sole restaurant on the piazza which served as his second office and his primary watering hole. He nodded to Marcus, the head waiter, and took his usual outside table. "Buongiorno, Marcus."

"Buongiorno, Signore."

"Latte macchiato, per favore."

"Si, Signore," Marcus replied.

Montanari gazed out over his piazza, idly watching his fellow Romans going about their business in the early morning freshness. It was too early in the day for tourists to be prowling off-the-beaten-path back streets and squares. His latte arrived, along with two sweet rolls he hadn't ordered but would eat.

He sighed contentedly ... this was the Rome he loved. The Eternal City. Rome, above all other European cities, lived in her own dimension. Founded by the son of a god, Rome's richness and variety, from Imperial times forward, overwhelmed one's sense of being. Layers of nearly three millennia of the living and the dead were everywhere around you as you experienced a magnitude of history unequaled anywhere else.

Breaking in on these lofty reflections Montanari's cell phone chimed for his attention.

"Si, pronto." The dreamy look in his eyes was immediately replaced by a hawk-like wariness. He switched to English when he saw who was calling him. "How goes it, Vado?" he asked.

Vado was a senior inspector for INTERPOL and worked out of the NCB in Rome. Montanari and Vado had worked together on various cases over the years and, although they worked for agencies totally independent of each other, both men realized that two sets of eyes and ears were better than one.

Vado, a dedicated INTERPOL employee, had been permanently assigned to Rome's National Center Bureau. He was a gifted investigator and had caught the eye of both the Pope and

Montanari on more than one occasion when he had run to ground guilty parties who had made off with items in the Vatican's vast collection of religious art and relics. Vado's skill and diligence had resulted in his being unofficially designated the go-to guy when it came to protecting the Vatican's cultural holdings and repatriating any oeuvres d'art that had been separated from the Mother Church.

"Busy as ever, Roberto."

"Anything of interest?"

"Some chatter over the past three weeks. INTERPOL command center in Washington, DC, picked up conversation regarding the future possible theft of a religious object in Italy. It was passed on and given to me to follow up on."

"And where are you now, Vado?"

"Sulmona, in Abruzzo, Generale."

"The Italian hinterland?" Montanari asked. "What could possibly be of interest in Abruzzo, Vado?"

"There is a small church in Lanciano which holds The First Eucharistic Miracle ... admittedly not the Shroud of Turin or the head of Saint Peter, but a significant religious relic, nonetheless."

"Any developments or leads?"

"Si, Generale," came the reply. "It seems we may have more than one party interested in the object in question."

"How so?"

"There is a group of pilgrims from Neuchatel, Switzerland in the region. Some member or members have been asking around ... a bit foolishly, I might add. One of their leaders got knocked on the head but was very secretive about what had happened to him. Oh, he was also grasping a scrap of paper with the map coordinates for Lanciano written on it. How stupid is that?"

"And the other interested party?" Montanari prompted.

"That one is a bit more complicated ... and dangerous. They will be my bigger concern."

"Shall I send someone from my office to Abruzzo to assist you, Vado?"

There was a stilted silence at the other end of the phone. "Ah, no, Generale," came the slow reply. "It is nothing I cannot manage on my own."

Montanari sighed, "I'm sure you have everything under control, my friend," he soothed, "but in the event that the unexpected happens, I'd be only too happy to assist. Agreed?"

"Ciao, Generale."

*****

# CHAPTER 13

Hardy was first on the van that morning, taking his usual seat up front. He wanted to observe the reactions of all his fellow hikers as they climbed aboard the van, seeing the switch in drivers for the first time.

The mixed responses to Bernardo's presence were interesting. Lucy and Amy gave a polite "Good morning," and went to their seats looking slightly puzzled. Dennis and Teddy were so busy with each other they actually said, "Morning, Giuseppe." Kelvin gave him a brief nod as he stepped into the van, and Peter did the same. Hal stopped dead on the step and said, "Who're you?" The Bradford twins were a bit more dramatic: Tillie froze, looked around, and barked, "Where the hell's Giuseppe?" Winnie gave her a shove from behind, along with a dark look, and they took their usual seats.

"Everyone," Hardy announced, "we have a new driver, as you can see. This is Bernardo. Say 'hello,' Bernardo." Bernardo looked in his rear view mirror, a warm smile lighting up his enormous face, and nodded a greeting to his passengers.

"Bernardo is my regular driver for my Italian trips. He had to cancel earlier due to an emergency at home, but since that is no long a problem he is back with us. I'm sorry for any inconvenience this may cause you, but my contract with Bernardo is very clear about my commitment to him. Giuseppe understood the situation and graciously accepted his being replaced. At any rate, switching drivers won't affect our schedule or the quality of the trip. Thanks for your understanding."

The only reactions worth noting were the pursed-lip looks exchanged between the twins. Amy and Kelvin looked rather smug; everyone else seemed indifferent to his announcement.

*****

Fifteen miles later, driving through the Sangro Valley, they arrived in Villetta Barrea in the heart of the Abruzzo National Forest. Once on the hiking trail the group headed into an ancient wood of beautiful black pine, traveling above the Sangro River. After several zigzags the trail crested the top of a hill, exiting the pines.

Before them yawned the natural, limestone amphitheater of the Camosciara, the heart of the first protected area in the Apennines. The open, meadow-like area, a mountain prairie, was abloom with Great Yellow Gentians, peonies in a variety of colors, and Red and Martagon lilies. Here and there they glimpsed the rare Venus Lady's Slipper orchid, found only in select areas of the Apennines and Alps.

Dense beech forests, the beech tree being the prince of Abruzzo's high elevations, many of them centuries old, are home to the Marsican Brown Bear, Apennine wolves, the chamois of the Abruzzo, lynxes, deer, and Golden Eagles.

As they approached the turnoff of Trail G6 they heard a full noise that seemed to come from all directions. The turbulent waters of the Scerto River and waterfalls, hidden by the trees, dominated their surroundings. They headed due south on Trail G6, an old mule track following the river, and entered the beautiful Scerto Gorge which had been carved between steep cliffs. After several hairpin turns and a steep hike through dense, shady woods dappled with occasional sun, running with streams and small waterfalls all around, they reached a clearing in the forest and saw below them the Waterfall of the Nymphs, its many fairy-like strands sifting and misting their silvery way down the rocky face of the deeply crevassed gorge.

"This is so incredibly beautiful!" Teddy whispered, reverently. Dennis halted beside her and snapped off several pictures. She leaned into him with her head on her shoulder.

"Glad we came?" he asked, putting his arm around her.

"Yes," she replied dreamily. "I feel a million miles away from Philadelphia and our lives there ... I wonder if I even want to go back. I'm just so at peace here, Dennis."

"You want to live like a hermit?" he teased. "A simple cell chiseled into a mountain side somewhere?"

His teasing broke the spell. She sighed. "You know me better than that, my love. I like my creature comforts, as do you. But," she added, "it will be hard to go back to city living. Maybe we won't ..."

"Italy would be a great place for you, Teddy. The Italians have always been at the forefront of textile and fabric design." She looked up into her husband's face, questioning. "I mean it. Your creative genius would really thrive here. I'm not sure what your husband could find to do, though."

Teddy turned to face Dennis. "Seriously? You mean you'd even consider it?" She laughed like a child then, and he loved her for it.

"To see you this happy? Yeah, I'd consider it," he smiled, pulling her into his embrace. "But now we'd better catch up with the group before they come back looking for us," he said, pulling her along.

There wasn't much to lunch, really. It was Tuesday and not a market day in Sulmona or Villetta Barrea. The hikers started to munch on their energy bars and dried fruits. Hal looked especially grim as he ate his meager lunch, washing it down with bottled water.

Hardy pulled a fresh loaf of bread and dried salami out of his back pack and started passing the food around to everyone.

"Bernardo brought this for us for our lunch," he said. "The salami and bread are made by his cousin in Scanno." A chorus of 'Thank you,

Lord' and 'Fantastic!' was heard as the hikers enjoyed the plunder Bernardo had contributed. The stoical starve-in-silence mood of the group had been replaced by Carpe Diem.

"Is tomorrow the day we go to Pescara, Hardy?" Hal suddenly asked. "And by the way, this salami is delicious!" A chorus of agreement followed Hal's proclamation.

Hardy took a minute to swallow a mouthful of nuts and dried apricots. He nodded. "It is, Hal. We've been hitting the trails steadily, so tomorrow seems a good time to take a break. We'll leave at nine, it's an hour's drive, so you'll have the better part of a day to spend in Pescara. So, for those of you who want to swim, get a tan, or eat seafood and enjoy a beach scene, tomorrow is it."

Hal looked pleased at this news, and Peter seemed keyed up a bit, too. In Hardy's experience it was always the ladies in the group who got excited about a day at the beach and shopping. At any rate, it would be the one day in the hiking tour reserved for anything but hiking. A throw-a-way day.

The group gathered up any food wrappers and water bottles lying around and stowed the litter in their packs. It was time to start the trip back to Civitella Alfadena. When the trail neared the base of the small waterfall Teddy suddenly exclaimed, "Oh, look! There! On that rocky ledge!"

Three Abruzzo chamois were poised at various heights of the rocky crag, looking down on the hikers. Two adult females and a smaller, juvenile kid. They were an inspiring sight and really beautiful to behold with their extraordinary tan coats, dark brown facial masks, dark hooves, and light-colored area on their throats. The graceful, straight horns curved back slightly at the tips, then downward. The small group stood motionless as it watched the hikers. The hikers stood motionless while they watched the chamois, mesmerized by the magic of the moment. Without warning, the lead female turned and scampered over the top of the ridge and the others followed. It all happened in warp speed. The hikers all started gibbering at once, like children.

"I didn't even get a chance for a picture," Dennis complained. "They were so amazingly fast!"

"And shy," added Lucy.

"The Abruzzo chamois is considered the most beautiful chamois in the world. It was almost hunted to extinction in the 1920's," Hardy explained, "and again during World War II. A major effort was made to protect and breed them, so we have close to eleven hundred chamois today in three different populations, the largest being here, in Abruzzo National Park. This particular species of chamois is actually a subspecies found only in Italy, so it has a small gene pool, which is one of its weaknesses. That, and the fact that the chamois competes with domestic livestock for grazing land. Under the Bern Convention the number of alpine meadows in their grazing range is being increased and kept off limits to foraging livestock. Hunting them is, of course, forbidden. Camosciara means 'land of the chamois,' by the way."

"What happened during World War II to decrease the number of chamois?" Teddy asked.

"Hard times. There was a shortage of food during the war, and the chamois have very tasty flesh. By the way," he added, "chamois always look downward when on guard and looking for danger. Which is why hunters usually try to stalk them from the heights above them, where they are undetected by the unsuspecting beasts." 'And that,' Hardy thought, 'is my trivia comment for the day.'

They began their return hike to Civitella Alfadena. When Hardy came to the G5 trail he took it, leading his group on a short, level trail to show them the Cascata delle Tre Cannelle falls, or Threefold Waterfall. The hikers split up, some to take pictures, others to find a cool spot in the shade.

Hardy left the group behind while they took a rest break and proceeded onto a short spur which led off from the main trail. He remembered a lovely, solitary overlook a short ways up from when he'd hiked it the year before and wanted to sit, quietly, for a few minutes while enjoying the view out over the valley.

He strode around the last bend in the trail and stopped, abruptly, staring in wonderment at the scene before him. There, sitting on a boulder at the side of the trail, was Kelvin

Gossett. Hardy heard a low, murmuring sound coming from the ex-priest and there, just a foot or so from where he sat also sat a brownish-gray wolf, on his haunches, with his head bowed, like he was listening to Kelvin.

For a brief instant Hardy thought he was imagining it all, but then the wolf looked up, saw Hardy, bared his teeth, and sauntered off. He was dumbstruck! Kelvin appeared not to be aware of Hardy's presence, so Hardy ever so silently backtracked around the bend and started to retrace his steps down the spur. After a short distance, however, he plopped down on a fallen tree and played back what he had just witnessed with Kelvin and the wolf. He knew what he had seen, but didn't know how to explain it. Had Kelvin, somehow, hypnotized the wild animal? What had he been saying to the beast?

Hardy had read once that in the time of Adam and Eve wild beasts had not had enmity toward humans. In the Garden of Eden, Adam and Eve spent a lot of time in God's presence, fellowshipping with Him, and the aura of God, the Shekinah glory, which is a visible manifestation of God, rubbed off on the humans a bit. Like a residue of God's glory. So the animals, seeing this remnant of God's glory on men, had somewhat of a reverence for humans.

However, as time wore on and people neglected their fellowship with the Lord and the aura of God left them the wild creatures' relationship with man changed, as well. Hardy thought that must be the explanation behind St. Francis of Assisi's affinity with nature and its creatures. St. Francis had, reportedly, dedicated his life to emulate the life of Christ so, logically, his life being so close to that of the Lord he must have had God's aura about him which would account for his special relationship with animals.

Hardy ran through all this in his mind and it seemed to make perfect sense. Except that he, Hardy, had witnessed a 'St. Francis moment' now, in the present. Just then Kelvin came around the turn in the trail; he stopped when he saw Hardy. Hardy hardly knew what to say, after what he'd seen, so he tried to play it low-key and cool but instead blurted out, "What the hell was that all about? With the wolf?" he added.

Kelvin gazed at Hardy thoughtfully for several minutes, in no hurry to answer. When he replied, all he said was, "Some of my best friends are animals." And headed on down the trail.

*****

Hardy decided on a mid-afternoon caffeine break at a cafe near the wolf museum in Civitella Alfadena while everyone else in the group, with the exception of the twins, decided to visit the museum in the hope of catching sight of a wolf in a specially built compound.

"Not my cup of tea, looking at animals in cages," Tillie commented as she seated herself, uninvited, opposite Hardy. Winnie winced at her sister's rudeness.

"Tillie, I think Hardy wants to enjoy his espresso in peace." She made as if to walk off but Tillie caught her hand.

"Stay here, Sis," she urged. "I want to ask Hardy what happened to Giuseppe first." She stared expectantly at Hardy, waiting for him to speak.

"Tillie, dear," Winnie persisted, "I think we should wait and ask him later. Perhaps this evening after dinner he will have time to talk to us ..."

"I want to know now, though," Tillie countered, sounding petulant. Winnie started to apologize but Hardy interrupted her.

"Now is fine, Winnie." To Tillie, he said, "As I explained on the van this morning, I was obligated to fulfill the standing contract I have with Bernardo. End of story. I told Giuseppe I would give him a solid reference and recommend him to my business associates. And I gave him one hell of a severance bonus. He was happy with it; there were no hard feelings." He paused, then asked, "Why are you so interested in Giuseppe?"

The twins exchanged looks and both began speaking at the same time, "He was looking into ..." "We just liked him ..."

They both stopped, abruptly, and Winnie began again, "Giuseppe was looking into several things for us and was going to get back to us with the information. That, and he had a contact for us to meet about something that interests us."

'That's a bit vague,' Hardy mused. "And I suppose you'd like to know how to get in touch with him, is that it?" he asked.

"Yes, exactly," breathed Winnie.

"Not a problem," Hardy assured her. "I've got all his contact information in my room back at the bed and breakfast. Feel free to stop by for it."

The twins looked relieved, and happy. "That'd be great!" Tillie smiled. "And sorry about being such a snit ... it's just that we've been so excited about what we've learned and his helping us ... I was worried it had all been for nothing. Thanks, Hardy. We'll stop by around seven-ish, if that's OK?"

Hardy was truly surprised at Tillie's transformation to reasonableness, and relieved that what he thought was heading into a confrontation didn't.

"Hey, glad I can help you, ladies. And sorry that Bernardo's appearance threw you for a loop," he said, keeping it light. From what Bernardo had told him about Giuseppe's shady dealings he could only imagine what Giuseppe's con was with the twins. He didn't want to know.

*****

From the wolf museum the group hiked through woodland in the direction of Barrea Lake for a look at the man-made reservoir. The return loop,

Hardy told them, was pretty bland, but an easy hike, following along the Sangro River. They could return that way, he suggested, or take the direct road linking Civitella Alfadena with Villetta Barrea. The twins went for the direct route and were off in a flash, since they'd expressed an interest in taking in the Transhumance Museum in Villetta Barrea. Hal decided on the short route, as well, and followed in their wake.

*****

# CHAPTER 14

The group who climbed aboard the van for Pescara the following morning looked like tourists. Gone were the sturdy hiking shoes and fanny packs.

Winnie and Tillie appeared in brightly printed cotton sun dresses and sandals, wearing wide-brimmed hats, their bathing suits worn discreetly underneath. Amy and Lucy had on light-weight walking shorts, short-sleeve knit tops, sneakers, mesh sport hats, and smelled of sunscreen. In place of fanny packs the women carried either canvas or straw bags packed with the day's necessities for survival in a tourist spot.

The men, with the exception of Kelvin, wore shorts and short-sleeved shirts. Hal showed up in an outrageously loud Hawaiian print that screamed American. With his pork pie hat, in a clashing plaid, he was something else. Dennis and Teddy were dressed like twins, down to their matching canvas hats. Kelvin sported well-worn seersucker pants with a tee shirt advocating animal rights, while Peter managed to look Ivy League in tailored, tan cargo shorts and a short-sleeved button-down oxford shirt. Hardy had on his usual Ex-Officio shorts and a 'Durkin Tours' polo shirt.

On their way out of town Hardy had Bernardo stop at the Confetti Pelino Company, a family-owned company that had been making confetti since 1763. The business was the heart and soul of confetti country.

Olindo Pelino, one of the current owners, showed the hikers around the factory and gave them an explanation of what the various colors of the sugar-coated candies symbolized.

"White confetti is, naturally, used for weddings and the candies have Avola almonds in the centers. That is a standard that never changes. But we also make pink for a girl's christening, blue for a boy's, red signifies graduation from college or a birthday, green for an engagement, silver for a twenty-fifth anniversary, and gold for a fiftieth. In all of these we use different centers. Some hazelnuts, anise seeds, coffee beans, cinnamon sticks, chocolate, marzipan, pistachio ... you name it, but the weddings, always almonds." He was, understandably, very proud of his product and the heritage that supported it. "All made in the tradition of ancient confetti," he beamed.

The hikers went on a spending spree for the confetti. "Look at these flowers they've made with the candies!" Tillie exclaimed. "They've even fashioned entire bridal bouquets with confetti!" The scope of colors used and the creativity in the designs were endless; even the men were impressed, though the confetti tour was typically a 'girl' thing.

In addition to confetti, the Pelinos had branched out into an array of chocolate and nuts candies, and a variety of liqueurs made with locally produced flavorings. Everybody stocked up on these after Olindo gave out free samples. Then they were on their way to Pescara.

The hour-long drive from Sulmona to Pescara passed quickly. The group was relaxed: no effort was needed to sit back and enjoy the ride and anticipate their day off. The steady 'nic-nic' of Winnie's knitting needles and muted conversations continued until they reached the outskirts of Pescara. After winding through Pescara they arrived at Hotel Salus, located on the city's seaside promenade.

"Everyone, this is Hotel Salus, where the van will be parked the entire time we are in Pescara," Hardy announced. "The Salus has a private beach, on the Adriatic, of course, and Durkin Tours has an arrangement with the Salus to use the beach. You will, naturally, have to pay a slight fee to use their facilities, if you wish to rent an umbrella and sun bed. That fee entitles you the use of the chaise and umbrella for the entire day. I recommend renting a space; if you want to take a break and go shopping or grab something to eat you have your spot to come back to.

"Please, do NOT try to 'borrow' a chair because the hotels around here closely monitor their territory and who has rented what. Use of their facilities means you have access to their restrooms, always a good idea. Also, note that use of the beaches, alone, is free. It's the facilities that cost."

He pointed up the beach. "The port of Pescara is a short walk in that direction. It's where the fishing fleet ties up, and is also the ferry terminal for boats to Croatia and the outlying islands. If you want cheap, fresh, no-frills seafood that's the place to go. You'll find local fishermen with small, beachside huts where they cook up the catch of the day very reasonably. Or, if you prefer, there's an endless array of more up-scale seafood restaurants all up and down the promenade.

"I urge you to try one of the local white wines, Pecorino-Terre di Chieti, a fruity white that goes really well with seafood. If you're drinking red wine, the local Montepulciano d'Abruzzo is the way to go."

He paused, "Lots of boutiques for you ladies. Also, if you're in the mood to pamper yourself there is an excellent spa at the Victoria Hotel, just two blocks away. First class, but pricey."

He mentally checked if he'd forgotten anything. "Oh, and the front desk staff at the Salus is very friendly and helpful ... just be sure to tell them you're with Durkin Tours. OK? Right, then … we'll be here all day, and leave tonight at eight thirty. I'll be having dinner at Ristorante Murena at half past six, in case anyone wants to join me in an all-around great seafood restaurant. It's two blocks up that way," he pointed, "right across from the beach."

The group filed excitedly off the van, each member pausing to look up and down the beach and out at the gorgeous, sparkling, deep-blue Adriatic.

"The water is exceptionally clean, but a little brisk, for those of you who like their swims tepid," he warned. "One more thing," he added, "there are vendors called marrocchini who prowl the beaches trying to sell whatever goods they may have. They're not necessarily Moroccan, but probably are in this country illegally. They sell lots of 'knock-offs.' Buying from them involves a risk, because they are illegal. If the police catch you, you can be fined. Having said that, if you do decide to do business with them remember that you NEVER pay the price they quote you. This is a bargaining proposition. Play hard to get. They'll give you a song and dance about how unreasonable you are … walk away. They'll come after you. What you seek is a meeting of the minds here; you don't want to rip them off, since a Euro or two is significant to them, but they still want to sell you something. If you are approached by a marrocchini and aren't interested, just shake your head and wave them off. They know the drill."

"Well!" Tillie declared, "I'm heading for the spa. Coming, Winnie?" she asked her sister, flouncing off in the direction of the Victoria Hotel.

"Right behind you, Tillie," Winnie answered. To the rest of the group she said, "Have a wonderful day, all," and to Hardy, "we'll see you around six thirty." Leaving her co-hikers with their mouths almost agape at her unexpected friendliness, she hurried off after her sister.

"Who was that?" Amy asked. "Has her body been inhabited by someone new?"

Hal snickered. "A pleasant change, at any rate," Hardy said. "Anyone else planning to meet me at the Murena for dinner tonight?"

"I'll be there," Amy said.

"We want to spend the evening on a date," said Dennis, "so don't expect us."

Kelvin and Lucy nodded their assent; Hal and Peter bowed out, separately. Hal said, "I'm going to meet a relative of my mother's in town and want to leave things open. You know, maybe be asked to dine with the family."

"I've got an old friend to look up in Pescara, so I'll probably be tied up pretty much the whole time we're here," Peter explained. That said, Hal and Peter headed off in different directions.

"Right," Hardy said. "Well, then, enjoy your day in the city. See you at the van at eight thirty."

Amy, Lucy, and the Fujimotos ambled off to rent their space on the beach for the day.

Kelvin fell into step with Hardy. "Where are you headed, Hardy?"

Hardy pulled up short. "To the Piazza Rinascita, known locally as Piazza Salotto; it's a local hangout. Why?"

"Mind if I join you?"

Hardy almost said 'yes,' but reconsidered. "Franciscan, right?" he asked.

Kelvin looked puzzled for a moment, then understanding dawned. "The wolf thing? Yeah, Franciscan is close enough," he replied, smiling.

Hardy looked smug. "I figured. I'll see that scene in my mind until the day I die. It's been driving me nuts. Sure, you're welcome to come with me. I'm just going to have a latte and people watch for a while. Relax."

"Sounds fine by me," Kelvin said, as they set off for the city's largest and most important square.

*****

# CHAPTER 15

Hal scuttled along the streets of Pescara, following the prompts from his GPS. Right here, straight two blocks, then left, left again. He stopped, finally, in front of an unremarkable store front in the middle of the block on a side street in the old commercial district. The faded sign overhead, paint chipping away, read, 'Colucci e i Figli: Importazione e Exportazione.' The 'sons' had never happened, but the 'i Figli' had been left on the sign, now a faded dream. This was the place: Colucci and Sons Import and Export. He took a deep breath and stepped inside.

The interior was dimly lit and slightly gritty; the front windows were so fly-specked and smeared that they admitted little natural light. An old wooden counter with a scarred surface filled one side of the room. On it was an old-style telephone, outdated adding machine, and cash register that shouted 1940's.

Behind the counter a rather plain woman, in a simple, frumpy dress in her middle forties eyed him suspiciously. Hal wasn't the usual walk-in traffic. She didn't move, didn't breathe, as far as he could tell. Her features, somewhat in shadow, reminded Hal of a frightened rabbit ... soft brown eyes, dollop of a nose, and small, dour mouth.

Hal waited for her to say something and, when she didn't, he spoke. "Good morning. My name is Hal, Hal Lambeth. I'd like to speak with Sal Colucci." When she still said nothing, he added, "Signore DiSalle sent me."

At mention of DiSalle's name the timid woman came to life, all five feet three of her. She nodded eagerly, "Si, Si, Signore." Her eyes took on warmth. She tried to smile but only half of it worked. On the left side of her face, due to what looked like the result of a stroke, the smile pulled down at the corners of her eye and mouth. What she meant as a smile was instead a grimace. He hoped she didn't notice his recoil to her appearance. Motioning for him to follow, she ducked, waif-like, through a doorway leading to a back room. He noticed she used only her right arm, while the left hugged her side in deformity.

It was a dingy back room. It took a few seconds for Hal's eyes to adjust to the light level as they wound their way through a dusty, musty store room containing stacks and rows of wooden crates and heavy-duty cardboard boxes. A rectangle of light in the distance grew larger and larger until, at last, they stepped through a doorway into a narrow alleyway that ran behind the block of buildings. They crossed the narrow passage and entered an apartment through its back door that exited onto the alley.

"Zio!" she called out as she walked through a sprawling, old-fashioned kitchen. "Ciao, Zio Sal?"

"Si," came a response. "Io sono qui." (*I'm here.*) A heavyset Uncle Sal, in his fifties, shuffled down the hall towards them, his slippers slapping the tiled floor as he walked. "Chi sei?" he asked Hal, watching the young woman disappear back the way she'd come. His eyes back on Hal, he repeated, "Chi sei?" (Who is it?)

Hal figured Uncle Sal wanted to know who the hell he was, so he started his introduction. Extending his hand, he said, "Hi, Signore Colucci. My name's Hal Lambeth ... Signore DiSalle said I should call on you. About some business," he added.

Recognition dawned on Colucci, finally, and he took Hal's hand in both of his and shook it heartily. Then he cheek-kissed him.

"Please to come in to my home," he said, switching to English. He ushered Hal into a somewhat shabby living room. "Please," he said to Hal, "sit down." He motioned Hal onto a forest green camel-backed divan with cushions lopsided from failing springs. "Would you care for something to drink? Espresso? Grappa?"

"Grappa would be nice, thank you," Hal answered.

While Colucci went to pour two grappas Hal studied his surroundings. The few throw rugs scattered on the tile floor were threadbare, the drapes at the floor-to-ceiling windows faded and sagging. The white, voile center panels had an intricate pattern of twining vines but had yellowed with age and someone had attempted, unsuccessfully, to mend small tears here and there. There were two overstuffed armchairs arranged at ninety degrees to each end of the divan where Hal sat, in somewhat better condition than the divan but spotted with grease or wax. A low, acrylic coffee table completed the fourth side of the furniture arrangement, and it was piled high with magazines, newspapers, and a partially-solved jig saw puzzle. Other than the long windows, the only lighting in the room was an old brass chandelier hanging in the middle of the ceiling from a brass chain, and a wrought-iron standing lamp at one end of the divan. A bookcase containing odd bric-a-brac filled the wall opposite the windows; one door led to a hallway, the other to the kitchen from whence they'd entered.

"Salute," Colucci said, as he handed Hal his grappa.

"Salute," answered Hal.

Colucci smacked his lips from the grappa. "Signore DiSalle ... Armando ... he told me he was sending someone, an American, to see me. So, what can I do for you?"

*****

# CHAPTER 16

The Bradford twins arrived at the Victoria Hotel by ten thirty, and by ten forty-five were submerged in the process of being purified and relaxed in the hotel's Wellness Center. Passing through a ritual of moist warm steam in the steam bath, on to the dry sauna, they finished in a cool cloud combining aroma and color therapy. The metamorphic progression of temperatures caused increased perspiration, which resulted in deeper mind-muscle relaxation.

Next, they were ready for a massage. Tillie opted for a holistic relaxing massage, designed to 'balance the harmonies between mind and body' using essential oils. She chose oil of lavender tweeked with just a hint of neem. Winnie decided on a Shiatsu massage, the Japanese technique using finger pressure on different parts of the body to loosen mental tension. She figured it would also help with her occasional headache and circulation problems. Neither twin was disappointed.

"Oh ... my ... God ..." Tillie oozed. "I feel soooo damn good I don't ever want to move. I just want to lay here and feel like this. Forever."

"Mmmmmmmm," Winnie answered back.

"What I don't get is why we only do this when we're on vacation," Tillie said.

"Too expensive," came her sister's reply.

"That's just it ... that's my point, Winnie." There was a prolonged silence.

"What's your point?" Winnie finally asked.

"Would our health insurance in the States cover going to a spa like this?" she asked.

Winnie joked back, "You're kidding, right?"

"No," Tillie answered her, "I'm not. You remember those Swiss hikers we ran across in Scanno? Well, I overheard them talking about spas in Switzerland they've visited and, get this, their health care coverage allows them to actually spend time at a spa and it's covered by their health insurance."

"Are you sure you heard right, Tillie?"

"Quite sure, Winnie. The government considers preventive care, which is what spas and massages are, a viable form of health care. In other words, you spend money to stay healthy instead of spending it to get well once you've become ill. Makes all the sense in the world. It's cheaper to do it that way, in the long run. Plus, you have a healthier, happier, hence more productive population. It's humane and brilliant."

"If Swiss people are so darned happy why is there such a high rate of suicide in Switzerland?" Winnie challenged.

"The suicide rate in Switzerland has actually been on the decline," Tillie replied. "Initially it was pretty high, I think, because the country legalized assisted suicides, but it's been going down for the past thirty or forty years. Still high, though, I admit."

She paused to turn over, adjusting her towel. "Several recent studies have found a correlation between happy places to live and high suicides, and unhappy places to live and lower rates of suicide. And they THINK the reason is because a discontented person living in a happy place feels more disenfranchised and miserable because of the contrast between what they feel about themself and what they see in those around them. And this makes one want to end it. Conversely, if an unhappy person lives in a place where the misery index is higher, they are less likely to kill themself because he, or she, thinks everyone else is equally unhappy and doesn't feel so bad about their own situation. You know the old adage: misery loves company."

"Well, I must say, Tillie, dear, it does make sense. Everything you said. Most interesting, too ..." and she drifted off to sleep.

*****

# CHAPTER 17

Peter stopped at the first car rental company he came to, Europcar, and rented a fully automatic Alfa Romeo Giulietta for the day. He used a false passport and fake U.S. driver's license, along with a false address to process the rental. That done, he headed west out of Pescara to where he picked up the A14, which would take him to Lanciano. He drove carefully and steadily, being heedful of the speed limit and traffic signs. It wouldn't do to attract attention to himself or, worse still, get flagged by a cop. He entered the coordinates of his destination into the Alfa's GPS, 42°13'49"N, 14°23'25"E, and followed the directions dictated by the navigation system.

Peter made good time to his destination in Lanciano, the San Francesco Sanctuary of the Eucharistic Miracle. Surprisingly, the large old church, totally nondescript, was located on a small side street of buildings packed closely together.

He circled the block once to scope out a parking spot and eased the Alfa Romeo into a space a block and a half from the church's front entrance. He checked to be sure he had his lightweight 4'x 4' tote that zipped itself into a four inch square when not in use, put a sunscreen up in the dashboard to block any view through the windshield, and locked the car, pocketing the keys. His heart was beating like a timpani and he purposefully slowed his step to casual and took slow, steady, breaths to steady his heart rate and his nerves.

He entered through the ancient portal of the narthex and paused inside to dip his fingers in the holy water font and, genuflecting, made the sign of the cross. The pipes from a giant organ occupied the balcony overhead. He advanced slowly up the aisle on the Epistle side of the church, on the aisle to the right of the pews.

Two thirds of the way up the aisle he slid into a pew and sat at the end near the side wall. He put on an air of meditation, but his eyes were scanning the nave, noting the number of worshippers and their places. Morning prayers had been going on since 10:30. It was now 12:20; the church would close in ten minutes and reopen two and a half hours later.

The crowd began to thin out as the worshippers left in anticipation of the church's closing. Moving slowly, fluidly, Peter escaped into an opening in the side wall underneath the ornate wooden lectern and quickly mounted the stairs to the stand used for the reading of the Epistles. Once inside, he crouched down in the darkness to wait.

After several minutes Peter heard the heavy wooden door at the front of the church scuff shut and the bolt being thrown. The interior double doors closed and footsteps padded faintly over the church's tiled floor as the priest in charge did a brief inspection for anyone or anything out of place. Satisfied, he knelt before the altar, crossing himself, then rose and exited the back of the apse through a door to the sacristy. Total quiet, but he continued to wait.

Peter looked at his watch. One fifteen. Now. On his knees he looked over the side of the lectern, his gaze sweeping back and forth in the interior of the sanctuary. All was still.

Wasting no time, he rose and descended to the floor of the nave and moved quickly to the area behind the altar. There, on a marble platform above the altar, resided the ornate monstrance containing The First Eucharistic Miracle. For an instant he was wonder-struck, awed, and then frightened by what he was about to do.

He shook off his feeling and climbed the marble stairs leading up to the glass case harboring the sacred relic. At the top of the stairs a platform allowed him to actually walk around the displayed reliquary, viewing it at eye level, only a foot away.

The feeling of awe struck him, anew. He stared at the speckled, yellowish, almost transparent piece of flesh, a piece of heart muscle, it had been determined, with a wrinkle down the middle. The flesh of Christ. The five, amber-colored globules of dried blood were displayed in an ornately designed goblet. The blood of Christ.

Doubt gnawed at him. What the hell was he doing? Then he remembered Helen, his wife, recently dead from a most hideous cancer. The struggle of her sickness; the incredible pain and sorrow. The devastation of the drugs. Hospice. The memory of it all rushed back on him in such a powerful wave it almost doubled him over. 'Oh, Helen.' The love of his life. His partner, friend, soulmate. They'd had such plans, such hopes. Of a good and loving life together. All shattered; all stolen. Stolen. He remembered why he was standing in front of the relic, and jerked back into the here and now.

After donning a pair of heavy latex gloves he quickly removed a small glass cutter from a pocket on his cargo shorts; from another pocket he took a powerful suction cup with a handle. Pressing the cup in place and testing it to be sure of its stability he applied the glass cutter to one of the glass panels encasing the relic and worked his way, slowly and firmly, around the perimeter of the panel. When he'd traced the entire outside edge he gave a healthy 'pop' to the four outer edges of the panel with his fist, breaking the glass at the cut lines. Gripping the handle of the suction device, he carefully lowered the cut glass panel to the base of the monstrance, leaning it against the side of the platform.

He paused and took a deep breath. The hard part was over, the precious relic ready to be his. Peter unzipped his expandable tote and shook it out to its full size. Unceremoniously, he reached inside the glass display and took hold of the almost-gaudy ostensorium, pulled it from its resting place, and deposited it in his tote. He angled it a bit so the cross at the top wasn't sticking out from the top of his bag. He disengaged the suction device from the panel of glass he'd cut from the monstrance and put the glass cutter and suction cup in his cargo pockets. He removed his gloves and stuffed them in the bag with the relic, glanced around to make sure he'd left nothing, and descended the stairs quickly.

He made for a recessed area on the Gospel side of the church; a small door led to the street where he'd parked his car. As he entered the recess he felt a tap on his shoulder. He spun around and found himself face to face with the leader of the Swiss hiking group.

"You!" Peter rasped. As an automatic reflex he swung the heavy tote containing the relic at his confronter, hitting him in the head with a sickening thud. The man crumpled to the floor and laid still, a red stain spreading on the tile floor around his head.

Without a second glance or thought Peter strode to the side exit, opened the door, and stepped onto the narrow sidewalk running along the side street. It took his last ounce of self-control not to break in to a run as he headed for his car, but to do so would have been foolish. There were few people walking, but the street traffic was a steady stream. He walked in measured steps; it felt like slow motion. He reached the Giulietta, drenched in sweat.

He was starting to shake and fumbled with the car keys. Thank goodness for automatic locking systems; he'd never have been able to fit the key in the lock. How would he manage the ignition? He stowed the stolen relic in the car's trunk, closed the lid, and slid into the driver's seat. Taking several deep breaths, he waited for the shaking to subside. Was he being watched? Had anyone noticed?

He glanced in his side and rear view mirrors for a glimpse of where he'd come out of the church. Nothing. He heaved a sigh of relief. He removed the sun shield from the dash and stashed it in the rear seat. His hand trembling slightly, Peter inserted the key in the ignition and started the engine. He sat for a moment longer, collecting his wits. He signaled, eased the car into traffic, and activated the GPS. Thank God he didn't have to think about how to find his way back to Pescara.

Several blocks from Saint Francesco's Peter heard the first sirens blaring, heading in the direction from which he'd come. Panic threatened to seize him, but he fought it back, reciting a Hail Mary. Aside from the Swiss hiker everything had gone just as planned. Perfectly. In his memory he heard the thud as he conked the guy on the head, saw the blood pooling on the tile. 'Did I kill the guy?' he wondered. His face hardened, then. 'Fuck him. He was in the wrong place at the wrong time. Poacher!' Nonetheless, the irony of what he'd just done versus the meaning of what he'd just stolen did not escape him.

He recalled Kelvin's words from the discussion the group had that second night during dinner when Winnie had broached the subject of stealing religious relics: "Your soul would be forfeit," Kelvin had said. Is that what he'd done? Lost his soul?

*****

# CHAPTER 18

When Kelvin's cell phone buzzed he looked to see who was calling and stepped away from the table where he'd been having coffee and a chat with Hardy on the piazza. This was one call he needed to take, he knew. The person on the other end never called for idle conversation.

"Si, pronto," he answered.

"Ciao, Vado," General Montanari began. "I assume you are not aware of what has happened in the last hour?"

"And what is that, Generale?" Kelvin, alias Vado, asked.

"That matter you were investigating in Lanciano? The First Eucharistic Miracle? It's been stolen, my friend."

Vado felt as though he'd been kicked in his solar plexus. "What! How?" Montanari had his full attention.

"Apparently, someone hid in the church while it was closed over the lunch hour. He cut a glass panel out of the relic's display case and made off with it without being seen. Well thought out. Went off without a hitch, except for one small problem."

"What was that?" Vado asked.

"He left a man lying in a pool of blood in the nave. Head wound. He's been rushed to hospital, but it's touch and go if he'll survive."

"Identity?"

"That's the strange thing," Montanari remarked, "The victim wasn't carrying any identification papers, at all. Pockets were completely empty, except for some gloves and a small hammer."

Something was tugging at Vado's memory. "Can you describe him?"

"Mid to late forties, slight build but muscular ..." Montanari began.

"Does he have a scar running down his left cheek clear to his ear?" Vado interrupted.

There was a startled silence on Montanari's end of the phone. "How did you know?" he asked incredulously.

"Just a hunch," Vado replied

"Who is he?"

"Well," Vado hedged, "if I'm right, he's the guide for the group of Swiss hikers who are on some sort of pilgrimage combined with hiking to churches and hermitages. And if I'm right, he's the guy I told you about we found knocked on the head in the church by Lake Scanno. The guy who had the map coordinates for the church of San Francesco written on a piece of paper he was grasping in his hand when we found him."

Montanari processed this information for a few seconds. "Then the other guy, the guy who actually stole the relic, is the 'other party' you referred to as dangerous?"

"Yes," Vado answered tersely.

"You got that right, didn't you, Vado? I'll let you know if I get more information. By the way, my colleague has one of his men tailing an American in a tour group hiking in Abruzzo ... a Signore Hal Lambeth ... know him?"

Vado squeezed his eyes shut, shaking his head. "Si, I know him, Generale," he replied, "he is one of the hikers in the group I've joined while pursuing the Lanciano investigation. What's he done?"

"Well, that's just it, nothing, yet. But he's been seen meeting with a known capo from Sulmona who deals in drugs that are shipped into Pescara from Albania. He was followed in Pescara and my colleague is waiting for a report about where he's gone and who he's seen today."

"Who's the capo?"

"Armando DiSalle. Shall I keep you informed?"

"I would appreciate that, Roberto," he answered.

"An addendum to your Mr. Lambeth is that he is also being tailed by an underworld figure on a Vespa ... a woman we think is a member of a Camorra clan."

"Are you sure about that, Generale?"

"Si, Vado. In fact, she followed your group to Pescara today; your friend is under her constant scrutiny, I'm afraid." Montanari hesitated. "The woman tailing Signore Lambeth is an unsavory sort ... more than that, she is suspected of at least one assassination in Naples."

"Marrone! Holy Mother! Who is she?"

"She sometimes works for DiSalle. Sometimes the Albanians. We know her as Black Maria," Montanari replied, "for a variety of reasons, none of which bode well for Signore Lambeth. I'll be in touch, Vado."

"Ciao, Roberto. Grazie," Vado answered, and rang off. 'Damn, Hal!' he thought angrily. 'Of all the stupid, brainless stunts to pull!' The thought of Hale Hal getting involved in the drug trade with a mob figure in Abruzzo would have been ludicrous on its face. But the fact that the chubby moron had actually made contact with the mob was serious and alarming. Hal probably had no idea he was in jeopardy ... dealing with a man like DiSalle was treacherous for an experienced criminal; Hal was a mere babe ... and if the Albanians were involved, which they most likely were, forget it.

Vado/Kelvin slipped his cell phone in the pocket of his seersucker slacks and stood, thinking. Hardy, still sitting in the café, was eyeing him suspiciously. He needed to get away and check up on the members in the group. Hardy would probably help him. No, not yet. He'd certainly have to bring Hardy in on who he was at some point, but it was still too soon.

He put a not-overdone smile on his face and returned to where Hardy was sipping espresso. "Something's come up," he said disarmingly. "I'm afraid I've got to find an internet café and send some e-mails, pronto. Do you know of one in the area?"

Hardy studied Kelvin's face. Calm, relaxed; it gave nothing away. 'Why do I always feel like people aren't who they seem?' "There are several nearby," he told Kelvin. "The closest is across the piazza and one block up on the left. Can't remember the name of it, but you'll recognize it when you see it."

"Great, thanks. Well, I guess I'll see you tonight at half past six, then. Enjoy."

He strode off in the direction Hardy had indicated for the internet café. When he was sure he'd been swallowed up in the crowds milling about the square, however, he changed direction and made his way to the Victoria Hotel. He approached the manager of the Wellness Center and flashed his INTERPOL ID. The manager was instantly wary.

"I need to confirm that two sisters, Winnie and Tillie Bradford, have been guests of the Wellness Center this morning, Signore."

Signore Delrosso scanned the names in the appointment log. "Si," he nodded, "They checked in at ten forty-five this morning for relaxation treatment and massage. They are still here." He checked his watch. "They should be finished momentarily. Would you like me to tell them you would like to speak to them?"

"You're sure they're still here?" Kelvin persisted. "They didn't slip out somehow?"

Signore Delrosso gave a puzzled look to the man standing before him. "No, Signore. Why would they do that? They pay for the full treatment; they get the full treatment."

Kelvin was relieved and frustrated at the same time. Not the Bradfords? He'd been so sure ... their furtive meetings with Giuseppe, those deadly knitting needles ... who else, then?

He started to leave, turned back to the appointment desk, said, "OK, thanks," and left.

Signore Delrosso watched him walk away, shaking his head. Then the typical Italian response: shoulders shrugged, arms out level bent at the elbows, palms up, slight jerk, eyebrows raised. Translation: 'Idiot.'

*****

The next place Kelvin headed was the private beach in front of Hotel Salus. He stood at the edge of the hotel's terrace next to the beach searching the mass of bodies stretched out in the sun. His eyes scanned over the crowd several times, then he began again, methodically looking row by row. He recognized the wide-brimmed hats Lucy and Amy wore, sitting at water's edge, the Adriatic lapping their feet. 'I can check you two off,' he told himself. Now where were Dennis and Teddy? He continued his search, starting to panic as he ran out of bodies.

"Hey, Kelvin," said a voice at his side. He almost jumped. Almost. He turned to see who had called to him and was relieved (he hoped it didn't show) when he saw the Fujimotos heading in his direction, the first flush of a sunburn glowing across the bridges of their noses. 'They've been sunning, alright,' he noted.

"Did you decide to join us?" Dennis asked.

"Uh, no. I'm looking for Hal. You haven't seen him anywhere, have you?" he queried.

"Not since we arrived this morning. Why?"

"Oh, I thought he might be interested in a quaint little restaurant I ran across a while ago," Kelvin said, lamely. "No big deal, I guess," he added.

'What's he really want, I wonder,' Dennis thought. "Sorry we can't help. Want to join us for a drink?"

"No ... no, thanks. I've been hitting the espresso most of the morning and I'm jittery. I really need to exercise some of the caffeine out of my system. But thanks. See you later," he added, and walked off. 'Where to now?' he wondered. The only members of the group unaccounted for were Hal and Peter. Had he got it all wrong? Apparently.

*****

Hal was feeling really pleased with himself. The meeting with Signore Colucci had gone well. Very well. It was all set up. He just needed to have the funds wired to Sulmona before the tour was over and give the cash to DiSalle; Colucci and his network would take care of the details. He'd just wait to receive the goods in Winston-Salem as part of a shipment of specialty pasta from Abruzzo. Piece of cake.

After Hal left Colucci's he wandered aimlessly, but in the general direction of the beach. His thoughts focused on the eating establishment he planned to open now that he'd have enough money to do it right. His mother's legacy, God rest her soul, would have been sufficient for a small café, but Hal's dream included a larger establishment that employed a chef, and the funds from his transactions with DiSalle would provide all that he needed. He started across the street and drew up short as a Vespa sped past, narrowly missing him.

*****

Peter was completely calm and in control of himself by the time he reached his destination in Pescara. An outside observer would never in a million years guess he had just stolen one of the Vatican's most precious, sacred relics and possibly killed a man.

The place of business he sought was located on a one-way street in a run-down section of the city's center. He didn't like one-way streets; they meant he only had half his normal options, so he parked around the corner and strolled to a seedy looking store front and entered, nonchalantly.

Five minutes later he was back outside, heading for the Giulietta. He did a rapid, thorough surveillance of activity on the street around him, saw nothing out of the ordinary, opened the trunk, hoisted his carry-all out, and closed the trunk so it latched. All slow. All casual. All easy. With one final glance around, he walked back to the uninteresting entrance in the middle of the block and entered with his prize.

*****

# CHAPTER 19

The Federal Reserve Wire Network, known as Fedwire, is a real-time funds transfer system run by US Federal Reserve Banks to enable financial institutions to transfer funds electronically, both within the United States and internationally. This network is used for funds which are also time-critical and large-value amounts. The daily value of transfers sent over Fedwire averages between 2.3 and 2.6 trillion-with-a-T dollars. The number of payments per day varies between 504,000 and 573,000. Day in and day out.

These transactions are monitored by the Office of Foreign Assets Control (OFAC), an agency in the US Treasury Department under the auspices of the Under Secretary of the Treasury for Terrorism and Financial Intelligence. Included on its watch list are 'terrorists, international narcotics traffickers, those engaged in activities related to the proliferation of weapons of mass destruction, and other threats to the national security, foreign policy, or economy of the United States.' Big Brother is always watching where the money goes and following the money trails. Especially if the trails lead to suspected or known narco terrorists.

When Hal Lambeth instructed his bank in the United States to transfer fifty thousand dollars to an obscure bank in Sulmona, Italy, a red flag went up due to the large amount of the transfer. When OFAC discovered that the local name given to receive the money was one Armando DiSalle, another red flag went up. Not only was Armando DiSalle a known mob figure in Abruzzo, he worked with an Albanian drug lord by the name of Murat Krasniqi. Yet another red flag.

When a red flag goes up on a person or organization, the INTERPOL office in the country of origin is notified. After being thoroughly checked out, the item is logged then flagged in the INTERPOL network. At that point, it is up to the desk jockey who processed the flag to determine whether any additional parties are notified, i.e. another country or agency. Because there were not one but three flags on Hal's transfer to Sulmona the INTERPOL office in Washington, D.C. notified their agent in the field of the other country involved, in this case, Italy.

*****

"You gotta be kidding me," Kelvin Gossett ejaculated when he was notified of Hal's pending transfer. "He might as well dress like Bozo the Clown with a big red nose and wear a sandwich board proclaiming 'I sell drugs.' If this transaction goes through he's a dead man. When the bank in Sulmona notifies DiSalle of the transfer he'll know Hal is a total boob who screwed up and have him killed. Hal won't even see it coming."

He guessed it was time to let Hardy know about what Hal was up to ... see if they could talk some sense into him before it was too late. It was only fair he let Hardy in on it since it could impact Hardy's business reputation and the safety of the other hikers. Damn! He looked at his watch. They were all meeting for dinner in half an hour, with the exception of the Fujimotos, Hal, and Peter. He had time for a call to Roberto Montanari.

"Generale, its Vado."

"Si, Vado."

"I've just had news from INTERPOL in Washington, D.C. about the hiker, Hal Lambeth, you mentioned earlier today." Montanari said nothing, waiting expectantly. "Signore Lambeth has instructed his bank in the US to transfer a large sum of money to a bank in Sulmona for an Armando DiSalle."

Montanari sucked in his breath at the news. "Mio Dio, that is signing his death warrant." He gave a long, low whistle. "What will you do? Can you talk to this fool? How soon will the transfer go through? Can it be stalled?"

"The transfer will be delayed, but only for twenty four hours."

"Do you have a plan?"

"If the transfer is cancelled altogether, how will Lambeth explain that to DiSalle? And if it goes through, he won't have to ... any suggestions?"

"None you'd like to hear." Call terminated.

*****

# CHAPTER 20

Some view the International Monetary Fund (IMF) as a band of unscrupulous global criminals, enacting policies self-serving to the greedy ends of the power elite.

It was in 1990 that the IMF, in all its wisdom, imposed its 'economic medicine' policy on Belgrade, plunging industry and agriculture in Kosovo into bankruptcy. Similar macro-economic reforms were imposed on Albania, with devastating social and economic consequences. Albania's banking system was wrecked, its economy shattered. Yugoslavia soon followed. Serbs and Ethnic Albanians were ground into abysmal poverty, and the rate of unemployment in Kosovo swelled to seventy per cent. The Balkans collapsed economically.

Ethnic tensions simmered, and the Kosovo Liberation Army (KLA) became the employer of choice for thousands of young men leaving their teen years. The KLA grew to a standing paramilitary force of thirty thousand men equipped with the latest and best arms and technology. In the absence of traditional employment opportunities running drugs, smuggling weapons, and prostitution became the normal commodities for trade.

Decent, normal people emigrated from the area in the tens of thousands, the hundreds of thousands, looking for a life free of extreme violence and extreme poverty, leaving behind a depraved, nightmare state.

After the IMF made its 'strategic' move the West stood back and watched at the ensuing chaos unleashed on an entire region. With the corrupt Democrat Party (PD) at Albania's helm, state institutions were transformed into criminal enterprises, many of them run by the politicians who were in power.

An extensive black market economy and regional border trade unfolded involving narcotics, oil, and armaments … an economy fed by the international community's sanctions and embargoes. The economic instability and misery fostered and encouraged an environment of illicit trade. The obscenely nouveau riche arising from this miasma of monetary policy gone haywire were the drug barons in Albania, Macedonia, and Kosovo, with ties to the Italian mob.

American and European business interests followed the developments in the Balkans closely, poised to take advantage of the unfolding situation. Western oil companies (Occidental, Shell, and BP) coveted the abundant, unexplored oil deposits in Albania. Other investors from the West had their eyes on the large reserves of precious metals yet undeveloped. German mining interests lobbied for a piece of the action.

Massive amounts of narco dollars, financial proceeds from the drug and arms trades, were funneled into the development of other illicit activities, such as an enormous prostitution trade between Albania and Italy. This vast quantity of tainted monies created a climate which allowed various mafias the ability to buy up assets of the State via privatization programs. The corruption of these programs led to a vast network of real estate dynasties in the hands of the elite criminal classes.

Allowing these social perversions to succeed in Albania is a government which is directly involved with the wickedness from the highest official on down, in spite of Italy and other neighboring countries protesting these officially-sanctioned criminal activities. The Prime Minister of Albania actually repealed the tough anti-trafficking laws in 1998, and freed many criminals from prison, allowing them to re-establish their bases and set up business. Allegedly, the Prime Minister, his body guards, and his wife all had interests in various aspects of the drug trade.

The economic vacuum created by the IMF and its shills has enabled the multinational territory of Albania, Kosovo, and Macedonia to become one huge drug warehouse, where the amount of drugs is weighed in tons, not kilograms. At any given time there are seven tons of heroin in stock, with an unlimited supply constantly available.

The Golden Triangle ... Afghanistan, Iran, and Pakistan ... produces eighty per cent of the heroin sold in Western Europe. It travels through the Balkans, under the guidance of the Albanian Mob. The trade route, originating in the Mid-East and parts of Central Asia, has a safe transit route through Montenegro and Albania, sanctioned by the powerful political elite, and on into Italy by boat.

*****

Adnan Lumani was orphaned at age twelve by the socio-economic upheaval of the early nineties. His parents were brutally murdered in their home one evening by a band of thugs who broke in for plunder. Finding nothing of real value they turned to killing, instead. It became the night's form of entertainment for the band of brutes. Adnan avoided detection by crouching in his wardrobe behind some old drapes that hung there, but he never escaped the sounds of that night.

For the next four years Adnan lived on the streets of Shkodra, Albania, surviving by his natural intelligence and, as his body developed, by brute strength, as well. At sixteen, Adnan had several claims to fame: he was adept at a particularly brutal form of street fighting, quick on his feet, and could wield a knife with deadly results. He kept a chain secured around his waist which he could easily release and this became a weapon to be feared since he had finely sharpened the edges of many of the individual links so that the chain sliced as well as gouged.

He was also very clever ... cleverer than the other punks who roamed the streets, so it was only logical that Adnan rose to the top of this heap of disenfranchised humanity as a leader, of sorts. At the age of sixteen Adnan Lumani, all five foot ten of him weighing in at one hundred and seventy five pounds, cut a handsome, somewhat unwashed figure ruling a four-block area of Shkodra and vying to expand his territory. His gang of eight, also orphaned teen-age boys, were devoted to him and more than a little afraid of his wrath. A good combination, Adnan thought.

This 'band of brothers' had life down to a basic routine. They'd claimed a large apartment in a semi-abandoned apartment house in the old Pjaca neighborhood near the city center. The gang was protective of the other residents of the building, but extracted a 'reasonable fee' for leaving them alone and fending off unwanted intruders. Part of this toll was a daily pot of something hot to eat, usually a stew or soup with dumplings, which the inhabitants took turns providing, gladly. The rest of their food came from stealing and scrounging. They were careful not to lay the burden of their foraging on local vendors, wanting to foster good will in their domain, so they took their plundering elsewhere.

'Opportunity is what you make of it,' Adnan often reflected. And so, one mid-afternoon on a chilly, damp day in April as he was scouting out new turf on Rruga Berdicej he came across a significant, pivotal opportunity.

Prowling down a winding alleyway he heard angry voices which turned into shouts as he approached. Peering around a corner where the alley junctioned with a walkway he witnessed a burly, heavily dressed man grab a smaller, foxy-looking guy by the neck and start to squeeze. The little man fought back, desperately, but the assaulting bull had the advantage. It would soon be over. 'Not even a fair fight,' Adnan thought.

Without thinking, he picked up a chunk of mortar lying by his foot and, with a sure aim and strong arm, lobbed it at the big buy. The flying mortar connected with the massive head with a resounding 'clunk' and the guy dropped like a stone, loosening his grip on the other man's throat as he fell.

Coughing, and gasping for breath the victim wheezed, "Who the hell are you?" He was dressed like a businessman in a well-cut suit, tailored shirt and expensive tie; he wore an expensive cashmere topcoat and a Patek Phillipe wrist watch. Adnan didn't know what a Patek Phillipe was, but he did recognize a high-dollar item when he saw it. For a second he considered stealing the guy's watch. His breath fully recovered, the guy asked, again, "Who are you?"

Adnan's gaze left the watch and settled on the man's face. 'Class,' he decided. The guy was coifed and clean, and exuded forcefulness in his manner of speech. "Adnan ... Adnan

Lumani," he replied, almost adding 'at your service,' but caught himself.

"Well, Adnan Lumani," the stranger said, "it seems you have saved my life from this big piece of shit." He lodged a neat, quick kick in the fallen man's ribs; there was no response. "And killed this big piece of shit in the process," he laughed. The small man looked Adnan up and down, noticing the under-sized, grimy clothes and scuffed shoes. 'Intelligent,' he judged, from the quick brightness of Adnan's liquid brown eyes. 'Eyes that don't miss much. And brave,' he added. He introduced himself. "My name is Krasniqi, Murat Krasniqi ... you have heard of me?" he questioned.

Adnan shook his head, "No, I have not."

"Do you live around here, Adnan?" Murat asked.

Again, Adnan shook his head.

"What are you doing here, then?" Murat demanded.

At this, Adnan lifted his head, looking directly into his inquisitor's eyes, "Saving your life."

Krasniqi threw back his head and enjoyed a really good belly laugh. His laughter alarmed Adnan. He lived in a world where laughing was distrusted and not expressed. Sensing this, Murat sought to allay the discomfort his outburst had caused the young man.

"Yes," Murat replied sincerely, "you did save my life. I owe you a huge debt of gratitude. And,

Adnan Lumani," he promised, "I am a man who repays his debts." He hesitated only a moment before removing his Patek Phillipe, which he offered to Adnan. "A small token of my gratitude."

That beautiful watch. For a brief moment Adnan looked at the watch, then his gaze swung to Murat's face. Placid. Confident. Well-fed. 'How do you get to be all those things?' he wondered.

"Go on, take it," Murat urged. "You earned it. Put it on."

Business Adnan understood. He quickly took the watch, feeling the rich, smooth, sleekness of gold and platinum extravagance. The timepiece caressed his rough, calloused hands. Such a watch!

Krasniqi watched Adnan closely. Suddenly, he understood the young man who stood before him; knew his whole history. He'd seen hundreds with the same background but this one stood out. He had real potential.

"Put it on," Murat ordered again. Adnan did so. It was as though some sort of pact had been signed; an unspoken agreement reached between the two of them; a bond established.

"Where do you live, Adnan Lumani?" Krasniqi inquired. When Adnan told him, describing the apartment building where he and his gang lived, Murat laughed again. "I own that building," he chortled. "In fact, I own that whole block."

He thought a moment. "Perhaps, Adnan, you can help me. I understand that there are gangs roving through that area and the surrounding neighborhood, and they're breaking into buildings, setting fires and stealing. Would you and your friends keep an eye on my properties? Sort of act as my real estate manager in the area? You can, of course, continue to live in the apartment as my guests. In fact, there is another apartment vacant in the same building, on the third floor ... you can occupy that one, as well. What do you say?"

For once, Adnan didn't know what to say. He thought about the past four years of constant struggle to get to his present station in life, if you could call it that, and here was this dude offering him a big step up, an immediate promotion, just because he'd brained his assailant with a rock. A Golden Opportunity. So he said, "Yeah, sure." And then, soberly, "Thank you, Murat Krasniqi."

*****

One week after the incident on Rruga Berdicej a small convoy of black Mercedes-Benz M-Class SUV's pulled up in front of Adnan's apartment building and a security team entered the building with a smallish, well-dressed man floating in their midst. When Adnan answered the sharp knock on his door he found himself looking into the savvy face of Murat Krasniqi. He was surprised, and so pleased he almost smiled.

"I would like you to accompany me, Adnan," Krasniqi explained. "I have business to discuss with you."

Riding on the soft leather rear seat of the Mercedes next to Krasniqi was a dream. He rarely rode anywhere except for the occasional bus. It was so easy to forget the brutality of life from the perspective of the back seat of a Mercedes. With tinted windows. The suspension in the car made it ride like a cloud, the interior was so soft and gleaming he was afraid to touch it and leave a smudge. 'What was it like,' he fantasized, 'to go through life in a cocoon like this car?'

Adnan had asked around about who this Krasniqi guy was and what he'd found out had impressed him. Krasniqi was a big-time criminal. One of the new elites in Albania. Fabulously wealthy from a drug-and-arms smuggling network he controlled from Shkodra over to southern Italy. Not a man to be crossed. And this was the man whose life he'd saved.

The fleet of SUV's drove for ten minutes, up and down the surrounding streets, past apartment buildings, commercial buildings, several banks, a hospital, a playground, parking garages, a church ... and finally Murat spoke, "Everywhere we've driven since I picked you up, I own," he stated matter-of-factly. "And this isn't nearly all of it," he added. "I have a large, complex business, Adnan. I need help with the running of it." He turned on the rear seat to face him. "Will you come to work for me?"

Adnan was caught completely off guard and said nothing for several minutes. "But you know nothing about me, Zoti Krasniqi," he offered.

Murat's hand waved Adnan's comment aside. "I know where you've come from. I can see what you've become. I realize what you can be. And," he added, "you saved my life ... that of a complete stranger, when you could have simply walked away."

Adnan, overcome, didn't trust himself to speak, so he simply nodded his head.

"Good!" Murat pronounced, clapping Adnan on the shoulder. "That's settled! Now, we must get you cleaned up and looking sharp. New clothes ... suits, casual, an entire wardrobe. You must visit my barber ... get your hair under control ... do you mind?" he asked, suddenly realizing he must be overwhelming the young man beside him.

Then he continued, "And you're probably wondering about your gang ... they'll be looked after, too, Adnan. I'm putting them on my payroll to watch over my investments in the Pjaca. But I want you to live on the grounds of my estate. You'll have your own place, of course, but I need to have my right-hand-man near me at all times. Agreed?"

*****

# CHAPTER 21

Hardy's hikers, such as they were, were a beached out, bedraggled bunch when they showed up at the Murena for dinner that evening. The scent of coconut suntan lotion and sea salt commingled in the space they inhabited. The ladies had all done some shopping in the boutiques along Corso Umberto I and small side streets nearby and the results were tasteful designer sundresses with straw or UPF cotton hats to match.

Dinner was a low-key affair since almost half the group was engaged elsewhere. The other half was subdued ... that's what a day in the sun will do, coupled with some wine and a good massage thrown in.

"I just want a shower," Amy moaned. "I love the sea but the salt water makes me feel soooo grungy, especially my hair. I can't even comb it."

"Why didn't you use the public showers along the beach?" Kelvin asked.

"Well," she grimaced, "I saw some little kids peeing in them while they rinsed off and decided I'd pass."

The waitress came over to take their orders. The Murena, located on the waterfront near the port, is a seafood restaurant owned by fishermen who literally carry their daily haul off their boat to the restaurant next door. The items on the menu are no frills, but fresh and excellent. The group ordered an assortment of appetizers which included skewers of calamari, linguine with clams, gnocchi with scampi, and a fresh risotto.

Winnie looked around her. "Not much atmosphere, as far as Italian restaurants go. I imagine Dennis and Teddy found some candlelit, cozy place to put their heads together," she sighed

The Murena definitely would not be called romantic. Plain, homely, clean, bright, lots of windows ... all of the above, but not romantic. A throw-back to the 1980's. The TV harping in the background was a bit of a turn-off and a real conversation killer. Hardy finally asked the owner to mute the volume, which he did, and the group's conversation seemed to explode in the silence.

Their fellow diners at that time of day consisted mostly of two local families with children in tow. At one table the kids were quiet and well-behaved; at the other, not so good, so that dinner was occasionally interrupted by a piercing shriek from the table across the room.

"Ye gads, that drives me nuts," Tillie whispered after the latest shrill outburst. She cast an ominous look in the direction of the offending table, but no one there seemed to notice or care.

"It's hit and miss here, sometimes," Hardy said. "Just drink some more wine and you won't notice."

Outside, darkness was falling across the Adriatic. End-of-the-day ferries were arriving at Pescara from Hvar or Split, Croatia, while others were heading out to sea to a handful of destinations. The fishing boats were all tied up, but lights from pleasure craft twinkled on the vast now-black expanse of sea. Their meal arrived and everyone was busy for a while just digging in.

"Divine," purred Tillie. "This is the freshest seafood I've ever eaten. No wonder Mediterranean people live so long."

"I wanted to try the fish soup, but it looks like a meal in itself," Amy observed.

"It is that," Hardy agreed.

In the grand scheme of things it was a quiet meal of simple, fresh seafood and wine. The Trebbiano d'Abruzzo was a local white wine that was neither expensive or that great, but it went well with the seafood and they consumed several liters during the meal. So much so that, after sorbet and coffee for dessert, everyone was pretty chatty.

Unexpectedly, Hal arrived just after dessert, looking extremely pleased with himself. 'Moron,' Kelvin thought.

Hal started a detailed description of his day spent with cousins living in Pescara. "They've done well for themselves," he boasted. He went into a lengthy explanation of where, exactly, his cousins lived. To anyone familiar with Pescara, someone like Hardy Durkin, for instance, it was obvious Hal's story was concocted and patently untrue.

'I wonder what he's trying to hide and why,' Hardy asked himself.

Hal's over-explaining was so obvious everyone at the table was growing uncomfortable with it. It just didn't ring true but he was so busy spinning his yarn that he didn't notice the embarrassed looks passing between his travel mates.

Winnie finally stemmed the tide by interjecting, "Has anyone seen Peter anywhere?" No one had, and right then, as if by magic he appeared, all smiles, seemingly without a care in the world. 'Which is all wrong,' thought Hardy. 'What happened to the stiff, proper, New England gentleman?'

*****

# CHAPTER 22

Kelvin caught his cell phone on the second chime after the group had arrived back in Sulmona from a tiring but satisfying day in Pescara.

"Pronto."

"It's me, Vado," said Montanari. "I have an update on the American in your tour group who contacted DiSalle in Sulmona and it is not good, my friend."

'Why am I not surprised?' Kelvin asked himself. Aloud, he said, "O.K., Roberto, let's have it."

"He was seen entering the business of an import/export owner in Pescara earlier today, one Sal Colucci. Colucci is a known associate of our friend, DiSalle. They've worked together for years. Colucci runs a bona fide import/export business, but it's mostly a cover for the illegal drugs he smuggles in from Albania under his business' umbrella. Once the drugs are in Pescara he passes them off to DiSalle. DiSalle then puts the drugs in his pipeline to Milan, and one of the crime families in Milan gets the drugs on the street. Precise, smooth and, so far, impossible to track."

"Who is the point of origin in Albania?"

"A very unpleasant man by the name of Murat Krasniqi. Actually, his adopted son, a young man who was orphaned by the war, name of Adnan Lumani, handles the day-to-day operation of goods coming in to Italy. We've never been able to find a hook into Lumani, either."

"Grazie, Roberto. Ciao." The Albanians ... Hal was in such deep water ... he was drowning and had no idea.

*****

Although it was fairly early, Hardy thought he was settled in for the night in his room at Sei Stelle when there was a sharp rap on his door. 'Do I ignore it?' he wondered. The knock came again, this time more insistent.

"Who is it?" he asked, his lack of eagerness for company apparent in his voice.

"It's Kelvin," came the reply, "I need to speak with you."

Inwardly, Hardy groaned. It sounded like this would take a while, and he really wanted to go to bed. He opened his door halfway and was surprised to see a worried, pinch-faced Kelvin exuding anxiety. He didn't ask for Hardy to invite him in, but brushed past him into the room, leaving Hardy, open-mouthed, to close the door. What was this all about? Kelvin's explanation began as Hardy turned to face him.

"I know it's late, but this couldn't wait. First of all, I'm with INTERPOL, and I've been tracking a potential religious art theft ..."

"What!" Hardy exclaimed. "Is your real name Kelvin Gossett? And how do I know you're really with INTERPOL?"

Kelvin had his identification out to present to Hardy before the question had been asked. Hardy took his time examining the photo ID and accompanying badge. His first response was anger.

"What the hell do you mean insinuating yourself into my hiking tour? And why the hell didn't you tell me at once?" he fumed. Having spent some of his fury, a calmer head prevailed. "Are you stalking one of my clients? And what's this sacred relic you're pursuing?" He stopped then, waiting for answers.

Kelvin, at Hardy's outburst, put his arm up in self-defense to ward off the impact of Hardy's angry questions. He had dreaded Hardy's reaction, fearing a temper tantrum and deserving one, but Hardy's ire was quickly spent and replaced by a cool calm.

"How could I tell you I was with INTERPOL" Kelvin asked, "when I still don't know who I'm after? For all I know, it could be you." At this suggestion Hardy almost choked on his wrath. "I know, I know," Kelvin apologized, staving off another outburst, "I realize, now, that you're not the person I'm after, but at first everyone was suspect. Surely, you understand that."

He paused to re-organize his thoughts. "Hal is a problem," he said, abruptly. "He's not the person I'm tracking, at least I don't think so, but he's got himself into an extremely dangerous situation and is too stupid to see it."

"Hal?" asked Hardy, "what could he be up to?"

"Hal," affirmed Kelvin. "He is being tailed by the Italian Carabinieri. He's been seen making contact with a capo in Sulmona who's involved in drug smuggling with an Albanian drug lord. He has no idea the people he's dealing with, and could easily end up dead. He was followed today when we went to Pescara. There's a known assassin tailing him on a Vespa."

This conversation got more alarming by the second. Albanians. Capo. Dead. Hardy couldn't even begin to see all the repercussions from a drug dealer captured in their midst. Nor all the negative exposure it could mean to his hiking business, but the unfolding scenario boded an ill wind, he was certain. In his three years as tour operator and hiking guide Hardy had never had a breath of scandal or question of impropriety in his business. He'd had a few minor injuries, which was to be expected in his line of work, but nothing extraordinary. And they'd all been handled very professionally.

His clientele, many of them repeat customers, were all aboveboard. He'd never even had inappropriate liaisons between his clients, to his knowledge. And now a drug dealer ... possibly a murder? The fallout from something like this could ruin, overnight, everything he'd worked so hard to establish. His name, in the tour business, would be anathema. More importantly, though, was Hal's safety. Could they still help him, or was it too late for that?

"How did the Carabinieri ever suss out Hal?" he asked.

"By accident, apparently. The capo, Armando DiSalle, has been under investigation for drugs for some time. It seems that Hal made contact with him at his address in Sulmona, which put him in the cross hairs of the Italian police. He was added to the list of people of interest, so when he went on walk about in Pescara today he was followed to the business of one Sal Colucci, who has an import/export business. His main routes of trade are across the Adriatic, into Albania. A particularly nasty drug kingpin in Shkodra, Albania, is one of his main clients. Connect the dots."

"And this so-called assassin following Hal," he asked, "wouldn't happen to be a young, dark-complexioned woman, would she?"

Now it was Kelvin's turn to be surprised. "That's right," he said. "Her name's Black Maria, a pretty nasty number from near Naples. How would you know?"

"I saw her tailing Hal yesterday in the Piazza in Sulmona. Are you sure she's a hired killer?"

"No question."

Hardy digested the scenario Kelvin had laid out for him. "But that doesn't prove that Hal is involved in the drug trade. It seems a pretty big leap to me."

Kelvin regarded Hardy with sympathy. 'Classic denial,' he thought, 'but who can blame him? One minute he's leading a tour of peaceful hikers in rural, idyllic Italy, the next he's embroiled in a drug deal which is destined to go seriously wrong.' Aloud he explained, "That's not all of it, Hardy. The US Treasury Department, the part that monitors terrorism and illegal transfers of funds, has a bead on Hal, as well. It seems he has authorized his bank in the States to transfer a large sum of money to a bank in Sulmona, in care of Armando DiSalle, the capo. Therein lay the danger to Hal: when DiSalle learns that Hal has his name as designee for the money he'll realize he's dealing with a total screw-up and have Hal killed. He has put DiSalle and, by extension, the Albanian gangster and his entire operation in jeopardy. The repercussions will be deadly, all down the line."

"How do you know about the wire transfer?"

"Treasury notified the INTERPOL office in Washington, D.C., and they passed the information on to me. The intel is good, Hardy. Hal is in serious trouble, and we've got to do something."

Hardy stared at Kelvin, not seeing him. A hired killer after Hal ... they would all be implicated to some degree, especially if someone, i.e. Hal, got put in jail or was hurt, or even killed.

There'd be interrogations ad infinitum, knowing the Italians. Everybody would come under suspicion. Delays. Confusion. Inconveniences. Lots of bad press, too. Kelvin was watching Hardy, recording his thought progression as it registered on his face. Denial; shock; anger; resignation; determination. Hardy finally spoke, "O.K., Kelvin," he said, "what do we do?"

Kelvin was visibly relieved. He had counted on Hardy's support to confront Hal. "We need to see Hal, tonight. Let him know we know. Tell him he's under surveillance. And tweaking the devil's nose."

*****

Hal Lambeth was one cool customer, or so he thought. When Kelvin and Hardy stopped by his room to confront him about his 'alleged' drug dealing he put on his best poker face and played 'The Don' just like in his favorite movie, The Godfather. His benevolent smile and deprecating attitude toward what Kelvin relayed to him about being under investigation by the police frustrated Kelvin. Hal just wasn't getting it, it seemed. Hardy stood by, saying nothing. Kelvin wanted to kill him; he finally snapped.

Kelvin pulled his chair directly in front of where Hal sat and hissed, "Listen, you fat piss wit ... the anti-terrorism unit in the US Treasury has flagged your drug-money wire transfer to the Sulmona bank. INTERPOL notified me. We also know that you've pegged Armando DiSalle as the receiver on this end. When he finds out what you've done ... basically put a bull's eye on him ... you're a dead man. He'll realize he's dealing with a nitwit who is a danger to him and his network. If he doesn't kill you, the Albanian drug lord who supplies him with illegal drugs will have you terminated, so either way, you've had it. DiSalle has had a mafia assassin tailing you for days." That got Hal's attention. The façade disappeared; in its place was a terrified, pudgy man who suddenly developed a bad attack of flatulence. Hal's situation, put in those terms, alarmed Hardy even more.

"So what's going to happen to Hal?" Hardy asked. "Will the cops give him protection?"

"Not likely," Kelvin responded. "If they do it will blow their entire operation against DiSalle and the Albanian drug lord. They won't risk all the months that have been put into the job on a two-bit, wannabe gangster. Hal is a throw-a-way for them; collateral damage." He was being unnecessarily cruel and knew it, but the effect was exactly what he wanted.

Sweat was pouring down Hal's face; his shirt had two enormous wet splotches around each underarm, his hair was plastered to his head. He was so scared that when he spoke his teeth almost chattered. "What about I just cancel the wire transfer?" he asked. "Then there's no way DiSalle's name gets flagged; I just walk away like it never happened."

For a moment Hardy looked optimistic, but Kelvin dashed his hopes. "If you tried to cut and run DiSalle would figure you for a snitch and have you capped. What they do to snitches isn't pretty."

At that revelation Hal cringed with a really bad gas pain and let rip. "Dang, Hal," Kelvin complained, "take an Alka Selzer or something." It was pathetic to see Hal's transformation from an elegant 'Don' with savoir-faire to a simpering, overweight, flaccid boob.

Kelvin almost felt sorry for him, but not quite. "I've been trying to think of a way out for him, and the only thing I can come up with is for him to wear a wire and meet with DiSalle. Get him to spell out the shipping arrangement and pick up for Hal's stuff; get it on tape. Get him to name Colucci. That way, DiSalle gets nabbed and put away, for a while at least, and the police would probably give Hal a pass for cooperating ... after all, he's not the one they want. It's the big fish: DiSalle. And Colucci, too, if it comes to that."

They both looked at Hal ... could he pull it off? In the world of real criminals Hardy had his doubts that Hal would be able to pass muster and play the part under duress. The profuse sweating was a dead giveaway. The farting was another thing ...

*****

The revelation of Hal's criminal dealings and its implication for Hardy's tour group agitated Hardy to the point of his needing to take a stroll and think it through. He left the Sei Stelle shortly after eight thirty and cut through the piazza. Just as he approached the far side of Piazza

Garibaldi he spied Black Maria riding her Vespa very slowly up Via Marselli, as though waiting for someone behind her. A light-colored cargo van with a furniture company logo emblazoned on its side followed about forty feet behind, its headlights blinking on and off like there was an electrical short in the wiring.

Hardy decided to tag along, an easy feat, since both vehicles were traveling so slowly. A short distance up Via Marselli the Vespa turned right and then took an immediate left. The street was much quieter in a mostly residential neighborhood of large houses that had been divided up into apartments. Half-way down this street Black Maria hesitated, flashing her lights twice, then proceeded to turn down an alleyway off to the right. The van, its lights blinking in some sort of bizarre code, followed.

At the entrance to the alley Hardy paused and listened. He could hear the phut-phut-phut of the Vespa's engine, but the van's engine had been turned off. Staying well in the shadows, Hardy crept up the alley. He could hear the murmur of voices. As he crept closer he could make out a woman's voice that he assumed was that of Black Maria. It was low and coarse.

"E 'la porta verde. Assicurati di bloccarlo quando si è fatto. Lascio DiSalle conosce i farmaci sono arrivati sani e salvi," she said. ("*The green door. Drugs for DiSalle.*") Kelvin needed to know this.

With a dismissive wave, Black Maria revved up her Vespa and left, leaving two thuggish-looking men to unload the van. Hardy waited several minutes and stole closer, hoping to get the license number of the van.

Suddenly, something bumped his leg. Hardy liked cats, usually, but they didn't like him. This cat was no exception. After the first bump, an exploratory pass to see what Hardy was, the cat turned back and this time attached himself to Hardy's right leg with its very sharp claws. Hardy gritted his teeth; the cat dug deeper. When he could stand it no longer Hardy tramped on the cat's tail and shook his leg in a flying sweep. The cat went flying through the air and let out a loud 'Reeoww' when it landed with a solid thump. The men at the van stopped unloading at the noise.

"Chi c'è?" one of them asked. Who's there? Hardy froze, deep in shadow.

"Chi c'è?" the man asked again, much louder.

The cat darted out of the alley just then and scampered under the van, hissing. The men laughed and went back to their task.

It was too dark to see the license plate of the van where it was parked during unloading. Hardy would do much better getting the license number as the van passed under a street lamp, but which way would the van exit the alley? Would it come out past where Hardy hid in the shadows, or take the same route Black Maria had taken on her Vespa? Hardy reasoned that they would leave the same way they'd come in because it was a route they knew. They obviously didn't know their way around Sulmona or they wouldn't have had to follow Black Maria to the storage shed, so they wouldn't be familiar with the way she'd taken when she left them.

Hardy backtracked out of the alley to the residential street. There was a streetlight where the alley intersected it. He hid behind a large bush that overgrew the sidewalk there and waited. Five minutes passed. Ten. He was beginning to berate himself for being in the wrong place when he saw the blink-blink of the van's headlights heading his way. He breathed a sigh of relief and his face broke into a smile: he'd guessed right.

\*\*\*\*\*

Back at the Sei Stelle Hardy found Kelvin in his room. He drew Kelvin a rough map, giving directions to the alley where DiSalle stored his drug shipments that came into Sulmona, and also furnished the license number of the van used to transport them. Kelvin was impressed with Hardy's prowess; he'd given him pure gold. He couldn't wait to report to Montanari.

\*\*\*\*\*

# CHAPTER 23

The breakfast table the following morning was abuzz with news of the heist of the sacred relic from the Church of San Francesco in Lanciano. Meals at Sei Stelle were served in a bright, pleasant room with a large checkerboard tile floor, and a high, pie-crust ceiling that gave the effect of a trompe l'oeil. The long narrow table, draped in a starched white cloth, was laden with plates of fresh, homemade sweet rolls, bowls of yogurt with fruit in season, jams, honey, and pots of steaming coffee. To the regular, daily fare had been added a charcuterie platter with butter and hard rolls.

"Somebody just waltzed right in and stole the thing, in broad daylight," Winnie was expounding.

"It wasn't that simplistic, dear," Tillie admonished her twin. "It was well-planned, so they say."

Kelvin listened and watched as each member of the hiking group espoused an opinion or comment about the theft of The Eucharistic Miracle. His face was expressionless, but inside his bowels were churning he was so angry. To him, the theft was an act against God Himself, a blasphemy. He took its plunder quite personally. Hal, he noticed, was unusually pensive this morning after the session he and Hardy had put him through last night; everyone else was pretty much according to character.

"How far is this Lanciano place from here?" Teddy asked.

Hardy stepped up to the plate with the answer. "It's just over sixty seven miles," he informed her, "but the roads are secondary so it takes about an hour and a half. Actually, Lanciano is much closer to Pescara, where we were yesterday, than Sulmona. According to the article in La Repubblica, the relic was actually stolen when we were in Pescara."

"Can you read Italian, Hardy?" Dennis asked.

All eyes swiveled toward Hardy. He was self-conscious under their gaze, but nodded. "I get the gist of regular stuff, but anything technical or specialized, forget it." He made good on his promise to Kelvin not to divulge Kelvin's attachment to INTERPOL or his interest in the stolen relic.

"How many people were involved in the heist? Did the newspaper say?" pursued Amy.

"The working theory appears to be it was someone operating alone. The police think he hid out in the church after morning prayers and did the deed while the church was closed over lunch."

Just then Peter arrived for breakfast, greeting everyone as he slid into his seat. He helped himself to coffee and a fresh roll. "Have you heard about the robbery yesterday, Peter?" Amy asked him. "A sacred treasure of the Catholic Church was stolen ... it's in all the papers."

Peter continued buttering his roll while he answered, "No, this is the first I've heard of it. Where did it happen?"

"Not far from Pescara, while we were there," she told him.

"A pity," he commented, pouring more coffee.

'Pity?' Kelvin mused.

"But really," Amy continued, "why would anyone want to steal a relic from a church, for heaven's sake? I know we discussed the idea of The Church monopolizing religious artifacts, but what could any person want with such a thing?"

There was a brief pause which Peter finally ended. "Maybe whoever stole The Eucharistic Miracle thought he had a better use for it than the church," he said rather dismissively. His air of nonchalance seemed a bit overdone. Normally, Peter was a very restrained person; this morning he was almost voluble.

Peter's last comment caused Kelvin's head to jerk, slightly. 'Now that's interesting,' he thought, 'he wasn't at the table when we were discussing what had actually been stolen. Amy told him it was a sacred treasure, and he claims he knew nothing of the robbery prior to coming down to breakfast. So how did Peter know The Eucharistic Miracle is the relic that was taken? And just where was Peter yesterday when the theft took place? He said he would be visiting an old friend in Pescara, but how do we know that's the truth?'

"There was one other piece of information about the heist in the news," Hardy added, his voice steady. "A man was found in the church sanctuary, where the relic was kept ... he'd been hit on the head and was unconscious, lying on the floor near one of the side entrances. The carabinieri think he tried to foil the thief and was struck down in the process." There was total silence around the breakfast table as this latest bit of news was digested.

Teddy finally asked the question on everyone's mind. "Is the guy still alive?"

Hardy hesitated intentionally to heighten the suspense, and also to allow him time to study the faces around the table before answering.

"The man was in critical condition and not expected to live last night. However, as of this morning his condition has been upgraded and the doctors expect him to regain consciousness. When, no one knows for sure. If the man pulls through he will no doubt be able to give the police a description of the culprit, barring any form of amnesia, of course."

The hikers had expected bad news about the man assaulted during the robbery, but relaxed, visibly, when Hardy apprised them of the morning update. All except for Peter. He seemed to tense up and his forced smile became wooden and robotic when Hardy mentioned the possibility of an identification. His reaction was not lost on the ever-observant Kelvin, either.

*****

Hardy pulled Honey aside after breakfast was over and the others had departed. "How's it going?" he asked nonchalantly.

"Great!" she replied.

He pulled her further into the niche in the wall where the aqueduct ran through. He lowered his voice and tried to shield her with his body. "Remember the other day when we were in the Piazza and you pointed out the dark woman you'd seen following Hal?" She nodded. "Turns out she's a hired killer." Honey sucked her breath in an audible gasp; her eyes bulged.

"What!?"

Hardy hastened to explain. "I'm not trying to frighten you, Honey, but I sure as hell don't want you getting involved in anything dangerous ..."

"What is an assassin doing following the goof in the hat?" she demanded. "What's going on, Hardy?" She was frightened. Suddenly, sunny Italy had been over-shadowed by something dark and ugly.

Hardy really didn't want to have to lay the whole scenario out to Honey; it would only alarm her more, but she deserved some explanation since she was the one who'd pointed out Black Maria to Hardy to begin with.

"Hal has gotten himself involved with some really bad people, Honey," he said. "Idiot that he is," he added. "I need you to keep this a secret for now; don't even tell your uncle. And for Pete's sake stay away from that woman ... her name is Black Maria, by the way. If you see her around, don't even notice her or let her think you're on to her in any way. Can you do that?" Honey was lost in thought and didn't answer. Hardy shook her, gently, by the shoulders. "Honey. Can you do that?" he asked again.

She shifted her gaze to his face and refocused on what he was saying. She nodded. "Yes. I won't tell anyone," she promised. Hardy was seized by a sudden desire to kiss those trusting lips and did so. His impulsive action left both of them startled for a brief moment, then Honey leaned forward with a seductive smile and they kissed again, a longer, lingering kiss.

A certain physical reaction below Hardy's waist forced him to break off the embrace. "You're dangerous!" he told her. "Before I forget that I'm responsible for a hiking group I'd better be going. But I'd sure like a rain check for later," he said.

"You got it!" she smiled.

He started to leave, and turned back to her, "Remember, Honey. Say nothing and be very careful. See you tonight." And he was gone.

*****

Hal went back to his room after breakfast. He felt sick to his stomach and knew it was stress.

How the hell had he got himself into this mess? Greed. Pure and simple. The money from his mother's estate wasn't quite enough to do what he wanted to pull off his restaurant idea and he thought he could make a quick windfall in a one-time drug deal. How damn dumb could he be? Kelvin and Hardy thought he was a loser; he was so ashamed.

He almost doubled over as another gas pain hit him. Jesus, Mary and Joseph! He'd never broken a law in his life and here he was, involved with a mob capo in Italy who was hooked up with a real villain in the Balkans. Someday, he might be able to laugh at his idiocy ... where was the damned Alka Selzer?

He gulped down a glass before the fizz had finished, and let out a tremendous belch. There, that felt some better. Every time he thought about wearing a wire to record DiSalle he had a panic attack. 'Please, God ... is there no other way?' he wondered.

God. Hal hadn't thought about him in years, let alone 'talked' to Him. He was desperate. Maybe he should at least try. What do I say? 'I screwed up, God.' He didn't think that would work, somehow. Then he did something he hadn't done since catechism ... he knelt down by his bed and made a teepee of his hands, and prayed. "Dear God. It's Hal ... Hal Lambeth. My mom really liked you. She said you were always there, so ... I need to talk to you. I'm in a lot of trouble and I need help, so if you can show me what to do, I'd greatly appreciate it, God. Thanks." He wondered if it was his imagination, but he felt strangely better, and calmer. And hopeful.

*****

Giuseppe turned up at Sei Stelle when breakfast was finished and he and the Bradford gals went off to the sitting room to confer tête-à-tête. He was a bit greasier looking than usual and smelled strongly of stale tobacco and sweat. He was unmindful of the uncomfortable looks thrown his way by Lucy and Teddy, who went out of their way to avoid crossing his path. Winnie and Tillie, however, were delighted to see the former bus driver and grabbed a sweet roll and cup of coffee for him before herding him into the lounge area, gabbling with excitement.

'What on earth are they up to with that shady character?' Hardy wondered. He had developed a major distrust of his former employee, and for the life of him couldn't fathom Giuseppe's connection to the twins. He only hoped that there wasn't something unsavory going on ... something questionable or even illegal. He grimaced at the thought. On top of Hal's attempt at drug smuggling he didn't need anything else to go wrong on his tour. He tried to stay positive.

"We leave in ten minutes, ladies," he called to them. They were busy listening to something Giuseppe was relaying to them, and Winnie appeared to be taking notes, but they gave him a wave of acknowledgment that the message had been received. He gave a curt nod of greeting to Giuseppe before heading out the door.

*****

# CHAPTER 24

The area around the Navelli Plain was the hiking destination for Thursday, and after a day off the trails spent sunning and shopping in Pescara everyone was ready to roll. Kelvin made his apologies, saying he had to nurse a blister on his foot; everyone else boarded the bus and headed for the village of Prata d'Ansidonia, about an hour away in the direction of L'Aquila. The hike scheduled for the day would take about six hours and be a fairly gentle exploration of the high Navelli plain, along with several old villages. The route would traverse forest, grassland, and quiet countryside following ancient sheep droves and mule tracks.

They set out from Prata d'Ansidonia at a leisurely pace, still in a languorous state from the previous day spent in the sun and salt air. By the time they made the tiny village of Tussio the group had shaken off its sluggishness and hit a steady, easy stride.

"I feel like my head is full of cobwebs," Lucy commented, keeping pace with Hardy on the tratturo, which was littered with recent signs of sheep using the path as they headed for flat summer pastures just above the vast plain below. She had turned a deep reddish-bronze in the Pescaran sun and the highlights of the rich colors glowed from her skin in the full morning sunlight. With her muscular long legs and sculpted upper arms she looked much like a warrior-goddess striding in the midst of an ancient landscape suited for catching thunderbolts and dancing with mountain nymphs. She had pulled her shiny, dark hair back into a pony tail, which swung rhythmically as she walked along.

"I should know better than to consume quantities of wine after a day in the sun," she yawned. Abruptly, she changed the subject. Lowering her voice, she said, "Hardy, my sixth sense is telling me that there's something fishy going on with certain members of our hiking group. I know it sounds weird, but I'm usually right when I get these impressions."

"Sixth sense?" Hardy queried. "Where does that come from?"

"My hair," she replied, simply.

Hardy broke stride to see if she was serious. She was. "Explain that to me."

"I know it sounds bizarre," she began, "but there have been lots of studies done about the relationship between a Native American's hair and his ability to perceive beyond the reality of our five senses."

Hardy's silence prodded her to explain. "For instance, during the Vietnam war young Native Americans were selected for their ability to track through rough terrain. These were men who had proved their skills and stealth many times over. They were even tested once they'd been inducted into Special Forces. But after they'd been officially signed up and had their hair cut short, army style, they lost these innate abilities.

"The military couldn't figure out what was happening at first ... they lost quite a few scouts and trackers before they noticed the correlation between the haircut and the loss of skills.

"To take it a step further, the military paired up two Native Americans with the same skills and tested both of them rigorously before any hair was cut, and they found that both men tested equally in their skill set. Then they would cut the hair of one of the pair of men and retest for the same skills. Without fail, the recruit with the haircut would fail the same tests he had scored high on before having his hair shorn.

"As a result of all the testing, it was recommended that all Native Americans be exempt from the mandatory haircut. In fact, it became required policy that all trackers keep their hair long."

Hardy was still skeptical. "Is there a scientific basis for this hypothesis?"

"Actually, yes," she continued. "Our hair is seen as a part of the central nervous system ... exteriorized nerves, if you will. Kind of like highly-evolved antennae. Our hair becomes an information highway to our brain; it also emits electromagnetic energy from the brain into our environment.

"Cutting our hair hampers the sending and receiving of transmissions with our surroundings." She paused before adding an additional comment. "It was disorienting and cruel to force Native American children to have their hair cut when they were made to attend government schools. God only knows how much it handicapped them."

Hardy, who considered himself somewhat practiced at trivia, was stunned with Lucy's revelation. He'd never heard anything like it, yet it made sense. Maybe that was the reason Sikhs never cut their tresses, and Orthodox Jews kept all their hair. Of course, Sikhs also wrapped their long locks up in a turban, so their hair wouldn't be transmitting much all bundled up in a towel. Still, Lucy's explanation fascinated him with all its implications, and he determined to test her theory, starting immediately.

"I'm going to quit shaving for the duration of our trip," he informed her, "and see if I notice any difference."

"I somehow think it will take more than that, Hardy," she rejoined, "to increase sensitivity to your environment." She smiled encouragingly, "But it's a start," she said.

'And it got you off your suspicions about things not being as they seem in our group,' Hardy thought.

*****

Immediately after the hiking group departed for their day's jaunt Kelvin went to the nearest car rental agency near the Sei Stelle and procured a small Mercedes A160 with automatic transmission and headed to Pescara. He had to trace Peter's movements in Pescara yesterday, if possible.

He left his rental in the same parking lot the tour bus had used the day before and began a methodical exploration of the streets nearby. He carried a pocket-size street map and, working on a grid system, searched up and down the streets, stopping at all car rental offices he ran across. At his third attempt he got a hit when he produced a picture of Peter that he'd surreptitiously taken with his cell phone at breakfast two hours earlier.

"Yes, he rented a car from me yesterday," the young women behind the counter finally admitted after Kelvin flashed his ID. "An Alfa Romeo Giulietta ... only his name wasn't the one you gave me." She pulled a stack of rental agreements out of a manila folder and began to rummage through them, talking aloud to herself as she did so. "No, not that one ... no, this was the foreign lady ... no ... ummm, no ... ahh, this is the one!" she exclaimed triumphantly, holding the paperwork for Kelvin to see. "You see," she said, "this man's name was Banning. Arthur Banning, from New York. But he looks just like the man in the picture on your phone."

Kelvin took several pictures of the rental papers, and asked her to also make him copies. "Did he happen to say where he was going?" he asked. No such luck. He was correct: Peter/Arthur had made no mention of his destination; however, the completed paperwork indicated that he had traveled a total of one hundred fifteen kilometers, enough to make it to Lanciano and back and allow for a few minor stops or diversions along the way. "Can I see the GPS from the car he rented?"

The clerk searched through the paper work before her. A perplexed look on her face was a harbinger of bad news for Kelvin. "It seems the car he rented was completely serviced after he returned it to us. As part of the servicing the electrical system was disconnected. I'm afraid all the GPS information is lost. Sorry."

Kelvin was sorry, too. It would have been a big break towards building his case against Peter. He thanked the helpful clerk and was on his way to Lanciano moments later.

*****

Honey volunteered to shop for the bread and pastries that morning and set out, ostensibly heading for the bakery. In truth, she had spotted Giuseppe conversing with the dark-skinned woman after his meeting with the Bradfords and, ignoring Hardy's warning, had decided to follow the lady assassin when she and Giuseppe parted company. It was her first attempt ever at sleuthing and she found it thrilling and not terribly difficult. Maybe she'd learn something valuable to report back to Hardy. Hardy. She blushed remembering his kiss earlier.

The prospect of an affair during her summer in Italy seemed like something out of an eighties novel. He was so good looking; still, she didn't want to lose her head over him like some school girl and end up feeling the fool.

Musing about Hardy broke her focus on tailing Black Maria. When she looked up ahead, Honey saw what she assumed was Black Maria passing in front of a cut-flower vendor's booth with bunches of fresh blooms stuck in buckets of water setting on the pavement all round the booth. Suddenly, her quarry was swallowed up by the crowd of market goers on the Piazza and Honey sped after her, abandoning caution.

*****

Black Maria knew she was being followed by the blond from the Sei Stelle as soon as she left Giuseppe standing outside the bed and breakfast. He was her source of information for the hiking group's daily travel destinations, which allowed her to keep track of the flaccid fool she'd been assigned to tail.

The blond wasn't a threat but Black Maria was feeling rancorous today and she decided she'd teach the silly girl a lesson as well as have a bit of fun. Once inside the open-air market she increased her pace, weaving in and out of the narrow aisles defined by the vending stalls. Predictably, her pursuer quickened her pace, becoming reckless. Black Maria gave a satisfied, mean laugh. She always felt a cruel gratification when the cat became the mouse.

She ducked behind a butcher's stall where she had stashed her Vespa and, wheeling it onto the nearby street, kick-started it, gently revving the engine until it purred evenly, all the while watching for her prey to emerge from the market crowd at the intersection.

Honey finally emerged from the Piazza and rushed into the crosswalk looking in all directions, craning her head for a glimpse of the dark-faced woman she'd been following. There was no sign of her on the sidewalks in any direction. Perhaps the assassin was still in the bustling piazza. She started to return to the market. From the back of her mind she heard a faint buzzing which rapidly turned into the roaring of an engine. Honey suddenly felt a crushing pain in her left leg and was thrown several feet, back onto the sidewalk. She glimpsed a figure shoot by on a Vespa before losing consciousness; her last thought was that she'd miss her rendezvous with Hardy that night.

*****

# CHAPTER 25

Hardy and company stopped for a rest break once they reached the ruins of the Bominaco Castle, one of the high points on their trek. The main part of the castle had been built in the thirteenth century as protector of the nearby monastery and village. The round sighting tower, built two centuries later, was the only part of the castle that had been preserved.

The views of the surrounding mountains were wonderful, particularly the main peaks of the Gran Sasso in the northeast and the Navelli plateau spread out below. From above, the broad valley was a patchwork of brown, amber, light and dark green squares broken by an occasional farmhouse or olive grove with the mountains a formidable backdrop to the entire setting. Raptors soared overhead, looking for their lunch in the fields below. Conversation was sporadic. For the most part, everyone kept to themselves, soaking up the sun, fresh air, and blessed peacefulness. The incessant insect buzzing was soporific. Heads were lulling.

"Everyone," Hardy announced, "I hate to break into your siesta, but if we don't move on we'll be dozing through lunch and be late meeting Bernardo for the bus back to Sulmona. Plus,

.'t want to miss our lunch date at a farmhouse restaurant."

were groans and muted protests as the hike. roused to their feet to continue their hike. A short distance away, down a steep, stepped path, they came to the Oratory of San Pellegrino, a plain looking little church built in a lovely location.

"This little chapel was founded by Charlemagne late in the eighth century as part of a Benedictine monastery in honor of San Pellegrino, who came from Syria to preach Christianity. He was martyred here, where the church stands. Legend has it that a pilgrim appeared to Charlemagne in a vision requesting the chapel be built. Saint Pellegrino is buried under the stone to the right of the altar."

"The door's locked," Hal informed them. "Says here to call this number for a guide."

"That would be Chiara," said Hardy. "She is an English-speaking guide who lives nearby ... it takes her about five minutes to get to the church ..."

At that moment a very spry lady in her late forties, not much over five feet tall, rounded the corner. Dressed in a long pale green linen skirt with a matching sleeveless linen tunic top and a dozen gold bangles tinkling around her left wrist she paused when she saw the group.

"Buongiorno. May I help you?" Her intelligent, dark brown eyes sparkled with warmth and humor.

"Buongiorno. Chiara, isn't it?" Hardy inquired. "We met last year when I came through with a group of hikers."

She nodded, smiled. "Would you like to see inside the Oratory?" she asked, producing a key from a large side pocket.

"If it's not too much trouble," Hardy said.

"No ... no trouble at all. I was just coming to enjoy the frescoes. I do that often ... sit and marvel at them."

She stepped lightly to the door of the chapel and, with a healthy twist of the rather large, ornate key, opened the heavy, creaking door and entered, motioning for the group to follow. The gasps of wonderment that came from the hikers spread a look of pleasure across Chiara's placid face. "They are quite lovely aren't they?" she whispered.

"My goodness, they're exquisite!" Amy gushed.

They had stepped into a rectangular nave topped by a vaulted ceiling; all of it was covered, completely, by marvelous frescoes representing the sacred history of the Childhood of Christ, the Passion, the Final Judgment, and the life of Saint Pellegrino. The frescoes are considered the most spectacular in Abruzzo, more than fifteen hundred square feet of them in rich reds, golden ambers, and vibrant earth tones.

The subtle, gossamer-like lighting from the two small rose windows and the slit openings on each side of the sanctuary contributed to an otherworldliness and ethereal quality of the spiritually sublime. They had, in fact, stepped into another world. This was the world of living church history, the walls of the church a painted book for the illiterate peasants who worshipped there, a book portraying the liturgy, sacraments, the life of Christ, and the lives of the saints. A giant rendering of Saint Christopher with his knees exposed stood guard next to the entrance directly over the stoup. The monks had included a Monastic calendar with signs of the zodiac, probably painted for liturgical use. Was that because they were also lovers of the sciences, or because it would help them keep track of the correct liturgy to use for a particular month or day?

"Who painted all this?" Hal asked Chiara.

"We think it was done by monks, primarily three monks, referred to as Masters, although an inscription by both the dragon, there," she said pointing, "and that griffin, on the right, claim Abbot Teodino as the author of the artwork, dated 1263.

"The three monks had different styles and training, and are referred to by the frescoes they painted. Maestro dell'Infanzia portrayed the story of Christ as a child. Maestro della Passione painted the story of the Passion. And Maestro Miniaturista was responsible for painting the calendar with the months, zodiac signs, and lunar phases.

"If you study the Passion you'll notice that scenes from Christ's crucifixion and resurrection have not been included. This is because the monastic theology of the time believed these two critical moments were to be lived, not represented: The Church offers the Eucharist in the form of communion to renew Christ's sacrifice, and the evangelical life of the monks, in loving and serving others, shows Christ's victory over death."

"These frescoes are a labor of love," Lucy said. "To be in the middle of nowhere, creating such a splendid place of worship ... an act of love for their God and fellow man."

She wandered over to an unforgiving wooden bench and sat down to contemplate a brotherhood of Benedictine monks living out their faith, a living faith ... what was it the Bible said, 'Faith without works is dead.' But all around her, here, in this tiny chapel existing in virtual obscurity, a community of monks had brought the love of God to a simple population. They had been the enlightened ones, studying the stars, reading the tomes of civilization, toiling in the earth, tending their vines, healing with their herbs ... they had brought the love of Christ to an illiterate, pagan land by being living examples that 'God is Love.'

How the Magnificat must have resounded within these walls during Vespers ... 'My soul doth magnify the Lord. And my spirit hath rejoiced in God my Savior ...' Yes, she could hear the song of adoration as the monks, immersed in lives consecrated to their Creator, lifted their voices to God as incense before His throne.

The atmosphere was still redolent of spiritual tranquility, even these many centuries later, brought on by continually being soaked in the glorious praises of the Benedictines so long ago. No one spoke. Members of the group either walked slowly around the vaulted hall savoring the painted depictions of Christian history or sat, awestruck, in their own religious ecstasies.

Finally, it was time to depart. Hardy donned his backpack, which signaled the others that they needed to be on their way. He handed Chiara a twenty-Euro note. "For the upkeep," he told her. They filed out, silently, reverently, still suffused by the heavenly calm of the chapel, not quite ready to switch time zones and rejoin the world.

*****

# CHAPTER 26

Hardy led them, single file, downhill to the fortified village of Caporciano, one of the localities for saffron production on the Navelli plain. All was peaceful, except for a Vespa that revved its engine as it swooped past them on their way in to the village.

On the edge of the little town they arrived at a farmhouse just before noon for lunch. Set amid a checkerboard of fields planted with olive trees, vines, wheat, and pastureland, the white stucco house, restored and given a new red tile roof, was abustle with activity.

In one of the outbuildings wool from this season's sheep shearing was being cleaned and carded in preparation for bundling and shipping. A distant field of wheat that had been harvested was being cut into straw prior to baling. Two young boys, in their early teens, dressed in cargo shorts and tee shirts, were hoeing and weeding a large vegetable garden on the south side of the house. The dark olive of their skin indicated this wasn't their first day working under the Abruzzo sun. They laughed and joked back and forth, making light of their labor.

A cream-colored Abruzzo sheep dog sauntered toward them as they made their way up a gravel drive, his tail wagging and a look of greeting on his noble face. He immediately began to herd the newcomers toward the loggia at the side of the house. A second sheep dog slept in the sun, too drowsy to be bothered with another job.

"These are such great dogs," Hardy said, scratching the working animal behind his ears. "They're called Maremmas or Pastore Abruzzese. They've been bred for centuries to protect sheep from wolves and bears. They're always this whitish color, for two reasons: one, the sheep feel better that the dogs are the same color as the sheep, and two, when it's dark at night the shepherd can easily distinguish his sheepdogs from a dark wolf." The dog raised a playful paw as Hardy stroked his head. "They make fantastic guard dogs, but without the vicious temperament typical of guard dogs."

They had been herded to the veranda, which was set as an outdoor dining area. A screen door leading from the house onto the patio was suddenly thrust open and the lady of the house emerged, all smiles, wiping her large hands on an apron smudged with residue from today's menu.

"Signore, Hardy!" she called out, embracing Hardy in a bear hug, kissing him on both cheeks. She released him and stood smile at her other guests, vigorously many greetings. The Signora was a tall woman with the strength of an ox and the heart of a saint. The twinkle in her large, fluid, dark eyes was engaging, her laugh, for a lady of her proportions, a light, airy chime. Hardy was pleased by the reception he'd just received. He always looked forward to his visits to Agriturismo le 4a, a farmhouse restaurant otherwise known as Mama Celia's.

"Mama Celia," Hardy said by way of introduction, "is the best cook in all of Abruzzo." She beamed at him. "What delights have you prepared for us today, Signora? Never mind," he quickly added, giving her a wink, "just surprise us." He took a moment to introduce the members of his group, and directed them to a small extension built on the side of the house. "Wash room and toilet," he explained.

Mama Celia stepped back into her kitchen to continue the preparations for lunch. Hardy removed his backpack and was stuffing it out of the way, "Oh, and by the way, this dog's name is Aberto; the lazy one is Aida."

Mama Celia's teenage daughter, Simona, was their waitress for the duration of their meal. Simona had a slender, refined body. Her arms and legs were long and strong, yet elegant in movement. She was actually quite a pretty young thing; her genes had been spared the coarse features of a peasant. But she was shy, unlike her mother, and kept her gaze averted as she brought forth the food and drink. Several times different members of the hiking group asked her questions about her schooling or what she liked to do, but the olive skin of her cheeks would redden and she'd be gone in a flash, avoiding an answer.

Several carafes of red wine were placed along the length of the table, along with a thick soup of beans and summer vegetables, served cold, with hard-crusted bread. "This beats the hell out of gazpacho," Hal commented, wondering if he could ask for seconds.

"La cucina tipica abruzzese," Hardy responded. "Typical Abruzzo food," he translated when Hal threw him a questioning look.

Hal smiled, looking slightly relieved. "For a minute there I thought I'd eaten something I shouldn't have," he said.

The next course arrived: a tagliatelle with zucchini flowers and saffron. "For the most part," Hardy explained, "everything we're being served is grown and made here, on this farm. This wine, Montepulciano d'Abruzzo, is made from grapes that come from vines growing behind the house. The family has their own wine press and a recipe they've used for centuries. Celia buys flour from a local farmer, I think, but she makes all her pastas herself. The saffron is produced on the farm, as well."

"I read that this part of Italy is really famous for its saffron," Teddy said.

"You read right," Hardy affirmed. "This entire Navelli plain is the heart of saffron country in Italy. It's considered the best saffron in the world. And it's really expensive."

"Oh, yeah?" Hal chimed in, "like how much is expensive?"

"It sells for over three hundred dollars an ounce," Hardy informed them. "Much more expensive than illegal narcotics." He avoided looking at Hal when he added the last comment.

"Why is it so terribly pricey?" Lucy asked.

"Well, for one thing it's very labor intensive to produce. Saffron comes from the orange-red filaments or stamens of a certain kind of crocus flower. It takes four thousand flowers to make one ounce of powdered saffron. It is backbreaking work, too.

"One reason saffron produced in the Navelli is so special is that the bulbs are dug up every year, by hand, and examined for size and quality. Another reason is the climate and soil. About this time every year the plots of land where the crocuses are planted, small parcels, are prepared with sheep manure. The bulbs are planted in August, and harvest time is October. It's a fairly short season, but once the flowers start to blossom they have to be picked early in the morning, before dawn, while they're still closed, so that none of the stigma's powder is lost. Then, that same day, all the stigma's gathered have to be hand sorted and dried over a wood fire right away. They usually use oak or almond wood with a neutral smell so that the fire doesn't imbue a smell that ruins the flavor of the saffron. When that's all done the saffron is stored in the lady of the house's closet, considered the safest, driest place in the house.

"No one grows saffron full-time, since the growing season is only a couple of months long, but the average family can make an extra eight to ten thousand dollars a year with a crocus crop."

"Is this the only place in the world that produces saffron?" Dennis asked.

"There are several countries that are now growing saffron, but the best quality is here. Spain and India make a cheaper product, which is a very real threat to saffron production in Abruzzo since price wars have developed over the spice. That, and the fact that so many of the young people are leaving Abruzzo for better opportunity, and the older population that has always grown the crop is aging. The amount of saffron produced in this region has fallen dramatically, unfortunately."

Simona rolled in a trolley which carried a large tureen of wild boar stew with white wine, oregano, and sweet peppers. The aroma that followed her progression as she ladled out the savory, steaming portions was ambrosia.

"This stew is the Abruzzese peasant's version of beef burgundy," Hardy explained. "They cook it for hours, at a simmer, over an open fire."

A groan escaped from Hal. "This is unreal," he sighed, relishing the dish. "I've never tasted meat like this in my entire life. It is literally melting in my mouth, and the flavors being released are indescribable. What do they do to their pigs to get meat like this?"

"This particular pig was actually a wild boar. Whatever it foraged on in the forest determined the flavor, to a certain extent. In this case, I'm guessing lots of mushrooms and nuts. No hormones or antibiotics, you can be sure of that. And when they brown the meat it gets a nice crust on it. In the States, many times, the meat is so full of water they add during processing that it rarely browns like this. Browning the meat seals in all the flavorful juices, then they stew it for a long time to tenderize it," Hardy explained.

"Why do they add water to meat back home?" Tillie wanted to know.

"Mostly to add weight so you get less meat for more money. It ruins the meat, as far as I'm concerned. EU regulations on food protect and benefit the consumer, not the big companies supplying it. Food in Europe is a much better quality all across the board," he added, "more organics, less genetically modified crap.

"France is especially vigilant about its food sources. They try to keep some of the big US companies, Monsanto and Dow in particular, out with all their GMOs, but one of the former US ambassadors to France with ties to big-agra in the States tried to force France to accept

GMO products by threatening a trade war. It got pretty nasty. That was when Bush was president. The French burn the fields when they discover a GM field in their midst. They want nothing to do with the stuff. Spain, on the other hand, is a willing participant with the US, helping to promote GM foods and crops in their country."

"I thought GMO foods had lots of advantages," piped up Hal.

'You would,' Hardy thought.

Amy was aghast. "Hal, you can't be serious, surely."

He threw her a piqued look, then defiantly stuck out his lower lip. "What's wrong with 'em?" he demanded.

'This should be good,' Hardy mused.

"Well," Amy began, "did you know that cockroach genes have been added to tomatoes? Ostensibly, so they ship better and don't bruise as easily in transit, and to extend their shelf life. It's still in the experimental stage."

She continued, "Monsanto makes crop seed that's Roundup and 2-4-D resistant, which kills weeds as they sprout in the fields. Roundup, one of the most toxic herbicides ever developed, is now a part of our food chain, above and beyond what they used to just spray in the fields. Farmers can also use 2-4-D to spray fields claiming that their products are herbicide free, though nothing is said about the ground contamination. Recently sprayed fields are a health hazard ... even the farmers stay out of them after they've sprayed.

"So what's so bad about Roundup?" Hal chided her.

"You've heard of Agent Orange?" she shot back at him. "Roundup is the new Agent Orange ... its primary ingredient is glyphosate. Studies in the EU, Sweden, Argentina, and Columbia indicate a direct correlation to birth defects, non-Hodgkins Lymphoma, and cancer-related tumors." She rolled her eyes at Hal in disbelief.

"The toxic fallout potential to our bee and butterfly populations is staggering ... imagine what would happen to our food supply without bees to pollinate the plants." She paused to regroup. "An aside to that is that scientists contend all our food will end up being GM because as bees pollinate between GM and non-GM crops they will contaminate everything. The same goes for bird droppings."

"Eh?" Hal uttered.

"You know," Amy explained, "the birds eat seeds from a GM plant and poop in a non-GM field ... the poop mutates the non-GM crops through the soil."

Peter jumped into the fray. "I've been following the controversy over Arpad Pustzai's research. He's one of the world's leading plant genetic modification experts who's conducted independent research on the effects of rats that were fed genetically modified foods. The results of his studies were shocking: the rats had smaller livers, hearts, testicles, and brains, damaged immune systems, and had structural changes to their white blood cells which made them a lot more susceptible to diseases and infections. There was spleen and thymus damage, and an overall increased risk of cancer. Pustzai was vilified for his research, and fired from his job for exposing the results of his research. Must have stepped on some financial toes ... by the way, additional independent researchers confirmed Pustzai's results. Livestock that has been fed GM foods show a plethora of serious health problems ... sterility, cancers, lung, liver, and kidney disease, diabetes ..." By this time Hal's head was shrunk down into his shoulders, making him look like a huge turtle.

"And the consumers are kept pretty much in the dark about what they're eating," Lucy chimed in, "because the big-agra companies have influenced the US lobby in Congress to pass laws that prohibit full disclosure in the contents labels of the foods we eat. The government is even re-defining organic when it comes to labeling. It's OK to say a product is 'organic' even if a percentage of the final product has non-organic ingredients in it. We're sliding steadily down a slippery slope."

"One of the worst fallouts from genetically modified foods is what is happening in India," Dennis announced. "It's criminal, really. I read an article in Global Research that Monsanto convinced the simple, poor farmers in India via officials in the Indian government to use pesticide-resistant GMO seeds and when they did the seeds pollinated all over and converted all the crops to GMO. It even polluted the soils the seeds grew in so that now only GM seeds will grow there."

"Kinda like the bird poop example?" Hal asked.

"Exactly, Hal," he answered. "And now Monsanto controls the seed supply to these farmers. The Monsanto seed is expensive, up to ten times the cost of heirloom and native seeds, and the resulting crops require more water than the old crops did.

"Unfortunately, the farmers and the government agricultural extension agents were ill-informed about the increased irrigation requirements which are suitable for large plantation-like growing, while India grows cotton on small, family-owned plots. After even one year of drought many of these uneducated farmers were financially ruined by the combination of the high cost of the seeds, the requirement to use only Roundup-resistant seeds, low yield, and the high cost of irrigation due to the scarcity of available water. They couldn't pay for the first seeds they bought, and sure couldn't afford to buy seed for the next year. What resulted from the Indian peasants converting to GM seeds is a phenomenon in India called 'GM genocide.'"

Teddy spoke up, "There are reports that over a quarter million farmers have killed themselves, and blame has been directed to those damned seeds as one of the key reasons. Personally, I think GM seeds are the main reason. Entire families have been wiped out, literally."

"In my opinion, Paul Bremer, with his Order 81, tried to set the same stage for a Monsanto takeover in Iraq," Amy said. "The Iraqi farmers have been using the same seed strains in Mesopotamia for thousands of years, using seeds from the yearly crop for next year's planting or trading seeds with neighbors. I read in 'Common Dreams,' an article critiquing Bremer's policy, that under Order 81 multinational companies are allowed to sell their seeds under a structured market. Because seeds will cross-pollinate from field to field, companies can claim patent infringement of any crops grown and force famers to purchase seeds only from the multinationals, denying any native seeds from being marketed. It's a filthy, stacked deck against the poor peasants. They end up drinking field-grade herbicides to kill themselves. It's called 'suicide by pesticide.'"

There was a stunned silence around the table as these last comments sank in. The intensity level of the discussion had gotten almost shrill, and Simona hesitated as she approached the table to clear the dirty dishes. Lucy gave her a friendly smile and nodded reassuringly.

"I had no idea," Hal murmured. He looked like a balloon someone had deflated. He thought for a moment. "So, is most of the food we eat back in the States this GM stuff?"

"Unless it's organic," Hardy replied, "yes. Some grocery stores advertise that they don't sell genetically modified foods, like Trader Joe's, but for the most part GM foods have become the norm. I think there has been a huge increase in food allergies, and I expect the more serious stuff to present itself down the road."

One other thing was bothering Hardy. "Of course, another obvious consequence to GM foods is that they will, ultimately, cede control of our food supply to a few big companies. That, to me, is a really frightening prospect. Imagine food being used as a form of punishment or control."

He lifted his wine glass in a toast. It was time to change the subject. "Here's to a great GM-free meal in Abruzzo," he declared, lightening the mood as he did so. The others joined in with sated "Hear, hears."

Simona appeared with the final course, a dessert of chocolate-glazed almond cake with an apricot sauce and wild fennel pollen, accompanied by strong, black coffee.

"How do they think these foods up?" Teddy wondered, aloud. "I mean, how do you even collect wild fennel pollen? And who would ever think of using it in a dessert?"

"This sauce is unnn--believable," Winnie raved. "It's the most apricot-flavored apricot I've ever tasted. Like right off the tree."

Mama Celia appeared, drying her hands on a faded, sagging apron. Hal rose and crossed to where she stood. He took her hands, almost reverently and, raising them to his lips, said, "Dear Signora, I kiss the wondrous hands that have made the most fabulous food I've eaten in my life. And if you ever need a job, you can be head chef in my restaurant in America." He guessed she understood his sentiment, because she blushed with deep pleasure and gave him a bear hug that squeezed the breath out of him.

*****

# CHAPTER 27

The person Kelvin needed to see at the church in Lanciano was Father Aurelius, the senior priest and an old and dear friend of Kelvin's. In his late sixties, wearing the monastic crown of tonsure, Father Aurelius received Kelvin in his spartan study. "It is always nice to see you, my son," he said to Kelvin. "You are well, I trust?" he asked, his kindly face alight with a gentle smile.

"I am very well, thank you, Father," he responded. "And you?"

"God is good," he answered simply.

"Any idea who took the Miracle?" Kelvin asked.

Father Aurelius had to stifle a smile. "Never much for chit-chat, are you?" he asked wryly. The thought of the stolen relic made his stooped shoulders bow even more underneath his cowled black habit. A huge sadness stole over his features as he focused on the reason for his friend's visit.

It wrenched Kelvin's heart to see his mentor so downcast over the loss of the precious Miracle. The theft was a terrible blow to the elder man's faith in his fellow man, those he'd served and nourished his entire adult life. Kelvin could only imagine the disappointment and sense of failure the priest must be feeling.

When his friend finally found words to speak, he said only, "No, my son. I have no idea who could have taken it."

That was pretty much what Kelvin had expected him to say, and it grieved him to hear it. Still, he, at least, had what he thought might be a lead. A remote lead, but he would pursue it. He decided, however, not to mention his hunch to Father Aurelius; he didn't want to get the elder priest's hopes up, only to feel additional distress if his investigation didn't pan out.

Kelvin wanted to scold his friend for not securing the sacred relic; he'd warned him for years that something like this could happen, and now it had. But he dreaded the thought of compounding the priest's anguish with a lecture about securing church artifacts. Instead, he simply asked, "Was the church locked during lunch?"

"Yes, Kelvin. I bolted it myself that day. It seems the thief was hiding in the church, probably in the lectern." He hung his head and Kelvin could see the grayed tonsure encircling a wrinkled, dried pate. 'This is really aging him,' he thought, and his anger was suddenly re-ignited at the outrageousness of the crime.

"That is the shame of it," he continued. In response to Kelvin's questioning look the priest added, "God is able to protect what is His. I, in my vanity, thought that I could do it with a locked door. I put my trust and faith in a metal lock instead of my Creator." His despair was crushing; Kelvin tried to ease it.

"That is not entirely accurate," he contradicted his friend. "I know your heart. Yes, you locked the front door. But you didn't give up your trust in God by doing so, Father. You are trying to blame yourself, and you mustn't. The blame falls on the person who allowed wickedness to tempt him to steal." He changed the direction of the conversation, "Any news on the man who was assaulted and found in the church?"

"He is still unconscious, I'm afraid."

Kelvin left his friend alone with his thoughts and went to the sanctuary to examine the scene of the crime. He went first to the lectern where it was thought the thief hid while the church was being emptied of the faithful after morning prayers. He found nothing to indicate anyone had taken refuge there.

Next, he climbed the steps to the second, smaller tabernacle which had displayed The Eucharistic Miracle. It was immediately obvious how the perpetrator had cut the glass of the monstrance and simply walked off with one of the most precious religious relics in Christendom. And not a trace left behind to indicate who had pulled it off. He stood contemplating the plunder that had taken place, wondering at the spiritual darkness of someone who would do such a thing.

The small town of Lanciano, in Roman times, had been called Anxanum. Tradition says that the Roman centurion, Longinus, who thrust his spear in Jesus side, piercing his heart causing blood and water to flow from the Savior, was from this town. Hence, it was renamed Lanciano, meaning 'The Lance.'

After witnessing the events which followed this piercing, the darkening of the sun and an earthquake, Longinus came to believe that Jesus was the true Savior. More personal, however, was yet another sign. Longinus had very poor eyesight, but after touching his eyes with the water and blood from Jesus' heart his eyesight was totally restored. And this is the simple story of The Eucharistic Miracle: after touching the heart of Jesus one is healed and converted. Thus changed forever, Longinus became a preacher of his new faith, was martyred, and became Saint Longinus.

'And that's the true crime of this theft,' Kelvin thought. 'Not only did the thief steal something from God, but the crime denies His faithful the venerated object of the ongoing, continuous miracle of transubstantiation.'

\*\*\*\*\*

Kelvin's next stop was the office of the Lanciano carabinieri who were responsible for investigating the theft at the local level. He arrived just past noon and hoped to catch the lead detective in before he left for an extended lunch. Montanari, from the Art Squad in Rome, had placed a call to the head of criminal investigations in Lanciano paving the way for Kelvin's visit.

"Please accord Signore Gossett every courtesy," Montanari had requested. "He will be my eyes and ears until I arrive later in the day." And so Kelvin was welcomed into the local Carabinieri fold and had access to all the information available to date, which included a briefing by head of investigations, Tito Pacetti.

"We found no finger prints on the monstrance's base or the pane of glass that had been cut out," Pacetti informed him.

"Did you dust for prints in the lectern?" Kelvin asked. Pacetti shook his head. "It's just a hunch," Kelvin explained, "but send someone to check the entire lectern area. If il ladro, the thief, was, in fact, hiding out there until the church emptied I'm betting he didn't have his gloves on then ... probably didn't put them on until he started work on the monstrance." Pacetti lifted his telephone handset, spoke into it briefly, gave Kelvin a brief nod, and hung up.

"It will be done right away," Pacetti told him.

"How about over where the other guy was coshed? Any prints there?"

"No prints, only some blood spatter. The person he assaulted, if in fact that is what happened, took a pretty brutal hit."

"What's the latest on his condition, by the way?" Kelvin inquired.

"No change since earlier this morning."

"Any ID on the guy in the hospital?"

"None. Only a small scrap of paper with a series of numbers written on it that was removed from his pants pocket."

"May I see it?"

Tito flipped through a folder at the top of a stack of folders on his desk and removed a small plastic bag into which had been sealed a piece of paper. He handed the bag to Kelvin. It took only a quick glance for Kelvin to confirm what he suspected.

"I've seen this paper before, and I have a pretty good idea who the guy is, though I don't know his name," he informed Pacetti.

For the first time since Kelvin's arrival in the investigator's office Pacetti came to life. Hope started to blossom across his stiff-featured face. With an almost boyish eagerness he asked Kelvin, "What do you know about him? Where's he from?"

Kelvin relayed the information he had about the Swiss tour leader and the two times he'd run across him and his group on various hikes. He recounted the affair in the lakeside church near Scanno where he and Hardy had found him knocked out on the floor of the chapel and told him about the paper he'd found clenched in the man's fist.

"The numbers I recognized immediately," he told Tito. "They were the latitude and longitude for

Lanciano." He paused, wondering how much he should disclose of what he suspected. "This is only a guess on my part, but I think he had designs on The Miracle for himself. I think the same person who bonked him on the head near Scanno is the same person who rendered him unconscious in Lanciano. Merely a conjecture, as I said."

Just then Kelvin's cell beeped. "Excuse me," he said, stepping outside Pacetti's office to take the call. It was actually a text message coming through from Montanari, alerting Kelvin to some pictures to follow that had been taken the day before in Pescara. The accompanying pictures showed Hal Lambeth entering and leaving a low-rent-looking import/export business on one of the side streets in downtown Pescara. He could barely make out the faded painting on the sign over the doorway ... Colucci e i Figli. The shots of him entering were of a man somewhat hesitant about where he was going. The exit pictures gave clear indication that, whatever had gone on inside the business, Hal was one pleased customer when he left.

"Dufus," Kelvin muttered as he perused the half dozen or so photos. The first four pictures told Kelvin all he needed to know about where Hal had gone yesterday ... he scrolled quickly through the remaining photos and saved them to his phone. He poked his head back in Pacetti's office. The investigator looked up from his work, eyebrows raised, waiting for an update. Kelvin gave none.

"My thanks, Pacetti, for your assistance; you'll let me know about fingerprint results from the lectern? Also, if the Swiss regains consciousness?"

Pacetti nodded, "Si, Si, Signore," and waved him off.

*****

# CHAPTER 28

The two-toned siren blared on and on as it raced to an address just off Corso Ovidio. The echoes of the siren undulated off the stone walls of the buildings in the heart of the city, confusing those on the street as to the exact location of the ambulance.

It was just gone on one o'clock. Sulmona was, for the most part, in a semi-drowsy state after its midday meal, so the clanging of the ambulance was an annoying throb disturbing the city's daily somnolence.

Slowing slightly, the emergency vehicle made a hard right turn on Via Archibugi, careening as it did so. Via Archibugi forms a quiet piazza, a pleasant respite from the bustle of Corso Ovidio. The ambulance came to a stop in front of a grey limestone apartment building fronted with graceful arches, killing the siren as it did so. Two imposing men waited just outside a massive wooden door on the ground floor and, when the paramedics jumped out, gestured impatiently toward the entrance.

Carrying their equipment in brightly colored nylon cases, the medical personnel hurried into the apartment and were escorted by one man, followed by the other, down a tiled hallway and into a tastefully decorated dining room. A peaceful dignity pervaded the room. Its beautifully hand-painted tile floors were spotlessly clean, its high ceiling embellished with an intriguing trompe de l'oeil.

Despite the noonday heat, the room was comfortable, the floor-to-ceiling windows let in little heat due to the overhang of a wide veranda at the rear of the building. It was in every way a lovely place to dine, except for the body slumped over the table at the far end, its face buried in a tagliatelle with a rich cream sauce of mushrooms and pecorino. Capo Armando DiSalle had died of heart failure during lunch.

*****

Halfway home on his return from Pescara to Sulmona Kelvin's cell buzzed with an incoming call. When he saw who was calling him he pulled off the side of the road before answering.

"Pronto."

"Vado?" Montanari queried.

"Si, Generale. What's up? Have you news?"

Montanari peeled off a laugh. "I'll say. You know your American chap, Hal Lambeth? Between-a-rock-and-a-hard-place Hal?" He paused for effect. "You're not going to believe what I have to tell you," he stalled.

"For cripe sakes, Roberto! Out with it!"

Montanari laughed delightedly. "Impeccable timing," he continued.

"What? What!" Vado said, exasperated.

"The capo in Sulmona ... Armando DiSalle? Dropped dead of a heart attack while he was eating lunch. His snout landed right in his plate of pasta." He set off chuckling again.

Kelvin's mouth dropped open. He started to smile. Broke into a big-assed grin. "Well," he told Montanari, "I guess old Hal dodged a bullet." He chortled. "What about the import/export guy?"

"Wait and see," came the reply. "Maybe the sky will fall on Chicken Little!" Montanari was still snickering when the call ended.

*****

Kelvin filled Hardy in on the death of DiSalle when he returned to the Sei Stelle that evening.

"We should let Hal know he's off that hook, at least," Hardy commented.

They decided to head off to Hal's room to see if he was in. Before leaving Hardy's room, however, Kelvin asked, "Was Peter on the hike today?"

Hardy's antennae immediately sensed more than idle curiosity behind Kelvin's question. "Yes, he was," he answered. "Why do you ask?"

Kelvin's face tensed for an instant. 'Do I tell him about my suspicions?' he wondered. He considered Hardy's position as tour leader and the responsibilities that went with it. He remembered the different times on the trip when a crisis situation had arisen and Hardy's cool manner in dealing with it. And he thought back on how he'd had Kelvin's back when they had confronted Hal about the drug deal he was arranging with the mob. He had to give Hardy high marks for his performance in all his capacities. This, plus the fact that Hardy was a solid, honest guy who had a right to know what was possibly going on drove Kelvin to confide his prescient feelings about Peter.

"Hal aside," he began, "my main objective is discovering and tracking down the person who stole the religious relic from Lanciano yesterday. Recovering stolen cultural treasures is primarily what I do for INTERPOL."

"So? What does that have to do with where Peter was today?"

"Well," Kelvin began, "I have a feeling Peter may know something about The Eucharistic Miracle."

Inwardly, Hardy cringed. Did he want to hear this? "Know something how? What something?"

Suddenly, Kelvin was in two minds. Perhaps he should have kept quiet until he knew more. Had some proof. His intuition seemed thin and almost silly, right now. He sensed Hardy's ire heating up but it was too late to try to change the subject, so he went on.

"My first suspicions were directed toward the Bradford twins," he began, "because of their secretive dealings with Giuseppe and also their isolation from the rest of the group ... their attitude. I was almost certain they were the ones plotting to steal the relic. But when it was actually stolen they were in the Victoria Hotel getting a massage. Then, I tracked down Dennis and Teddy at the cafe on the beach, and Amy and Lucy were there, too, so ..."

"Wait just a damn minute!" Hardy finally burst out. "You went around checking on the members of the group? Spying on them?" he asked incredulously. "Are you listening to yourself? You're not even sure it's someone in my hiking group!"

Kelvin looked at Hardy in surprise. "Well, of course I was verifying where everyone was. That's my job. I'm an investigator for INTERPOL, remember?"

Hardy checked his anger. Kelvin was right, of course. He wasn't really a hiker on tour ... he was a policeman, of sorts, pretending to be a hiker on tour. He let his breath out slowly, and with it went his hostility.

He nodded. "And so?"

"We know where Hal was and what he was doing. He was up to no good, but he wasn't in Lanciano stealing a precious artifact and almost killing a Swiss tourist. Well, at least we can say that for old Hal." Kelvin paused a moment before resuming. "Peter, on the other hand, rented a car in Pescara and, I think, drove to Lanciano and stole the relic."

"And you think this based on what?" Hardy prodded.

"A hunch, at this point," he admitted. He'd know more once the results of the finger printing from the lectern came in. And if the Swiss hiker ever regained consciousness and could identify his assailant. Or they found what had become of the relic. Looked at like that, Kelvin realized how circumstantial his suspicion of Peter was.

"Pretty flimsy, if you ask me," Hardy said. "That's a hell of a leap to get from Peter-the-hiker becoming Peter the thief-slash-assailant."

Hardy was right, Kelvin saw. But he knew his hunch was right ... he just knew it. "I know there isn't any real evidence, yet. But it's early days. We'll see. In the meantime, don't mention this to anyone. I probably should have kept quiet, but thought you should be made aware of what I'm looking at." He made a move for the door. "Let's go inform Hal what a lucky little shit he is, shall we?"

*****

The lucky little shit, Hal, sat on his bed like Humpty-Dumpty while Kelvin broke the news to him about Armando DiSalle's unexpected death-by-heart-attack and what it meant to Hal. It basically got him off the hook from having to wear a wire, and also gave him time to cancel his wire transfer. The wire transfer that would have sealed his death warrant when it compromised DiSalle and his criminal organization.

Hardy watched Hal's face intently as Kelvin spelled it all out for him. What he saw was a kaleidoscope of emotions wash over Hal's visage: alarm, relief, awe, and finally, a tinge of amusement.

Hal's only verbal comment was, "Awesome!" He was visualizing the mighty arm of God sweeping DiSalle off the checkerboard of life, cancelling his chips, all for him, Hal.

"You still have Colucci to worry about," Kelvin was telling him, "and, possibly, the Albanian." For some reason Hal no longer seemed perturbed by the direness of his situation.

*****

# CHAPTER 29

After leaving Hal's room Hardy went back to his room for a quick wash up and change of shirt, then headed down to the front desk of the Sei Stelle to find Honey. She was nowhere to be found and for a second he wondered if he'd misunderstood about their date for that night. Seeing her Uncle Dante in the sitting room, Hardy decided, 'What the hell?' and approached him.

"Good evening, Signore Rafallo."

Uncle Dante looked troubled, Hardy thought, and was somewhat brusque when he merely replied, "Si?"

Suddenly, Hardy felt awkward and boyish. 'This is silly,' he told himself. He cleared his throat. "I was supposed to meet your niece, Honey, tonight, Signore, and I've not been able to find her. Has she gone somewhere?"

At mention of his niece, the proprietor of the Sei Stelle tensed noticeably and he gave Hardy a sharp, suspicious look. Normally gracious and outgoing to his guests, the inn keeper's response to Hardy's inquiry threw Hardy for a loop. 'What the hell is going on here?' Hardy thought.

"You haven't heard?" Signore Rafallo asked.

"Heard what, Signore?" Hardy replied.

Signore Rafallo read the sincerity in Hardy's question and his tone softened. "My niece was injured in an accident today. Near the Piazza."

Hardy was filled with dread. "What kind of accident? How?" He was afraid he already knew the answer.

"She was hit by a Vespa this morning. A hit and run."

"How is she? Where is she?" Panic seized him. It had to be the assassin, Black Maria. But why had she targeted Honey? Had she somehow felt threatened by her? He caught hold of his fear, forcing it from his thoughts. A cool calm took its place. Obviously, he reasoned, if Black Maria had meant to kill Honey, she'd be dead. The attack, then, must have been a warning. A damned vicious one. He clenched his teeth in anger at the senselessness of the assault. When he finally looked up he found Signore Rafallo studying him, a kinder mien on his face.

"Honey is fine," he assured Hardy. "Her left leg is broken and she is bruised and shaken, but the doctor says she will be pretty much back to normal in a day or so, except for the leg. She is being kept in the hospital tonight because of a possible concussion sustained when she was thrown by the impact."

"Which hospital, Signore?" he asked, impatiently.

He gave Hardy a knowing, kindly look. "There is only one hospital in Sulmona, Mr. Hardy," he replied.

*****

"What in all that's holy were you thinking, Honey?" Hardy asked, exasperated by what she had done in following Black Maria. "Tailing an assassin, even after I'd told you how dangerous these people are?" He looked at her lying in bed with her leg in a cast, and a bulky dressing taped over her right elbow where a large patch of skin had been peeled off when she hit the sidewalk. There were several smaller areas that had been skinned on her back and she sported a multitude of bruises, but her face, fortunately, had escaped damage.

She looked pitiful. And despondent. And her gorgeous eyes were glassy with pain. Hardy felt bad for berating her and softened his tone. "Gosh, I'm sorry, Honey. I don't mean to scold you ... that's the last thing you need right now, but this Black Maria is a vicious bitch, a professional assassin ... she could just have easily killed you."

"How do you know it was her?" Honey asked. "I didn't see who it was; whether it was a man or woman. It could have just been a ..."

"Will you stop, all ready," Hardy interrupted, his voice almost a shout. "You're not Nancy Drew and these mafia people don't mess around. They make lots of money doing illegal stuff and to them murder is just part of the business they're in. What they call 'cost of doing business.'" Lord, she was maddening! He wrestled with his frustration, finally getting it under control. "Anyway, you missed our date because of all this," he said, gesturing to include her, the hospital, the bandages, the cast ...

She gave a small smile then. "Thanks for coming to see me," she said, shyly. "And for the flowers."

"Our tour ends the day after tomorrow," he told her. "But I might be back before September with another group. When will you go back to the States?"

"School starts at the end of August, if I can get this cast off by then," she answered. "So I'm scheduled to leave on August 15th." Realizing that she wouldn't see Hardy in Italy again made her sad, and it showed in her face.

"Where's school?" he asked.

"I'll be starting graduate school at the Massachusetts College of Art and Design, in Boston. My areas of concentration are in fibers and jewelry design."

Hardy gave a low whistle. He was impressed. "That's a tough place to get into," he said. She was pleased that he knew it. "I live in Cambridge," he added.

This caught her by surprise. "Really! That's just across the river, isn't it?"

"Yes, it is. We'll almost be neighbors. The office for my tour company, Durkin Tours, is in Cambridge, as well." There was a longish pause that almost became embarrassing, but Honey was determined that the next move was Hardy's. Finally, he spoke. "When my tour season is over with I usually spend a month or so decompressing at my mom's house in Frankfurt, or sometimes I take a trip off by myself." He cringed, remembering the trip he'd taken to Corsica last year to relax and how that so hadn't happened. "Maybe when I get back to the States in late fall we can catch a movie or go out for drinks," he suggested.

Her face lit up. "That would be nice," Honey said. "And I promise I won't be tracking any mafia dons and miss it this time."

*****

# CHAPTER 30

Except for Winnie, the entire tour group was gathered at the breakfast table the following morning enjoying excellent coffee, fresh-baked rolls, and hot cereal with fruit and yogurt. Winnie skipped in several minutes late, bubbling with excitement.

"We got it!" she announced to Tillie. "The contract with the spinning mill in Teramo ... it's done! Giuseppe closed the deal with the owner this morning!"

Tillie's face broke into an ear-to-ear grin as she rose from the table to give Winnie a hug and dance a brief jig. They both looked so young and refreshed when they were happy, and they were definitely that.

Hardy's ears picked up at mention of his former driver. "Giuseppe? You mean that's what you were doing with him all this time? Arranging to do business with a yarn mill here in Abruzzo?"

"What sort of business?" Lucy wanted to know.

Winnie gave her sister a conspiratorial look. "It's OK to tell them now, isn't it?" Tillie nodded. "Well," she began, "you all know Tillie and I have a high-end yarn store in Sarasota, right? One of the deciding factors in our taking this tour, no offense Hardy, was the fact that it was in Abruzzo, a region of Italy that is the origin of some of the best wool yarns in the world. And the dyes they use here are highly prized, as well. Tillie and I decided to see if we could find a yarn mill to deal with directly and act as their sole importer into the States. With our connections in the yarn business over the years we've amassed quite a Rolodex of contacts of people who sell specialized yarns and figured we could be exclusive distributors. Giuseppe, dear that he is, has a distant cousin who knew a spinner in Teramo, so he helped us negotiate the arrangement, since neither Tillie nor I are fluent in Italian." She paused to grin and savor their accomplishment. "We're so excited!"

"And I thought you and Giuseppe were into something shady," Dennis commented. "Just goes to show ... you never know."

At Dennis' comment the rest of the hikers nodded their heads, collectively. Apparently, they all had harbored similar misgivings about the Bradfords and Giuseppe. Tillie started to take umbrage at this, but Winnie quickly jumped in to deflect her anger.

"Yes, I can understand that," she admitted. "We did sort of sneak around and put everyone off with our behavior. But," she added, "we felt we had to play our cards close to our chest on this. We had an edge on our idea and wanted to protect it. And I know some of you ... well, perhaps all of you, have been suspicious of Giuseppe. He looks a stereotypical Italian mobster, granted, but he's really been invaluable to Tillie and me in pulling off this deal."

"We discovered we really love Abruzzo," Tillie interjected. "We feel good about what we've arranged. It will help us, certainly, establish a thriving yarn business in the States, but it is also a boon to the mill owner and his family. And Giuseppe, too, of course. He will act as our agent here in Abruzzo. This spinning mill has been in the same family for six generations and they take immense care and pride in the yarns they produce. And the colors of the dyes they use are glorious. Winnie and I were so smitten with the colors of the wildflowers we've seen on our hikes here, and we wanted to have yarns dyed to replicate some of the colors ... the saffron dyes the mill uses are like nothing we've seen. We plan to use that color as the focal point of our collection.

"The Chinese have begun duplicating some of the Italian yarn techniques, much as they copy Gucci bags and Rolex watches. But the quality isn't there. Our contract with this family mill, if successful on our end, will virtually ensure its continued existence and, hopefully, facilitate a renaissance in wool artistry in the area that has been disappearing at an alarming rate."

Hal summed up everyone's reaction to this news. "Cool beans."

"Yes," Hardy added. "Congratulations, to both of you. And Giuseppe. We all wish you total success with your enterprise. This area of Italy has taken some big hits economically, and I think what you gals have pulled off is fantastic."

Flush with their success and the admiration of their fellow travelers, the Bradfords rushed off to the reception desk to await the contract being faxed from the mill owner. The rest of the hiking party, one by one, headed back to their rooms for a short break before setting out for the day's adventure.

Kelvin was the last to leave the table. He withdrew a plastic Ziploc bag from his pants pocket and very carefully picked up Peter's juice glass by the rim and dropped it into the bag. He made some notations on the bag with a felt tip marker and hastened to his rental car for a quick trip to Pescara and the regional police headquarters. Would his hunch pay off? The results of the finger print search in San Francesco's lectern had yielded some prints. The next step was to try and find a match, and Kelvin hoped Peter's juice glass from breakfast would provide it.

*****

# CHAPTER 31

Murat Krasniqi was in a rage. The only person not afraid of Krasniqi's fearsome temper was his adopted son, Adnan Lumani, who watched quietly as Murat paced the hand-loomed Persian carpets strewn across the floor of his opulent salon, cursing as he went.

Murat's lineage could be traced back to the warlike Illyrians indigenous to the area around present-day Shkodra in Albania. Ancient tribes from this area, conquered by Rome and exposed by this conquest to early Christianity, had supplied the Roman Empire with some of its best soldiers. Centuries later, after being overrun by Slavs, then Turks, and subject to Muslim rule, the legendary Prince Alexander, a native son, emerged to rule Upper Albania. Although he had been raised as a Moslem in the court of Murad II, to whom he had been given as a hostage by his father, the valorous prince embraced Christianity after freeing his people from Turkish rule.

Upon his demise, his people became disorganized and, once again, fell under Muslim rule, although they were never completely subdued but treated more as allies than subjects.

The two religions and races co-existed and, as had been the practice under Rome, the Albanians supplied the Turkish army with its best fighting men. Some Albanians converted to Muslim, while others joined the Greek Orthodoxy, but the majority remained Catholic, practicing their religion devoutly and maintaining their traditional customs and manner of life.

The purity of the lifestyle of these northern Albanians was an invitation for Franciscan missionaries to establish a foothold in the region and for Rome to show an interest in, and support for, the Catholic population against their Muslim oppressors. For centuries the Catholic Albanians have bravely defended their religion. It is a simple faith, but a vigorous one, and the same warlike spirit that fought with the Romans and Turks acts as defender of the faith today.

Murat's anger was directed toward one of his Italian business partners, Salvatore Colucci. Colucci, he had learned that morning, was complicit in the theft of the Vatican's priceless religious relic, The First Eucharistic Miracle. Colucci hadn't participated in the actual theft, but had received the stolen relic and had been given the job of smuggling the relic of adoration out of Italy and away from The Church.

"Blasphemy!" Murat roared. "Worse than that ... sacrilege!" he ranted. Adnan watched as Murat, Defender of the Faith, came forth. Genetic memory in action.

His friend, surrogate, and business associate may smuggle and deal illegal drugs and order unspeakable deaths to those who betrayed him, but he was a devout Catholic and would not, NOT, stand by and allow the evil stain of perverse greed of ANYONE with whom he was in business to touch or taint his Church. Murat, he knew, would insist on going to Pescara himself to deal with Colucci. To Murat, the trip to Pescara carried the same gravity and purpose the crusades had held for the knights en route to the Holy Land. He considered it his duty to journey to Pescara to rescue the holy relic from the Infidel Colucci, or at least prevent Colucci from having anything to do with its exploitation.

"Make the necessary arrangements. We leave at once!" he declared, having worked himself into a real lather.

"Contact Leski," Adnan advised. "Let him send someone to take care of it."

"This is something I will do myself," Murat insisted.

"Don't risk going to Italy, Baba," Adnan coaxed. "Leski can deal with it much quicker than you can travel there. Besides, I need you here for the new route we're negotiating through northern Italy." Adnan knew this would be the deterrent to Murat's 'pilgrimage' to Pescara.

Business trumped everything. But Murat was not to be dissuaded so easily.

"I can take my plane to Pescara and be home by nightfall," the elder man argued. "Reschedule the meeting with the Italians for later in the evening." Adnan started to protest but was cut short. "That's final, Adnan. I'm going to deal with Colucci personally." And that, Adnan realized, was the end of the discussion.

*****

# CHAPTER 32

Friday promised to be a stunning day for the tour group. They were headed back to Caramanico Terme to hike the Orfento Valley, one of the most beautifully wild and spectacular protected areas in Abruzzo. It was a longer and slightly more strenuous hike than any they had attempted so far, but dangling at the end of the hike was another delicious soak in the thermal waters at La Reserve, the area's most luxurious hotel specializing in a variety of treatments at their well-heeled spa.

Caramanico is an historic town, dating from the Middle Ages, perched on a hilltop between the Monte Morrone and Majella mountains in the valley of the river Orta and the Orfento, its tributary. The views down the valley from Caramanico, the largest town in the area, are fabulous. There are several beautiful churches in the town as well as an historical center featuring really fine medieval houses. Some of the most important Paleolithic remains in Italy have been discovered in the area. Surrounded by misted mountains, the town of Caramanico Terme sticks out above the green forests, a village of old stone and stucco buildings topped by the traditional red tile roofs.

Before setting out on their hike the group stopped at the Paolo Barrasso visitor center to register before entering the valley, as required by law. The path they traversed followed the edge of the valley, the river off to their left far, far below. As they progressed, the path lost elevation until the river was now quite close by. At this point they headed right on the fork marked for Guado San Antonio and had an easy walk on a perfectly graded old mule road.

The road rose gradually to grassy meadows full of aromatic herbs and a spectacular palette of meadow flowers. Red hellebore, sunshine-yellow hawkbits, white rampion bellflowers tinged with blue, purple thistles, pyramidal orchids ranging from pink to purple, delicate fern fronds, wild red poppies ... great swathes of color undulating with the summer breeze. Equally colorful were the various species of butterflies flitting from bloom to bloom, busily pollinating the feast of floral pigment, creating their own multicolored painting, the rare and protected Apollo butterfly prominent among them.

After reaching the highest point of their walk at Guado San Antonio and its sheer, stratified canyon walls dropping to the river below, they descended through forest back into the valley, visiting the refreshing spring waters of Fonte Rava Cupa before heading on to the refuge at La Cesa, where they stopped for a picnic in a serene forest of slender beech trees.

Conversation was light and sporadic among the hikers. There was a sadness creeping upon them as they realized that the real world was waiting to reclaim them in three short days, the fantasy escape to the primordial wilds of Abruzzo soon to be a tranquilizing memory.

Hardy had seen the curtain of gloom descend on members of his tours over the years as they faced the end of their sojourn with nature and knew they would soon splice their lives back into the grim reality of the matrix. That was the great deception ... that we were somehow meant to live our lives amidst the polluted confluence of physical and spiritual corruption. It always gave him pause to be thankful for the job he had. He'd occasionally carp about difficult clients, or the smothered feeling of playing parent/confessor, tour guide, and general dogsbody while on tour but the fact was he really loved doing what he did where he did it. After the brief stint he'd done years ago working as a techie for a computer firm he didn't want to have to face that kind of work environment ever again and understood the dread some of his clients were feeling right now.

The return journey to Caramanico Terme followed alongside the river through still forest, the path bordered by towering rock bluffs. The footpath descended and ran level with the river, narrowing to single file. Like a giant rock wave, the cliffs overhung the left side of the path. On the right was a steep and dangerous drop to the rushing stream. Giant metal eyelets had been driven into the sheer rock wall and a cable was threaded through them, thus providing a handhold for negotiating the treacherous stretch of trail.

Once past this difficult passage the trail widened and they crossed Ponte San Benedetto to the other side of the river and continued on to their destination. The valley had widened and the river broadened, and they passed peacefully through stands of graceful beech trees as they followed the river up the pastoral valley. They crossed the river again and began climbing out of the valley until a path off to the right, leading to Caramanico Terme, took them back toward the river and into the narrow gorge. A manmade runnel diverted off a channel of water from the river for irrigation purposes. The walls closed in, creating quite spectacular cliffs hanging overhead.

The peace and seclusion of the gorge seemed to stop time for the hikers, and they soaked in the ancient, pervading tranquility that lived and breathed all around them as they strolled in the hushed ravine. On the left, a feathery cascade tumbled down the length of the canyon face, sending a fine mist over the foot path, carbonating the air with its vitality. After a steep but brief climb up to the bridge arching overhead they were, suddenly, thrust back into the bustle of rural Italia, a stark contrast to the pristine cosmos left behind mere steps away.

Hardy always felt like Alice climbing up the rabbit hole. Kind of like when he went to a cinema and immersed himself in the microcosm of the movie for almost two hours, the end of which catapulted him back to the everyday world.

*****

The Pilatus PC-12 touched down at Abruzzo International Airport four kilometers south of Pescara at exactly 2:47 in the afternoon. Leski waited on the tarmac as the private jet taxied to a stop on the private plane runway, then drove the black Mercedes S-Class turbo-diesel to the stairway being lowered from the Pilatus and collected a casually dressed Murat Krasniqi before gliding off in the direction of Pescara.

"Has anyone warned him I'm coming?" Krasniqi wanted to know.

"No one, Murat," Leski assured him. "I told the driver to take the day off so I could meet you myself."

Krasniqi nodded his approval of Leski's caution. He seldom left Albania and almost never involved himself with the gritty side of his criminal operation, but the egregious nature of Colucci's collaboration in the theft of the Lanciano relic was anathema to Murat ... he would deal with it personally. And finally.

The Mercedes sped along the Via Tiburtina Valeria, a straight shot from the airport into downtown Pescara. Once they crossed the Pescara River the vehicle slowed as it made its way up Corso Emanuele and the old commercial center toward the Adriatic. Leski found the narrow side street he wanted, Via Palermo, and took a right, then left, and right, ending on the apartment-lined short street, Via Campania. He glided to a stop in the center of the block and rushed around to open Murat's door, but Murat had already jumped out. "Which is it?" he asked, wanting to know where Colucci lived.

"The red door," Leski answered, indicating an entrance with peeling coral paint offset by planters mounding over with colorful blooms trailing down the steps.

Murat pulled back slightly, waiting for Leski to precede him to the apartment. He felt in his light-weight safari jacket pocket for the Sig Sauer Mosquito he carried. Smaller than the 226 and chambered in .22 LR, it was Murat's pistol of choice. He pulled out the Sig, as well as the Gemtech Outback II silencer and screwed the latter into place, then held the firearm behind his back.

Leski rapped on the door. They waited a few moments, then he knocked, again. When the door swung open Leski shouldered his way in, forcing Colucci backwards, down the entrance hall. Murat followed, closing the door but leaving it unlatched. He caught up with Leski and Colucci where the entrance widened into a dingy foyer. When Murat stepped forward Colucci recognized him and began a belated "Welcome."

"Save it, Salvatore," Murat snarled at him. Stung by the rebuke, Colucci recoiled, a mixed look of confusion and uncertainty clouding his face. Then he saw the Sig, and the confusion was quickly replaced by fear.

"But why, Murat?" he dared ask.

"Because you mock God," Murat hissed, shooting him in the center of his forehead, the mid line of his chest, and each shoulder, thereby making the sign of the cross on his dead body as it crumpled to the floor in slow motion. They left him where he lay, and drove back to the airport. Leski deposited Murat back at the bottom of the steps to the Pilatus. "That was one short trip, Murat," he said by way of farewell.

"The conversation was one-sided," Murat replied, and hastened into the waiting jet. He turned back on the top step. "I want his warehouse searched, completely, for the relic. Let me know what you find." Then he was gone.

*****

The finger print analysis taken from the lectern in San Francesco was a disappointment for Kelvin. The prints found were too smudged to have any value for comparison, so that avenue of investigation terminated in a frustrating dead end. Further efforts were made to check for prints around the monstrance but no new evidence was forthcoming. The crime scene was a virtual blank, except for the injured Swiss hiker who had still not regained consciousness in hospital.

Kelvin worried that the trail had gone cold and the probability of recovering the religious treasure grew increasingly remote. Hardy's tour would end very soon and if, IF Peter was involved in its theft the difficulty of apprehending him would increase exponentially once he left Italian soil. These thoughts clambered around in his head trying to find a new pattern, a new toehold, anything that would add value to his dwindling investigation. When his cell buzzed he snatched it greedily, hoping for good news.

"Pronto."

"Have you heard, Vado?" Montanari asked. "Colucci is dead. Someone seems to have settled a score with him. I thought you'd like to know ... your man is off the hook."

Kelvin, at this point, could care less about the plump American gangster wannabe. "Thanks, Roberto, I'll pass along the news."

"You sound down, Vado. No breakthroughs with the Lanciano theft?" he asked.

"None, Generale. I am sure the American, Peter Fynch, is involved but I can't prove it."

"Faith, my friend."

"Ciao, Roberto."

*****

The light was back again, beckoning. 'Wait ... wait ... I'm coming,' Raymond Devaux cried out. He tried to run, but was held fast. The light started to fade down a long, dark tunnel. 'No, wait!' he called out. No one heard him. Why was that? And who had tied him up so he couldn't move? It was coming nearer, now, bobbing gently in the distance as it approached. A flashlight beam dimmed by waning batteries. He wanted so badly to sit up, to be noticed, but his body was leaden ... was it even his body?

Suddenly, the light flashed, disco-like, and for a brief moment he saw. His arms punctured by needles attached to IV tubes leading out of sight. His body in a narrow bed with side rails. A monitor of some sort nearby letting out steady, intermittent beeps. A blurred face topped by a white stiff cap peering anxiously at him, coming into focus for the briefest of instants, then fading away.

*****

"He was murdered, Hal. Assassinated, in cold blood." Kelvin was exasperated with Hale Hal. He'd tried describing Colucci's ritually shot corpse to him but all he got was a silly-assed grin. What was with this guy, anyway? "Unless there's some link back to you with Colucci and DiSalle, I think you can consider your case closed. I hope you realize how lucky you are, Lambeth," he continued. "Two mob guys are wiped off the board ... it could just have easily been you."

'Luck,' thought Hal, 'had nothing to do with it.'

*****

# CHAPTER 33

The final day of hiking for Hardy's group dawned hot and hazy. Days like this could go either way: a shower by mid-morning, or it could burn off as the sun climbed skyward. Their luck held. By the time they'd reached the beginning of the day's hike, one of the most beautiful villages in the region about twenty minutes from Sulmona, the air had cleared but the day promised to stay hot.

Anversa degli Abruzzi is a twelfth century medieval village perched half on a mountain, half deep in the valley of the Sagittario River, at around two thousand feet elevation. Like Scanno, Anversa degli Abruzzi is a village that was blessed by the riches of the wool industry and the houses, built from solid dressed stone, are a testament to that wealth. The buildings get their individuality from the various decorated doors, archways, windows, and portals chiseled artistically and intricately in stone, and stone is king as the building material. Even many of the roofs are fitted stone, though some are a beige tile made from the region's clay. Most of life's color in the town comes from the window boxes of trailing flowers cascading over wrought-iron balconies and terraces, and potted plants bursting with intensely flashy blooms. That, and the odd bits of laundry hung out to dry on abbreviated clothes lines or draped over handrails.

"I never see any litter in these villages," Lucy commented. "Rome is awash with debris in the streets, but every hamlet and town we've visited always looks like the street sweeper just went through ahead of us."

Peter quipped, "Cleanliness is next to godliness. Maybe it's a class thing; peasants are more apt to retain their basic belief system."

"Ya think?" Hal asked.

"I think it has something to do with immigration, as far as the bigger cities go," Dennis said. "That's where the majority of the third world illegals end up and they a) are usually a lower class person and bring their lower class values with them, and b) they have no love or connection to their adopted country and could care less if they trash the place." He paused. "It's only a theory, but one, I think, with merit."

"Probably all of the above," Amy summed up. "But Lucy's right. The villages all look like movie sets. It's so refreshing. The residents really care about where they live. We used to call it civic pride, although if we did so today we'd probably get labeled xenophobic or racist."

The group decided to take a look through the village before setting off on their walk. The ancient town sits on a small spur overlooking the magnificent Sagittario gorge and is completely surrounded by the massive stone peaks of the south-central Apennines, including one of Italy's tallest peaks, the Gran Sasso. Walking the narrow, meandering streets, and the stepped, cobbled walkways, they entered a simpler time where growing vines and saffron, and raising sheep for wool determined one's daily routine.

Anversa degli Abruzzi is an ancient fortified village. On the side of the little town coming from the direction of the hamlet of Cocullo the houses form a protective wall with a small opening that allows a narrow path into the heart of the historic center, the Piazza Roma. The village's daily life is played out in this square. The main church, Santa Maria delle Grazie, with its bell tower, ornate Renaissance portal, and beautiful rose window fronts the piazza. Above the church's circular window is carved a peculiar draftsman's compass entwined with two serpents.

Across the piazza, a time-worn triangular stone fountain spits a single spigot of water from the mouth of a black iron lion head. The elder men of the village gather outside the café with awnings proclaiming 'Bar-Panini' and catch up on the latest village gossip since they parted the afternoon before. Several large chestnut trees line the sidewalk across the street from the café.

Lucy pointed to the rose window above the door of the church. "What's with the snake thing, anyway?"

"Pagan symbols, probably," Dennis offered.

"There's a little village called Cocullo about ten minutes from here," Hardy began, in story-telling mode. "And Cocullo has what is called the Snake Festival every year to honor their patron saint, Domenico di Sora. It was held last month, as a matter of fact. The festival actually begins in March when the serpents are gathered from the woods around the village, and lasts two months, culminating in the procession. Then they let the snakes go back into the woods. During this Fest dei Serpari a statue of the saint, Domenico, is carried around the town's piazza covered with live snakes. A whole ball of them, wrapped around the statue. And they parade around with it. There are snake breeders who handle it."

"Ick!" Teddy said. "Sounds disgusting!"

"Creepy!" Winnie agreed.

"What kind of snakes do they use?" Hal wanted to know.

"Mainly grass snakes, green whip snakes, four-lined snakes, and Aesculapian snakes ... all non-venomous.

"What's the story behind the saint ... this Domenico?" Hal asked.

"He is regarded as a protector against snake bite, a curer of snake bite, and a defender against the evils of society. He also healed tooth aches and rabid dog bites. Tradition says that he rid the area of poisonous snakes back in the eleventh century. Actually, I think the snake rite goes way back. It was, initially, a pagan ritual and the Church came up with the current rendition as a means of metamorphosing the festival away from its pagan roots. The festival is really very popular ... people come from all over this part of Italy and it even draws foreigners."

"Does anyone ever get bit?" Hal just couldn't let it go.

"Probably, Hal. We're talking a nine-foot statue attached to a base on wheels draped with a writhing mass of snakes. It's really pretty bizarre. The snakes hiss and stick their tongues out and wriggle them. Some fall off the statue and slither away in the streets. People sometimes adopt them as pets ..."

"Enough, already!" Teddy fussed. "It makes my skin crawl just to think about it."

*****

The group decided it was too pretty a day to tour the church's interior, so they headed down into the lower part of the village, which is the oldest area that gives off a truly medieval air with its cobbled alleyways and endless narrow and closed turns. It is a maze of small streets, intersections, stairs that go up, stairs that go down, and narrow archways with fragments of blue sky appearing for the briefest of moments before the walls close in and you find yourself in a darkened, covered walkway. An unsettling place for a claustrophobe. Occasionally, there is an opening in the wall and you behold a breathtaking panorama of the Sagittario Gorge and the tiny hamlet of Castrovalva clinging to the ridge opposite.

Hardy led them towards the top of the village, up Via Castello to the ruins of a twelfth century Norman Castle, one of the symbols of Anversa degli Abruzzi, felled in a violent earthquake in 1706. The tower is all that remains amidst the rubble and strewn boulders of the rest of the castle. They gave the castle a quick pass and headed back down into town.

"There is a lot of clay in the mountains around this village," Hardy explained in his tour guide persona. "The tile produced here was prized pretty highly and there were quite a few potteries. The villagers use an earthenware pot, called a pignata, for cooking a local bean dish and the locals were given the nickname of pignatari. They also use the clay to make a ceramic whistle, called a cucu, which I think the shepherds use to call their herding dogs.

"After World War II the government introduced hydroelectric power to the Cavuto River. Since most of the potteries were located at the headwaters of the river they were forced out of business." He added, "But they're still famous for their award-winning smoked ricotta."

They were on Via delle Fornaci where one of the old potteries was perfectly preserved and still functioning. The potter, an elderly man in his sixties attired in dusty jeans, a shirt with tell-tale streaks of clay, and a battered beret sat at his potter's wheel spinning a rather elaborate three-tiered object with a long neck that looked suspiciously like a hookah pipe in the making. Pitchers, ewers, vases, and assorted bowls were displayed unceremoniously around his workspace and on some makeshift plank shelves attached to the stone wall behind him. In a round, tattered basket was a collection of small ceramic pipes which had been glazed in earth-tones.

"Whee! Whee!" Hal had blown on one of the pipes, generating an annoying sound. The old artisan winced and gave a slight shake of his head. Taking one of the whistles he coaxed a mellow, two-toned note out of it and smiled with satisfaction at the effect it produced.

"Oh, I want one!" Tillie exclaimed. "They're really quite clever, aren't they?" she asked her sister, Winnie. She sorted through the basket and picked out two to her liking. "How much are they?" she asked the old man, as much with gestures as with words. He cocked his narrow head at her as though the thought really cost him, and held up five fingers. Tillie fished in her bag for the Euros and counted the coins into his hand. The old guy nodded appreciatively, threw the coins in a small wooden box on the dirt floor near his right foot, and resumed his work at the wheel.

*****

Kelvin intended to drive to Pescara to poke around Colucci's warehouse in the hopes that the stolen relic would turn up. He flipped open his phone to give Montanari a call and hit the video button by mistake. A picture of Hal outside the importer's establishment flashed on his screen and he hit the delete button. The next one in the series showed the same foolish grin on Hal's face and he deleted that one, too. Also the third, fourth, fifth, six ...

Kelvin paused mid-delete. The man in the sixth photo wasn't Hal, nor in the seventh. He hit reverse and zoomed in on the face. Was he seeing things? He advanced to picture number seven again and zoomed in. There was no mistake, he was sure of it.

The man in the two pictures, walking into Colucci's, was Peter Fynch. And he was carrying a large bag with something fairly heavy in it. It had to be the Lanciano Miracle monstrance. There was no other logical reason for Peter to be visiting the shipping counter of a known mob connection with a large parcel in tow on the same day the relic was stolen. Kelvin peered at the time set the picture was taken. Within an hour after the treasure was reported stolen. No doubt about it. He was so excited he almost dropped his phone. He finally managed to hit the speed dial for Montanari and, when Roberto answered, Kelvin spelled it all out for him.

"We need to send a team over to Colucci's warehouse and search for the stolen relic," he told Roberto.

"No need, Vado. I was getting ready to phone you when you rang me. The Eucharistic

Miracle was dropped off at the police station in Pescara not more than ten minutes ago."

"What?" Kelvin caught his breath. "The relic has been recovered? It's safe?"

"Si, Vado. A messenger brought the relic to the main station and left it with the front desk. He didn't leave a name, but he is a small-time crook who does odd jobs for a guy named Leski. Leski works for an Albanian drug lord named Krasniqi. He was spotted arriving in Pescara yesterday but the tail lost them after they left the airport. It's probable Krasniqi has a lot to do with Colucci's demise, but we're not sure why. Then the relic shows up this morning. And yes, it's safe."

"What about the Swiss in hospital?"

"Still unconscious, although his nurse reported late yesterday afternoon that there was evidence of rapid eye movement ... always a positive sign." Montanari thought for a moment before adding, "What are you going to do now?"

"I'm going after Peter Fynch," Vado replied.

"Do you have enough to arrest him?"

Kelvin hesitated, "I have enough to make him talk," he said, "or run."

*****

# CHAPTER 34

They headed down to the Sagittario River, crossed it, and settled into a quiet trek up a steep, well-maintained mule path that climbed up through woods and passed beneath a rocky bluff, emerging onto a splendid vista as the trail opened out on top. After ten minutes more pushing upward they found themselves level with the tiny village of Castrovavla on the other side of the steepening valley. Now they were following the paved road, hanging to the side of the gorge, as it snaked toward the top of the ridge in a long switchback.

From a distance the road appeared to stop, abruptly, but closer inspection revealed its disappearance into a tunnel going under the ridge, reaching the town from the other side in a last curve up the mountain. The hikers were above the tree line of the gorge, the sheer rock face covered here and there with grasses and the occasional shrub.

"I've seen this place before," Teddy announced, pausing to look all around.

The rest of the group pulled up before taking the final, gentle climb to Castrovalva. "M. C. Escher made a lithograph of Castrovalva when he was here in 1929. It hangs in the National Gallery of Art in Washington," Hardy informed them. "The town was also used as the basis for a story on the BBC's 'Dr. Who' series."

The group stood looking up at the tiny village perched on the knife edge of a ridge and clinging to the side of the cliff.

"How does a town end up in such a place?" Amy wondered aloud. "Hanging on the side of a precipice. How on earth do you even build up here? This village existed long before the road was put in ... "

"It might have been started as a hermitage or something where the inhabitants wanted to be away from everyone," Peter offered. "And grew from that. The serenity here is marvelous."

"The location would certainly have discouraged attack or conquest," Dennis observed. "Imagine leading an assault on this place ... climbing straight up the side of a rock wall ... you'd be struggling to hang on to the side of the mountain, never mind launch an offensive."

"It's almost too steep to be used as a summer pasture for sheep," Hal added.

"The town was built as a fortified village before the year one thousand," Hardy explained. "It dominated the Sagittario Valley and controlled one of the entrances to the Peligna Valley, which is further up. It began as a strategic

outpost. There is some evidence to in⸍
a feudal lord had his residence at th⸜
of the village on a rocky outcrop."

The hikers followed the narrow stone footpath, worn through dried grasses, into the small central piazza where the post office and a café were open for business. A small church, its walls pale pink stucco, hosted a big clock telling accurate time positioned high over the wooden entrance door which was inset in a colorfully detailed portal. The church, Michael the Archangel, dominated one side of the square. A trim limestone fountain, off to the side, sporting a single spout from a stone rosette, was a constant invitation to take a drink or have a quick wash.

To the rear of the village a massive mountain rose as a backdrop; both sides of the ridge plunged into the depths of the gorge, the views down through the valley a spectacular, dizzying panorama.

"Very few people now live in Castrovalva, about thirty or so," Hardy explained. "There were close to four hundred residents at the beginning of the twentieth century. A lot of the houses in the village have been restored and are now summer homes for city dwellers."

The buildings were basically the same color scheme as those in Anversa degli Abruzzi: beiges and earth tones built of dressed rock with rock or beige tile roofs. In some places there were rocks placed over the tiles to hold them in place because of the fearsome winds that swept over he ridges. Here and there some of the residences had been painted pale ochre or salmon pink, evidence that that particular house was one of the refurbished summer getaways. Masses of bright kaleidoscopic blooms spilled over balcony railings and erupted from planters of all shapes, sizes, and mediums.

"Most of the streets in the village are walking streets, off limits to cars, and they are swept immaculately clean. Aside from the paved road and a wind farm beyond the village, little has changed here in the past ten centuries," Hardy said.

The decision for the hikers to stop for a mid-morning coffee at the little café on the piazza was unanimous. There were a few other tourists wandering about Castrovalva, but for the most part Hardy's group felt they pretty much had the place to themselves. It was a luxurious feeling to sit in the sunshine, much cooler at this higher elevation, and soak up the insouciant tranquility the little village exuded. Hardy stretched his long, tanned legs at a table outside the café, sipping his espresso appreciatively. He did a double take when he remembered he was working ... what a life! Teddy broke in on his thoughts.

"Dennis and I have been seriously considering a move to Italy," she began, taking a chair across from him. "I know you must have people say things like that from time to time when you're on a tour, but we really mean it. We've both been fed up with cities in general and Philadelphia, in particular."

Hardy had been leaning back with his face toward the sun, eyes closed lazily. "I know you know that there's a big difference between visiting a place while on vacation and actually living there full time. The language barrier is a big thing ... were you thinking of learning Italian? And you may be tired of the rat race in the States, but the pace of life here, the prevailing attitude of 'domani', tomorrow, can really drive you nuts after a while." He yawned, stretched, and sat up. "But I can't say as I blame you for considering it ... at all. I wouldn't live in that daily grind for anything."

Amy arrived at the table balancing a sweet roll on top of a café latte. "Oh, look," she said, pointing with her chin, "Kelvin's here." She plopped down her goodies and waved until he saw her and returned the wave. He strode across the piazza to where Hardy and company sat enjoying their coffee. He was tense and preoccupied, and he seemed to be looking for something.

"You made it!" Lucy sang out when she saw Kelvin standing next to Hardy. She had a coffee in one hand, postcards in the other.

"Where's Peter?" Kelvin asked without prelude.

His tone put Hardy on alert. "What's happening, Kelvin?"

"Some new developments. The relic has been recovered and is safe. Where's Peter?" he asked a second time, glancing around the piazza and the people in it. Kelvin was so intent on locating Peter he was oblivious to the other members of the group and the startled looks they gave him. They didn't understand this Kelvin and his abrupt demands and what it all had to do with Peter.

Hardy sat upright, his attention focused on Kelvin. "He's around ... what new developments?"

"The pictures ... on my cell phone ... I'd missed it earlier, but this morning I finally looked at the last two taken outside Colucci's and Peter was in them. Carrying a large bag with something heavy in it. Colucci's been murdered, by the way." He tossed out the last bit of information so casually he might have been discussing a leaking water bottle.

He scanned the piazza again and caught sight of someone, Peter he supposed, dodging around a corner far up the little street on the opposite side of the village square. "That's him," he said, heading off in pursuit. By this time Teddy and Amy were thoroughly alarmed by Kelvin's behavior.

"Why's Kelvin after Peter?" Amy asked. "What's going on? What's he have to do with the stolen relic?"

"And who's Colucci and why was he murdered?" Teddy wanted to know.

"All good questions, ladies," Hardy replied as he assessed Kelvin's mood. He couldn't just sit here. As casually as he could manage he stood, stretched as if he hadn't a care in the world, and sauntered in the direction Kelvin had taken. "Back in ten minutes," he said over his shoulder. He hoped.

*****

Peter was in the little café waiting for his espresso when he noticed Kelvin standing outside talking to Hardy. Instinctively, he'd ducked behind a display rack for chocolates and breath mints, but unmistakably he heard Kelvin's demand, "Where's Peter?" He knew Kelvin suspected him of being involved in the theft of the relic; he'd been loitering in the lobby of the bed and breakfast yesterday morning when he saw Kelvin bag his juice glass. For finger prints, he assumed, rightly. Something must have happened to send Kelvin in pursuit of him ... had they somehow found Colucci? Had he talked? Not likely. He was sure there was no trail from him to the Swiss hiker. Had he regained consciousness and talked? That was probably what happened. He was almost relieved at the thought of the hiker's recovery. And now the chase was on ... 'the game was afoot' as Sherlock Holmes would say.

He snuck out the rear entrance of the café and followed a walkway too narrow to be called an alley to where it joined the street at the far end of the little piazza. Just beyond the last house in the village Peter hastened down stone steps to a ridge he followed until he came to a track zig-zagging down the mountain, just before the black metal cross planted beside the trail.

Rejoining the old mule path, he passed above the road tunnel and eventually came to the paved road.

He felt exposed traveling the road and turned down the path to the gorge, hoping to lose himself in its shade and cover. His heart was beating furiously, so hard it made his head pound, as well. Behind him he heard running footsteps but he couldn't push himself any faster. The walls of the steep cliffs closed in on the trail; far below he heard the Sagittario River gurgling among the rocks and boulders, falling in cascades.

"Stop! Peter!" It was Kelvin, almost caught up with him. There was no place to go except forward; going over the precipice would be fatal. He turned, suddenly, to face his attacker, desperation etched in the lines of his face.

"It's no good, Peter," Kelvin told him.

"Good?" Peter sneered. "What do you know about good?"

"I know that God is good."

"Nooo!" Peter shrieked. "He isssnnn't!" His face was contorted with rage and pain and it spewed out in a tirade that had needed spewing for a long, long time. "He let Helen ... my Helen ... let her die! When he could have saved her, healed her ... but He let her die a horrible, gruesome death. Helen was good. She," he choked, "was the only good thing in my life. Gentle Helen." He reared back, balled his hands into fists and shook them skyward. "You let her die, damn you!" His head fell forward on his chest and he shook it back and forth like a wounded great beast.

Suddenly, Peter's body shook with sobbing that had been bottled up so long it had been putrefying his soul. The wracking sounds echoed through the narrow canyon. Kelvin stood in shock, watching someone who, only ten minutes ago, he wanted to put in prison. The wretch before him, fallen man that he was, evoked only pity and sorrow in Kelvin, and he started forward as if to comfort him.

But Peter would have none of it. He stepped back, toward the cliff wall, to avoid Kelvin's sympathy. A sharp, burning stab in the calf of his right leg caused him to scream, and he fell back against the rock face.

Kelvin thought Peter had twisted his ankle until he saw a snake slithering into a crevice in the cliff's face. Then he understood what had caused Peter's distress. He'd been bitten by a central Italian asp, or Vipera aspis francisciredi, the venomous viper indigenous to central Italy. Though not highly fatal, envenomation from this asp brings immediate acute pain, accompanied by severe swelling and discoloration. Its toxin can seriously impair vision and affect breathing. Already he could see Peter's leg turning a hellish color and edema setting in. Peter was in a tremendous amount of pain and losing it. He tried to rise and lost his balance, falling and rolling perilously near the edge of the ravine. Loose gravel failed to stop his roll and he pitched over the side and would have fallen to his death if Kelvin hadn't grabbed his left ankle and hung on.

"I've got you, Peter," he reassured him. "We need to get you to a hospital."

Peter, in the early stages of delirium, thrashed wildly and threatened Kelvin's hold on his foot.

"Hold still, Peter," he commanded. "I can't hang on to you if you fight me." Kelvin inched forward slightly, just enough to get his other, free hand anchored around Peter's foot. But he was too heavy for Kelvin and Kelvin was fatigued. He didn't know how much longer he could hang on. His sweaty hands were losing their grip.

"Let me go," Peter pleaded. "Please. Just let me fall."

Kelvin tightened his hold in defiance of Peter's request. "I will not," he asserted. "You and I will get down off this mountain together, Peter." But he could feel Peter's foot sliding from his grasp even as he said it. It was then that Hardy's bronzed, muscular arm shot forward, his big hand encircling Peter's ankle just above where Kelvin gripped him.

"On three," Hardy commanded. Together, at the count of three, they hoisted Peter back up on the ledge and lay him flat, elevating his head and shoulders slightly. Hardy removed Peter's watch and handed it to Kelvin to deal with, and removed Peter's shoes and socks so there would be nothing constricting in the area of the bite.

Next, he marked the perimeters of the swelling on Peter's leg with a pen. "How long has it been since he was bitten?" he asked Kelvin. When Kelvin advised him it had been approximately three or four minutes Hardy noted that on Peter's leg, as well. "There's no cell phone coverage here on the trail. I'll run back up to the road and try there. It's best to call in a helicopter; they can land on the road. The nearest decent hospital is in Sulmona. Can you stay here with him?" Kelvin nodded. "Did you see what kind of snake it was?"

Kelvin nodded, again. "It was a viper. About two feet long."

Hardy headed back up to the road at a run. Two-and-a-half bars of coverage registered on his cell phone and he called the Italian equivalent of 911. He explained to the emergency personnel there was a viper envenomation, gave them Peter's approximate age, size and weight, and told them they'd be waiting on the road to Castrovalva just before it entered the tunnel going under the ridge. He also provided the exact coordinates from his GPS. 'Thank God there's no wind,' he thought. A helicopter would never attempt to land on a narrow road perched on the edge of a ravine in the slightest wind, he knew. Peter was in no condition to walk, and needed to be kept in a supine position with his affected leg lower than his heart.

Next, Hardy rushed back to the piazza in Castrovalva and enlisted Hal and Dennis to help move Peter. He told them only that there had been an accident on the trail and a helicopter would arrive to take Peter to the hospital.

The path in the gorge where Peter lay was so narrow only two of the men could maneuver him back to the wider section of path where, in a four-man hammock carry, they managed to transport Peter back up to the road to await the arrival of the helicopter.

His leg had become grotesque and he was almost non-responsive when Hardy tried to talk to him. He was soaked in perspiration and moaned continually from the pain of the bite. Hardy took some disinfectant from his first aid kit and liberally doused the wound with it, but beyond that there was little else he could do to help Peter. He marked the current parameters of the bite area and again noted the time on his leg. The progression of the edema was alarming; he needed medical attention, and quickly.

The chukka-chukka-chukka of the medical helicopter on its approach from Sulmona was music to the hikers' ears. Peter's situation, they knew, was grave. Lucy and Amy had arrived on the scene and fashioned a sunscreen from two wind breaker jackets and held it over Peter to keep his head out of the sun. He was still sweating profusely, but at the same time he was shivering and his teeth chattered.

"Shouldn't we give him a drink of water so he doesn't dehydrate?" Lucy asked.

Hardy shook his head. "Nothing to drink, no tourniquet, no cutting into the bite ... I've done all I can do for him. When the medics arrive they can assess his condition and make those calls."

The chopper had come into view and hovered momentarily, judging the best place to land on the road. The flattest, widest spot was about a hundred feet away and it moved into position, preparing to land. The hikers turned away from the down draft and the flying dust as it descended and, once in place, two emergency personnel jumped down from the helicopter with a lightweight stretcher. With hardly a break in stride they loaded Peter on the stretcher and headed rapidly back to the waiting aircraft. It lifted skyward immediately and was soon out of sight.

Hardy heaved a huge sigh of relief. "Thank heavens. I hope he doesn't lose his leg."

"Better his leg than his immortal soul," Kelvin observed.

*****

# CHAPTER 35

Kelvin had gone on to Sulmona to follow up on Peter's care. He'd be taken to the private hospital, Casa Di Cura San Raffaele in Sulmona, initially, and then moved to Rome American Hospital in The Eternal City once he'd been stabilized. Recovering from a venomous snake bite, Kelvin knew from personal experience, could take quite a while, especially if necrosis developed.

Normally a moral hard-ass, he was rethinking Peter's state of mind and what must have been his motive in stealing the Eucharistic Miracle from the church in Lanciano. Clearly it hadn't been for financial gain, which took some of the sting out of it, at least. He hadn't known about Peter's wife, either.

The man had been in a deep state of repressed grief, resulting in anger. It had to come out in some fashion. Grief was a process, a progression of stages of emotion. Peter's had stayed bottled up early on and turned toxic.

Had Peter thought that the sacred relic, with its healing properties, could somehow resurrect his wife in restored good health? It seemed a stretch, but Kelvin thought it highly probable in Peter's frame of mind. It almost crushed his spirit to realize the depths of Peter's despair. How, then, do you prosecute a fellow human so devastated, so emotionally anesthetized? Where did mercy come into play? And forgiveness? Or did it? He checked himself. He was allowing his sympathy to overrule the truth. Peter had shown no remorse for his actions ... there had been no repentance. And that, Kelvin knew, was the beginning of redemption. He caught his cell phone on the second ring.

"Pronto."

"It's me, Vado," Montanari announced. "There is news from the hospital. The Swiss hiker has regained consciousness."

"And?"

"He has said nothing. He wants a representative from his embassy in Rome present before he talks."

That made perfect sense Kelvin thought, especially if he had something to hide and had, somehow, played a role in this whole business of the theft. "When will that happen?"

"The Swiss Embassy is sending someone later today, is all I know. What about your other American? Fynch ... Anything?" Kelvin recapped the adventures of the morning for his friend. Montanari whistled. "So, an eventful day for you. Sounds like your man is traumatized on many levels."

"Yes, he is," Kelvin had agreed.

"So, I'll let you know the precise time of the embassy's presence at the hospital, shall I? I imagine you'll want to be present, yes?"

"Very much so, Roberto. Thanks. I'm heading to San Raffaele's in Sulmona now to check up on Fynch. Ciao."

"Ciao, Vado."

*****

They had retreated to the terrace outside the little café in Castrovalva after Kelvin left them. Hardy took questions from the group about Peter, his involvement with the theft, and the Swiss tour leader, but reminded them there was a lot he didn't know. The initial shock and disbelief of the hikers had given way to a strange fascination with Peter's stealing of the precious religious relic, as well as a sorrow for his state of mind.

"I had no idea what Peter was going through," Lucy admitted. "I knew little about his wife dying, or how she died, or any of it."

"How could we have known?" Winnie rationalized. "He is such a very private person ... typical New Englander, I thought. Regional stoicism and all that. When it comes down to it, all we really know about each other is what each of us wants known about ourselves." She turned to Hardy. "Were you aware of Peter's loss? Do you do background checks on us before signing us up for one of your hiking tours?"

Hardy shook his head. "No, Winnie," he smiled. "I did know Peter's wife had died ... he mentioned it as one of the reasons for the hike ... a means of getting away, putting distance between himself and New Hampshire. But I had no idea what the circumstances of her death were."

Hal cleared his throat. "So what, exactly, did he intend to do once he'd stolen this relic," he asked. "IF, he stole it," he added hastily.

"We're not real clear on that, Hal. Peter's state of mind is very unbalanced right now ... I mean he's really 'out there.' According to Kelvin, Peter blames God for his wife's death. He was crushed when God didn't heal Helen. Helen is, was, Peter's wife. Kelvin thinks that Peter wanted to use the relic of the Eucharistic Miracle to try and bring Helen back to life, healed. I know, I know," Hardy said, putting up his hand to qualm the various reactions of amazement and pity from the group. "It all sounds really far-fetched to us, but it made perfect sense to Peter in his grief and desperation."

"Will he go to jail?" Dennis asked.

Hardy had been worrying over that issue, too, and pursed his lips before answering. "Who's to say, Dennis. There are still a lot of unresolved issues. The relic has been returned, unharmed, sure, but will the Church just give Peter a pass? I have no idea. They could show mercy, considering his emotional and mental state, and physical state, come to think of it, and let him off easy. They very well may. But there's still the matter of the guy in the hospital with his head in bandages ... Peter could be charged with assault and battery ... any number of things, probably. I'm not a cop or lawyer but, yes, he could end up doing some time."

He could see it in their faces. The men and women in his troupe were trying to come to terms with the fact that one of their number was not who they thought he was.

He was, in fact, a person from the dark side who had a streak of violence and larceny in his soul and had stolen and injured another human being. Someone not of their world had inserted himself as a harmless man of bonhomie into their midst when, in fact, he was neither harmless nor jovial. And they hadn't been able to tell. That was what really gave them all pause. Peter could just have easily been a mass murderer or a terrorist. Would they have known? Hardy had to think that yes, they would have known. For Peter was of their world, just temporarily crazy. He shared the same, basic values and beliefs as they did, but his beliefs had been suspended or temporarily hijacked by his grief and anger. Not like a real criminal or terrorist who lacked a system of mores and principles sympathetic to their own.

Hardy was relieved that everyone had taken the news of Peter's situation so well. There'd been no sniping, no recriminations, and no blame being leveled or tossed about. They were a good group, he decided. Instead of holding Peter at arm's length, noses being held in disdain, they were trying to give him the benefit of the doubt and be supportive of him. Yeah, they were a good group. He was proud of them.

*****

"So all this time Kelvin has been working undercover as an INTERPOL agent?" Winnie asked, incredulously. She looked around at her fellow hikers to see their reaction to what she'd stated. To a man, with the exception of Hal, who sat crumbling his bread stick while feigning disinterest, Hardy's hikers were astounded to learn that they had been infiltrated by INTERPOL since the beginning of their hiking holiday in Abruzzo. Of course, absent from the narrative was any mention of attempted drug smuggling by a member of their cozy little hiking group.

Hardy nodded. "I wasn't even aware of it myself until three days ago, when he came to me to explain his suspicions about the theft of the relic. At that time he hadn't narrowed down who he suspected and we were all possible villains." This produced a collective gasp around the table. It was the second time within hours the group discovered that one of them was not who they thought and it was disconcerting, to say the least.

WE were under suspicion?" Tillie demanded. She was so apoplectic at the thought of it that for once she was speechless.

"We ALL were," Hardy confirmed. "Even me. After all, I'd be a perfect candidate for something like that. Using my business to m country to country. Seemingly low tacts everywhere. It made sense that ɔect me." He paused. "You and Winnie were the original hunches, based mostly on your involvement with Giuseppe. That, and he mentioned something about your knitting needles being 'assassins' weapons,' Winnie."

That set Winnie back for a minute until she realized what he meant. "The sharpened points, you mean?" Hardy nodded. "Well, we're not allowed to transport any means of self-defense when we travel so I honed down my knitting needles, which I usually carry on me. I dare anyone to try and snatch my purse!" The image of fifty-six year old Winnie defending herself wielding a pair of razor-sharp knitting needles set everyone smirking and giggling.

"I find the whole thing incredibly exciting!" Amy thrilled. "I'm glad no one was killed, except for the two mobsters, of course, and I'm not really glad they were killed ..." she got flustered at her verbal entanglement. "Anyway, what I mean to say is, well, this is the kind of thing you see in the movies, and here we are ... part of it. My students will be amazed when I mention I was part of an international crime on my boring hiking trip, as they think of them." Tillie rolled her eyes at this outburst but didn't say anything unpleasant, as she wanted to do.

The hikers were finishing off their official 'last supper' at La Fiaccola, a wonderful trattoria in Anversa degli Abruzzi that served organically grown and prepared food. Set in the heart of one of Italy's most beautiful small villages, La Fiaccola is an intimate little restaurant, a favorite with the locals that serves typical Abruzzi cuisine. They had booked well in advance and were rewarded with a window table that gave fabulous views down into the gorge.

The group opted to eat family style, and had been deliciously inundated with heaping portions of food literally fit for royalty. The restaurant was famous for its award-winning smoked ricotta, and the attendant cold cuts had suffused their palate with subtle, local flavors, as well. A frittata, packed with asparagus, wild spinach, and mint had sent their taste buds reeling with delight. The house specialty, which had won a first prize at the annual Chef's Culinary Festival in Chieti, consisted of homemade gnocchi served in a sauce of La Porta del Parchi cheese, fresh basil and walnut. Lamb. Beautifully roasted vegetables. Borlotti beans. Fig and hazelnut tart. The experience of the meal went from ecstasy to ecstasy. They were intoxicated with good food and a perfect setting for eating it.

Hal, of course, especially enjoyed the feast but had become suddenly sober and somber. "I just realized something," he said. All eyes turned toward him, not knowing what to expect. Hardy feared he was about to confess to his association with the local mob and tried sending him a signal by shaking his head. Hal had been looking out over the gorge, but now he brought his gaze back to his fellow hikers. "We've been enjoying some of the most fantastic food I've ever eaten. In one of the most beautiful places I've ever been."

He paused a moment, trying to find the words to express what he was feeling. "The food is fabulous by itself. And the scenery is amazing, all by itself. But it's when you put 'em together that the magic happens. The history of where we are ... the rawness of nature ... its staggering beauty and majesty, the simple way people live here. Their struggle to survive in these incredible mountains. And the food, somehow, has all that in it."

Heads began bobbing around the table as the hikers began to understand what Hal was trying to say. Teddy closed her eyes, head tilted back, as though savoring ... tasting ... what he'd said. Her eyes suddenly opened, wide, and she was smiling. She got what Hal was saying.

"You all know I want to open my own restaurant, and I still do," he hastened. "But I don't think people in Winston-Salem would get it. I don't think any place in the States would really understand and appreciate food like this. How could they? Sitting in a city with foul air, nasty water, cars and noise all around. Stress. How can you taste the intricate flavors of this cuisine if you're stressed out and too busy to take time to eat?" You could tell Hal was figuring this out as he was saying it; he was talking to himself as much as to the group.

"What will you do, Hal?" Dennis asked.

He exhaled in a long, peaceful sigh. "I think I'm going to come back to Abruzzo and open a restaurant here." There. He'd said it, and it felt so right. There was hesitation around the table and then, one by one, they started to applaud him. Lucy even cheered. And he knew it was the right decision.

"I got an inkling the day we ate at Mama Celia's farmhouse when we hiked around the Navelli plain," he explained. "I remember hugging her and telling her if she ever wanted to come to the States she could cook in my restaurant ... what a ridiculous thing to say! Who in their right mind would want to leave that to come to the treadmill lives we live in the States? That's when I started to think it wouldn't work ... in Winston-Salem, I mean. And that I should come here. I won't be a big fish in a little pond, or any pond, but that's not what matters." Almost to himself he said, "No, what matters is that I'll be doing what I want, and I'll be happy."

*****

"So what kind of snake was it that bit Peter?" Teddy asked, wanting more information about Peter's fate over coffee at La Fiaccola. She almost shuddered just saying the word 'snake.'

"A poisonous viper, common to this part of Italy," Hardy said. He went on to explain, "It is also called a Central Italian asp."

"An asp!" Winnie exclaimed. "Like the kind that killed Cleopatra?"

"Nah, that was an Egyptian asp," Hal said. "They're in the cobra family and a whole lot more deadly."

"Will Peter be all right?" Lucy wanted to know.

"He should be," Hardy assured her, "but there's always a chance of tissue and muscle damage from the toxin. If they got him in time, though, he should be O.K. after several weeks."

"And if they didn't?" Lucy persisted.

Hardy shrugged. "Depends. I've known people who've lost a limb from snake bite if the necrosis isn't managed." There was a gloomy silence around the table as Hardy's words hit home about one of their fellow hikers.

"I had no idea there were venomous snakes here," Lucy said. "But you see snakes carved on the stone surround on the fronts of buildings, and there was a some kind of compass I saw in this village today with serpents entwined on it carved in stone, on a church, of all places ... it almost looked Masonic.

*\*\*\*\*\**

# CHAPTER 36

As promised, Roberto Montanari phoned Kelvin, a.k.a. Vado, to tell him the approximate time the representative from the Swiss Embassy would arrive at the hospital in Pescara to act as advocate for Raymond Devaux. He hoped the Swiss hiker's testimony would bring the whole Lanciano theft puzzle together but that wasn't the case.

Propped slightly up in his hospital bed, his head swathed in bandages, several IV tubes still attached to his veins at one end and monitors and fluids at the other, Devaux really had very little to say. It was an exercise in frustration for the investigator from the local carabinieri and also for Kelvin.

"Who attacked you in the church, Signori?"

"I don't know."

"You didn't see who hit you on the head?"

"No. I was hit from behind."

"Excuse me, Signori, but your head wound indicates you were struck down by someone facing you."

"I didn't see anyone."

"What were you doing in the church, Signori, over the lunch hour when the church was closed?"

"Praying."

"But everyone is turned out of the church when it closes. How did you manage to stay there?"

"I was kneeling in prayer; the priest must have missed me."

"You did not hear everyone shuffling out of the church and the door being locked?"

"No, I was praying."

"Did you see who took the Eucharistic Miracle, Signori?"

"No ... I ..."

"You were praying ... right."

On and on it went. The questions were asked, and then re-asked. And Raymond Devaux, in his boring, unchanging monotone gave the same answers, over and over and over.

The policeman questioning him became disheartened and felt defeated. He knew Devaux was lying, but couldn't prove it. Kelvin wanted to smack him up the side of his bandaged head. Devaux had them check-mated and he, Devaux, knew it. Without Devaux as a witness the case against Peter Fynch was much flimsier. Kelvin was fairly certain there was no love lost between Devaux and Peter, if in fact they knew each other, but if Devaux gave evidence against Peter it would, to a degree, implicate him, Raymond, as well. His refusal to testify cleared himself and also aided Peter.

Just when Kelvin could tolerate the song-and-dance no longer and he prepared to leave in disgust the door to Devaux's hospital room burst open and a bird-like woman with thin legs and arms rushed in. She was plain-looking in a faded denim dress, rather severe with her blunt-cut hair in a bob, and her face was void of any make-up, whatsoever. She clutched a shapeless canvas bag to her flat chest and gabbled, "Raymond! Raymond! C'est tu?" She collapsed to her knees at his bedside and buried her face against his arm, murmuring in her native French, "My dearest, I was afraid of this. I told you stealing the relic in Lanciano would bring ill upon us."

*****

Kelvin speed-dialed Montanari as soon as he exited the hospital.

"Pronto."

"It's Vado, Generale. I'm just leaving the Swiss at the hospital."

"Anything?"

"From him, nothing. Total denial and feigned ignorance. But just before I left his wife came rushing in. Apparently it's the first she knew where to find him. Anyway, she was speaking to him in French. About stealing the Eucharistic Miracle from Lanciano and the problems it would bring them." He paused. "It would be wise to add them to your data base of potentials, Roberto. They may be back."

"Grazie, Vado. Ciao."

*****

Leski dreaded making the phone call to Krasniqi. He'd heard the tirades before, even been the recipient of a few, but the call had to be made, nonetheless.

"Alo. Kush flet?" ("*Hello. Who speaks?*")

"It's me, Murat. Leski." There was a prolonged silence, so Leski continued. "There have been new developments on the Lanciano theft," he said. Silence still. "The Swiss person has been identified, but he did not steal the relic."

Murat broke his silence, his voice was calm, controlled, and deadly. "And how do you know this?"

"I have an informer in the police station in Pescara."

"Is his information good?"

"Yes, Murat." Leski paused. "There's more." He waited for Krasniqi to speak but was disappointed. He continued, "An American hiker has been identified as a person of interest in the theft. He has been taken into custody, but is in hospital in Sulmona. Under guard."

There was silence from Murat's end, but Leski could feel the energy of his ire building, coming through loud and clear. "Check further. If he is responsible, have him killed. Quickly."

\*\*\*\*\*

# CHAPTER 37

Kelvin sat in a cracked, vinyl, puce-colored armchair tucked in the corner of Peter's hospital room farthest from the window and the street sounds and heated air that wafted in through the semi-closed shutters. He'd been sitting quietly for over half an hour, waiting for Peter to awaken. He felt like a voyeur. The nurse had been in and out once or twice to monitor various screens, paying Kelvin no mind at all as she bustled about checking on her charge.

The sunlight that slanted through the shutter louvers created a striped study of light and shade on the white muslin bed coverlet. Why was it, he wondered, had he taken such a personal interest in Peter? Kelvin normally handled his cases very matter-of-factly and kept a measured distance from all those involved. But Peter ... it was different with Peter. Peter had stolen; he'd attacked someone ... but at heart Kelvin knew he wasn't of a criminal nature. He'd witnessed Peter's crippling despair and although that in and of itself didn't excuse his actions it explained a lot. Didn't erase it, but explained it. And he knew that Peter was salvageable and worth saving, so he was sitting in semi-darkness waiting to see which way it all would play out.

The sheets rustled as Peter stretched his restless legs. Kelvin sat forward and the springs in the lop-sided seat of the chair protested the weight shift. Peter's eyes opened at the sound of the squeak. "Is someone there?" he asked. Kelvin brought the chair forward into the room and parked it two feet from the bed where he could see and be seen. Peter caught sight of him and stiffened, briefly, closing his eyes and emitting a short sigh. When he reopened his eyes he asked, "Where am I?"

"San Raffaele Hospital in Sulmona." Peter nodded slightly as a sign that he was processing the information. "When the doctor is sure you're stabilized you'll be moved to the American Hospital in Rome. That way if you need any rehab care it will be available through the hospital. This hospital is fine, but it is regional. If it was my leg I'd definitely prefer a hospital in Rome." Again, the almost imperceptible nod. "Your leg should be fine, Peter," he added. "If the bite doesn't become necrotic you should have complete use of your leg in several weeks."

The leg in question was heavily bandaged and had a plastic tube leading from the wound, through all the wrapping, to a clear plastic bag hanging on the side of the bed. A gravity-fed arrangement. An occasional drop of bile-colored liquid would plop into the bag after making its way from where it had been anchored in the area of the snake bite. It was pretty gross looking, even for hospital excretions. An IV ran from the back of Peter's left hand to a monitor, and a second IV line connected a drip bag to a vein on the inside of his right arm. "My eyes," said Peter, passing his hand over his face. "It's as though I'm looking through water. Not very clear." Fear tinged his voice. Was he going blind?

"It's the toxin in the snake venom, Peter. It can affect your vision, but it should be temporary. The doctors do expect a full recovery for you." The tension eased from Peter's face at Kelvin's encouraging words.

At that moment a young volunteer, the equivalent of a candy striper, breezed into Peter's room bearing a large bouquet of brightly colored blooms in a vase of water and placed it on the stand next to Peter's bed where he could touch and enjoy them. Having done that, she gave him a beaming smile and sped off on her next errand. He reached out for the attached card, fumbling with his fingers, and knocked it to the floor. Kelvin leaned over and retrieved the card and handed it to Peter. 'Get well, Peter,' it read. 'We're all thinking of you.' Signed, Hardy & Co.

Peter sat, working his jaw muscles, trying to tamp down the emotions building inside but he lost the struggle and tears started to overrun the lower rims of his eyes and course down his cheeks, dripping onto his hospital gown. Kelvin rose and set a box of tissues beside Peter on the bed, and sat back down.

While he waited for the sobbing to subside he studied the broken man before him, mercy tugging at his heart for the wretch. His gaze clouded over as his thoughts wandered off, remembering a dark time in his own life when someone had thrown him a lifeline, enabling him to tread water, catch his breath, and find his footing again.

Presently, he heard Peter blow his nose and clear his throat. "It was awfully nice of the group to send me flowers. If you see them, please let them know it means a lot to me." Kelvin nodded. He looked straight at Kelvin then. "The Swiss tour guide ... is he ... how is he?" He'd been afraid to ask, but he had to know what, exactly, he'd done.

"He's regained consciousness, Peter, and his doctor says he can go home in a day or so."

Peter clenched his eyes shut and exhaled in a long, deep breath. For a moment he was afraid he'd begin weeping again, but didn't. He'd relived that moment so many times ... using the sacred relic to, of all things, wound a fellow human. It was a perversion, to use an instrument of God to harm someone and Peter had wondered just how dark his soul had become.

"Thank the Lord," he whispered. Then, louder, "I never intended to harm anyone ... never meant that anyone would get hurt." A tear spilled over the rim of his eye and he brushed it away, self-consciously. "I'm so ashamed at what I've done, Kelvin. At times I don't know who I am anymore. Or what I've become. If Helen ..." His voice cracked, then, at the mention of her name, and his face screwed up in abject misery. He shook his head, trying to chase away the thoughts that caused him such despair. "If Helen saw me this way she'd be appalled. What I've become ... this angry, bitter person ... is just the opposite of who I was to Helen. She'd be so disappointed in me. Oh, God, I've let her down."

His eyes focused on something Kelvin couldn't see. Something far away. Kelvin kept silent so as not to transgress into Peter's private world. He didn't need to be trampling about in Peter's wilderness with him.

The confession, when it came, was complete. Peter led Kelvin down the road map of his psycho-traumatic journey, which began shortly after the death of his beloved Helen and culminated in his stealing the Eucharistic Miracle from San Francesco in Lanciano and wounding Raymond Devaux in his getaway.

Up until he'd seen his wife's coffin lowered into her final resting place he had believed God for a miracle to bring her back to him, healed and fully restored. The sense of betrayal, when it didn't happen, consumed him. He vacillated between comatose sorrow at the loss of Helen and rage at God for letting him down.

Kelvin sensed that Peter had become unhinged, irrational. And it was in this mental and spiritual quagmire that the idea of making off with the monstrance containing Christ's body and blood in all their healing, death-defying power was birthed. It had been a simple plan involving only Peter, which is why it was successfully carried out.

"So, what happens now?" Peter asked Kelvin, when he'd finished his narrative. He expected the worst. Here he was, in Italy where The Church is all-influential, and he'd stolen one of its most treasured relics. Plus, he'd assaulted and seriously injured a man. In a Catholic church. In Italy. And he wasn't even Italian, but a foreigner who'd abused the trusting welcome of the host country.

"That's not for me to say, Peter," he responded. "However, I will tell you that the Swiss hiker has refused to supply any information, whatsoever, as to who or how he came to be bonked on the head. In light of that, the authorities probably won't be able to charge you for that since, according to the hiker, nothing happened. As for the relic … it has been returned, undamaged, so I don't know what The Church will want to recommend. Even though law enforcement is not under the jurisdiction of the Catholic Church in Italy, The Church still has a tremendous amount of influence. How they will use it, I have no idea."

He paused to let Peter process the information. "I will, of course, be called on to testify, since I'm the INTERPOL agent responsible for investigating the crime and bringing you in. I can't promise you how things will turn out Peter, but I will tell you this: I am going to recommend mercy to the court on your behalf." There, he'd said it. He had gone against every rule of conduct in investigating a crime. And he knew that he'd made the right decision.

*****

# CHAPTER 38

The hiking tour was coming to an end; they would leave the next day at noon. Hardy was heading out to return Lucy's trekking poles to the merchant who'd rented them to her and as he passed Hal's room he heard movement within. He had just seen Hal leave for some last minute shopping on Corso Ovidio and housekeeping had finished freshening the guests' rooms hours ago. Stepping up to Hal's door he gave a brief rap, then opened the door and was stopped dead by what he saw. Black Maria was searching Hal's belongings. She looked up as the door opened; when she saw Hardy a venomous hiss escaped her lips.

"Merda!" she shouted, flicking open a stiletto she'd drawn from the waistband of her slacks. She assumed a crouched position as she faced him, dancing lightly from foot to foot. Her lips curled in a wicked smile. She motioned for him to c'mon with the hand not holding the knife.

"I'd enjoy nothing more," Hardy said, "after what you did to Honey." He tossed aside one of the poles he was carrying and, using the other pole as a foil, assumed a fencing posture, perfected from years of training as a pentathlon athlete. Black Maria was briefly startled at his stance, but then grinned malevolently, egging him on. "If you insist," he responded.

Black Maria made her move immediately, lunging at Hardy with her sharp blade. He parried her move easily and followed with a remise that backed her into a corner. Hatred oozed from her eyes as she realized her vulnerability. She tried another jab and he knocked the stiletto from her hand with a hard rap on her wrist. She yelped loudly, cradling her right wrist in her left hand. His final lunge pinned her down and she spat Italian pejoratives at him so fast the spittle ran down her chin.

"You're lucky I'm a nice guy," he told her.

Hardy heard someone in the hall and gave a shout. Kelvin poked his head in the door.

"What the ..."

"Kelvin, meet Black Maria," Hardy said. "And call the police," he added.

*****

When Murat Krasniqi told Leski to have Peter Fynch killed if it were learned he was responsible for the theft of the Eucharistic Miracle he knew the job would fall to him and it was a task he would've liked to assign to someone else. But, knowing Krasniqi's wishes and his penchant to rage he thought it best that he, Leski, see to killing Fynch personally.

So on Sunday morning, the Lord's Day, Leski set out for Sulmona and San Raffaele Hospital, alone, to get the job done.

*****

Kelvin showed up for breakfast at the Sei Stelle on Sunday and found the hikers in a mixed state. There was a certain dread of returning to the regimented life back in the States while at the same time an anticipatory excitement about doing so. Thrown into the mix was a moody concern about Peter and his fate.

When he appeared he was given a not overly enthusiastic, guarded greeting but he detected no overt resentment from anyone. He did, however, feel as though he were being reassessed now that he was known as an INTERPOL agent.

"Hey, Kelvin," Hardy called out. "Joining us for breakfast?"

"Just a cup of coffee, I think," he replied, serving himself. He sat at the end of the table. The group felt as awkward as he did. "Peter asked me to thank all of you for the flowers and the note," he said. "It really meant a lot to him," he added.

There was a strained silence. You could see the conflict on their faces. Should they side with Kelvin-the-cop or Poor Peter? Kelvin helped them decide.

"I can't blame you for distrusting me after I posed as someone I wasn't." He wanted to tell them he wasn't just a policeman, that he was a human being, first, but didn't know how.

Winnie spoke first. "It was a bit of a surprise, Kelvin, you must admit." The others all nodded at her comment. "I feel as though I've been spied upon. Rather like having a Peeping Tom peeking in my window." She smiled to soften her words. "Not a lecher, but a kindly voyeur."

There was sniggering from Hal and Dennis, and a mild laugh from Amy. Tillie colored somewhat at her sister's gracious synopsis of Kelvin's behavior. He turned red, even to the tips of his ears, but didn't take offense and even agreed with what Winnie said.

Lucy wasn't quite as forgiving. "You did spy on us. Hardy said you considered all of us as possible suspects for the Lanciano job."

Kelvin gave a quick glance in Hardy's direction. "It's true," he admitted, "I did suspect everyone, at first. That's what investigators do."

"You should have declared yourself," she insisted.

"Like Peter declared himself?" Kelvin shot back in as gentle a tone as he could manage. He didn't mind taking his place on the hot seat, but let's be fair about it. His retort inserted a clearer perspective into what had become an impromptu hearing and the group, as a whole, reacted favorably to his self-defense.

Hardy had refrained from weighing in on the discussion up to this point but decided to jump in.

"Let's try and keep an open perspective. Peter definitely came here with an agenda, granted, in a totally irrational state, and Kelvin had his job to do. Personally, I think Kelvin has bent over backwards to be discreet in the way he's handled the situation. He's been more than fair with Peter ... kind, even." His words had the effect he'd intended. He saw the group as a whole visibly relax, including Lucy.

"Are we allowed in to see Peter?" Winnie asked.

"If you want to visit him, let me know," Kelvin answered. "I'll leave a list of your names with the carabinieri on guard outside his room and he'll let you in. I know Peter would welcome a visit from anyone at this table," he added.

*****

After breakfast the hiking group dispersed to their rooms to attend to packing, and reconnoitered an hour later for some last minute shopping in Sulmona. They headed down Corso Ovidio to a reputable gold jeweler and entered with credit cards drawn, figuratively.

The Sulmona of the early Renaissance was famous for its silver and gold smiths, especially for work done in Byzantine filigree. There are jewelers throughout the city who carry on this tradition of fashioning fine jewelry, making intricate earrings and pendants. One pendant, called the Abruzzese Presentosa, is a typical jewel done in gold or silver with filigree. The solid part of the presentosa is molded, but the filigree part is always handmade. It is traditionally 'presented' by a man to his fiancé or wife.

The establishment they'd chosen, though a bit on the pricey side, guaranteed all their gold products to be pure gold, whereas some lesser known jewelers sold jewelry whose gold content and quality was sometimes suspect.

Dennis bought a presentosa and presented it to Teddy, amid everyone's 'Oohs' and 'Ahhhs.' Then Hal decided to buy one for his little sister, back in the States. Hardy even purchased one for his mother, living in Frankfurt. When the jeweler explained that it was O.K. for single women to buy for themselves, Lucy, Amy, and the Bradford twins each bought a presentosa with ear rings to match. Single women really got off on using plastic, Hardy observed, as he watched them slapping down their credit cards like they were playing a trump ace.

After the jewelry store, the group split up into ones and twos, heading off in different directions to look for last minute items and additional picture taking opportunities.

*****

# CHAPTER 39

Her last minute shopping complete, Lucy had immediately headed over to the hospital to visit Peter. Good for his word, Kelvin had given the carabinieri in charge of guarding Peter's room her name and she was admitted without a problem. Peter looked so pitiful lying in bed; he oozed loneliness and hopelessness. He was awake when she walked in and seemed surprised but happy to see her.

"I didn't know if you would be up for company," she began.

He managed a shy grin. "It's good of you to stop by." He hesitated, and then continued, almost choking on his words. "I feel such a vile person and a total fool, Lucy. I can't even imagine what you and the rest of the group must think of me."

The pain on his face cloyed at her heart. Yes, he'd done something truly terrible, but from the depths of such despair who could say that in the same situation someone else wouldn't have done the same or worse?

"It's not for me to judge you," she told him. "None of us realized the tremendous burden of grief you were carrying. It doesn't excuse what you did, but it explains a lot. We all feel sorry for your personal loss, and deeply regret that we missed what was happening. I sensed your sadness but didn't want to intrude. I'm so sorry, Peter."

She reached for his hand that was free of IV tubes, then, and gave it a gentle squeeze. He gave the hint of a squeeze in return. They held hands in silence, unaware of life beyond Peter's room. Their hands had become a bridge spanning a crevasse of misery and anguish, transfusing Peter with hope.

Lucy broke the silence. "I've just decided something, Peter," she began. "I'm staying on in Italy a while longer, until we know what position the authorities will take with you."

Peter pulled his hand away in the beginning of a protest but Lucy took it firmly in her own again. She looked him squarely in the face before she spoke.

"Don't worry, Peter. No commitments. You're in a foreign country with not a soul in the world to be here for you. It's the least I can do. I'm sure you'd do the same if our situations were reversed."

The fight had gone out of Peter. His New England stoicism gone, he gave a curt nod of his head and merely said, "I accept, Lucy. And yes, if our roles were switched I would." He struggled trying to find the words to say and in the end simply said, "Thank you."

She was thrilled at Peter's acquiescence but kept it to herself. Now all she had to do was sweet talk the casino back home into extending her vacation time. And be the rock that Peter needed.

*****

Arriving at the hospital on the northern outskirts of Sulmona, Leski passed through the hospital's neighborhood a few times to get the lay of the land. He parked in a side lot of the hospital, reserved for staff, and walked through the main entrance, which was overshadowed by a contemporary portico constructed of metal grillwork.

Once inside he blended in with those people coming to call on loved ones, following along in the mainstream of visitors who led him, eventually, to the floor for critical care patients. Once there, it was fairly easy to determine where his quarry was being kept. The carabinieri positioned outside the room was a dead giveaway that a person of interest, i.e. a prisoner, was inside.

Leski found the men's room on that floor and ducked in the door, needing a strategy to decoy the cop. He emerged from the men's room a few moments later in a panic, yelling, "Un corpo! Un corpo in bagno!" ("*A body in the bathroom!*")

A nurse at the nearest nursing station came running. The carabinieri outside Fynch's door did several double takes before joining her. This left the door to Fynch's hospital room unguarded; Leski moved in.

He checked the name on the tag outside the door: Peter Fynch. This was his man; he could see him propped up in bed through the small glass window pane in the door. He entered Peter's room, drawing a small handgun from the rear of his pants and fitting it with a suppressor in one swift, practiced motion. Hardy was sitting in the visitor's chair and turned to see who had just arrived. When he saw the drawn weapon he started out of his chair.

"Who the hell are you?" he demanded.

Leski had not anticipated there would be anyone in the room other than Fynch and realized he suddenly had a big problem. He felt sick at his stomach. He wasn't a hit man, for starters, and now he had to kill not one, but two men. He motioned for Hardy to move over toward the bed. He was so intent on the situation in front of him he didn't hear the door open behind him and certainly didn't expect the searing, stabbing pain plunging deep in his right shoulder.

"Ayyeeee!" Leski screamed, firing a shot that went wild, taking out the infrared light over the head of the bed. The glass showered down on Peter, who tried to cover his face for protection. It was Winnie, attacking the killer with her infamous honed knitting needles.

Hardy saw his chance and jumped the killer, wresting the weapon from his hand and pinning him to the floor. Winnie's sharpened needle protruded from Leski's right trapezius muscle. She'd really nailed him.

Hearing a commotion from outside, the carabinieri rushed in; he was horrified at what he saw. He'd left his post on a ruse, he realized, and almost lost his charge because of it. Flustered, angry, and relieved, he took Leski off Hardy's hands, handcuffed him, and man-handled him out of the room, calling for backup as he went.

There was a stunned silence for a minute. "I hope I get my knitting needle back," Winnie complained, "I need it for the flight home."

Hardy cracked a big smile. "Sweetheart," he said, "I'll buy you as many knitting needles as you need. And I'll even pay to have them sharpened."

## Finito

42946203R10189

Made in the USA
Lexington, KY
12 July 2015